T0011705

Heavy Sinners MC:

Dare to Ride

Heavy Sinners MC:

Dare to Ride

Rae B. Lake

www.urbanbooks.net

Urban Books, LLC
300 Farmingdale Road, NY-Route 109
Farmingdale, NY 11735

Heavy Sinners MC: Dare to Ride
Copyright © 2022 Rae B. Lake

All rights reserved. No part of this book may be reproduced in any form or by any means without prior consent of the Publisher, except brief quotes used in reviews.

To the extent that the image or images on the cover of this book depict a person or persons, such person or persons are merely models, and are not intended to portray any character or characters featured in the book.

ISBN 13: 978-1-64556-450-8
ISBN 10: 1-64556-450-9

First Mass Market Printing February 2023
First Trade Paperback Printing February 2022
Printed in the United States of America

10 9 8 7 6 5 4 3 2 1

This is a work of fiction. Any references or similarities to actual events, real people, living or dead, or to real locales are intended to give the novel a sense of reality. Any similarity in other names, characters, places, and incidents is entirely coincidental.

Distributed by Kensington Publishing Corp.
Submit Orders to:
Customer Service
400 Hahn Road
Westminster, MD 21157-4627
Phone: 1-800-733-3000
Fax: 1-800-659-2436

Chapter 1

"What the fuck do you want me to do, Lisbeth? I don't shit money. We got motherfucking bills, and I make sure that shit gets paid."

"Yeah, you're always going to hold that shit over my head, aren't you? You think I want to be stuck here in the house with a baby at twenty-one? I could have been off doing my own shit, but your dumb ass couldn't be bothered with a fucking condom." She sucks her teeth and walks away from me.

It seems as if every day there's another fucking problem for her to bitch about.

"Lisbeth, it took two of us to make her." I try to keep my voice calm. The last thing I want right now is for us to have another huge fucking fight in front of Tia. I'd give my very soul for that little girl, but it seems Lisbeth doesn't feel the same.

"Yeah, well, you made me promises. You told me you would finish college, get a job, and we'd be straight." She turns around quickly and screams at me. "Look the fuck around, Darius. Does this look like we're fucking straight to you?" Her chest heaves up and down as she sucks in huge breaths. She's waiting for me to respond, but I don't have the fucking energy for it.

She says that shit like I'm not already on the road to giving her everything I had promised her. I got my degree, a good job straight out of college, and we're already living in a three-bedroom condo. Is it the most fucking luxurious shit that I've ever seen? No, but she doesn't need to do shit all day except take care of Tia.

Lisbeth tilts her head to the side, her nose flaring and the ring in her nostril making it look like she's a bull ready to attack. "What? You got nothing to say? Fucking figures."

I wish I could say I didn't see this shit coming, but I did. I knew what kind of girl I was getting involved with when I knocked up Lisbeth, and I thought she knew who I was.

She didn't.

She knew my name and thought with the last name, "Heavy," came all the spoils.

Marcus Heavy is one of the baddest gangsters in the state and happens to be the founder of the Heavy Sinners MC Club. Wherever he goes, money, power, and respect follow. Lisbeth expected to get in on *that* life. The problem is that I'd rather someone stick hot needles in my dick than be anything like that man. I fought like hell to make sure I'd never have to be part of that life, and Lisbeth resents me for it.

"Dada! Rocket ship!" Tia calls to me from the living room, where she's throwing her crayons in my direction. The small projectiles barely fly more than a foot in front of her. It doesn't matter, though. She laughs every time.

I pull off my tie and drape it on the back of one of the island stools. "You making a rocket ship, baby?" I slowly make my way toward her but stop short when I feel a crunch under my hard-soled shoes.

When I lift my foot, I see a bright blue crayon crushed into the light beige carpet.

"This the shit I'm talking about. Who the fuck is going to have to clean that shit up? Me. Tia, I told your ass about throwing those goddamn crayons around." Lisbeth storms toward the little girl.

"Hey, calm the fuck down. It's just a fucking crayon. You don't need to be yelling at her like that. She's a fucking baby." I step in Lisbeth's way and yell at her.

"That's the damn problem. You keep fucking babying her. She's spoiled and doesn't fucking listen," Lisbeth screams in my face.

"What the fuck are you talking about now? She's playing with her crayons." When I turn back to look at Tia, she's scooted back against the wall with big tears streaming down her face. My heart cracks at the sight.

"Fucking hell, Lisbeth. Whatever. I'm not going to do this shit with you." I lower my voice and walk around her toward the front door. I just need to get some fresh air.

"Leave. I fucking hate you, Darius. You ain't shit but a damn headache." She screams at my back as she follows behind me to the door.

I know better than to turn and yell back. We'd be fighting all night if I did.

I pull the door open and have to blink a few times for my brain to comprehend what I'm seeing. *What the fuck? A gun?*

"Special delivery, motherfucker."

The earth stops spinning in that one brief moment, and it feels as if my body may just float up from the ground . . . only to have the world come crashing down on my head like a plane from the sky in the next second.

The man in front of me brings the gun up and clubs me hard on the side of my head. I feel warmth gush down my cheek as I fall to the floor. Five men rush into my home and make quick work of closing the door behind them.

"Ahh! No! Help, Darius," Lisbeth screams as she runs in the opposite direction. Two men run after her. I roll over to my front and try to get my legs under me, but the other three men surround me and stomp me out—boots to my side and head. My skull cracks hard against the baseboard of the wall I'm pressed up against. Blood erupts into my mouth after one of them brings his foot down hard on my rib cage. The light in the room dims, and I can no longer hear Lisbeth yelling for me. Instead, all I can hear is the sound of my heart beating in my ears and the thump of boots coming down on my body.

I close my eyes for what feels like a second, but when I open them again, they've tied my arms behind me, and one of them is kneeling on my back. The sound in the room has returned, and I turn my head to see one of the men holding my daughter while the other three men are beating my wife. With every kick or punch, they laugh and talk amongst themselves, as if they don't have anywhere else in the world to be. They're not scared of anyone hearing us scream for help, not afraid of the cops—nothing.

"What the fuck do you want?" I wheeze, the sound gurgling through the blood in my throat.

"Darius, help! No, please, stop!"

"Daddy! Go-way! Stop! Go-way!" Tia kicks and screams at one of the men, but they don't let her go.

"Get the fuck off them! What the hell do you want?" I roar through the pain, frantically pulling and twisting the binds, but it's no use.

"What do we want? Payback, retribution . . . a good time," one of the men standing over Lisbeth replies. "You decide."

The men have their faces covered, leaving only their eyes visible, but I swear it seems as if they're smiling at me. This is a fucking joke to them. "Fuck you. I swear on my life I will fucking kill you for this." I roll again, and this time, I dislodge the man from my back. But he's on me again in an instant, and this time hits me with the butt of his gun before he settles himself down.

"Stop fucking moving, asshole. You're not going to get away from us. Don't make this any harder than it fucking has to be." He uses the barrel of his gun to trace a pattern on my head before he trails down my back and pokes at one of my ass cheeks.

"Get the fuck off of me." I kick up again.

He laughs and brings the gun back up. "Stay still, Darius. You're not going to want to miss this."

My eyes revert to my wife. Blood pours from her nose and mouth, and her cries have gone from piercing to pitiful.

"Please, stop. Get off of me," Lisbeth begs. Her short hair is matted down with blood.

"Mommy." Tia sobs hard and reaches for her mother, leaning far out from the man holding her arms. "Daddy, help!" Her little eyes swing over to me, and I can feel her begging me to save her. The weight of it is like a vice on my heart.

"You know, I think it's time we have a little fun. What do you think, Darius? Can we have a little fun?" One of the men standing over Lisbeth turns to me and asks. I look up at him, and though I'm not able to see his face, I try to remember what features I can see. They can't get away with this.

"No, please."

His hand goes to his belt. There is only one fucking reason for him to be taking his pants down. "Please, I'll give you whatever the fuck you want, but please don't fucking do this," I yell furiously, trying to get to Lisbeth.

"That's what the fuck I'm talking about. I bet this prissy bitch got a tight pussy." The other man moves closer, his hand moving to his belt as well.

"No, mmmnn, no." Lisbeth is barely conscious, but she must realize what's about to happen since she turns and tries to crawl away.

"Motherfuckers, what do you want?" I buck my head upward and try to use my legs to get the man above me off. His gun is pressed firmly to my side, but I don't care if he pulls the trigger right now.

"Darius, please . . ." Lisbeth begs one final time before the man above her rips her thin lounge pants off and rams himself into my woman like she belonged to him.

Lisbeth wails as she gets a burst of strength and tries to fight off the man. "No, get the fuck off of me."

I squeeze my eyes shut for a second, a deep roar of anguish forcing its way up my throat.

"Mommy! Mom! No, Mommy!" Tia cries hard, every once in a while, gagging from the force of her tears.

"Tia, baby, close your eyes. OK, sweetheart? Close your eyes for Daddy." I try to soothe her, but I feel like a fucking failure. There is nothing I can fucking do. I spent my whole life doing everything I could to make sure I wasn't ever in a situation where my family would be put in danger, and these motherfuckers burst in and rip my world apart.

Tia glances back in my direction before she slams her hands to her eyes and keeps them closed.

"Liz, I'm here, baby. I'm here." I turn back to my wife and watch her body rock hard as the man brutalizes her.

"Darius . . ."

"Please, I don't know what you want. Why are you doing this?" I beg, but none of them answer. All of them are focused on my wife, except for the man above me.

"Fuck, yes. Hurry the hell up. I need my turn." The other man standing next to Lisbeth is jacking himself off hard.

"We don't have time for this shit. It's not what we're here for. This ain't a goddamn party. Save that shit for your woman," the one holding Tia barks out. A wave of relief washes over me only for a brief second. It's almost over. They will be on their way soon, and I can get my girls the help they need.

"Hold up. Just hold up."

"Ah, no. Too much." Lisbeth's fingers claw into the carpet as the man above her fucks her harder and faster.

"Yes, are you in pain, pretty? I like that shit. Show me more."

I helplessly watch as the fuck pulls his dirty cock out of her before ramming straight up her ass.

Her scream echoes in the large condo, followed by the sound of the rest of them laughing.

"No! Lisbeth!" I bang my head against the ground, willing something to give. I can't take this. She can't take this. It must stop.

Lisbeth shudders hard, and she lurches forward slightly as vomit bubbles up and out of her mouth. She gags repeatedly, but the man doesn't stop; instead, he goes faster.

"Yes, a dirty bitch. Fuck, yes," he hisses.

Her face turns a dark purple, and I have to avert my eyes. Instead, I focus on the man's hands—the tattoos. I force myself to commit them to memory instead of the sight of Lisbeth being brutally raped. A few seconds more and the man roars out his climax.

"Can we fucking go now?" the one holding Tia asks.

Go? Where the fuck are they going?

He doesn't wait for them to answer him. He pulls some tape out of his back pocket and starts to wrap up Tia's mouth.

"No, what the fuck are you doing? That's my daughter. Get the fuck off her." Another wave of adrenaline washes over me when I realize they are planning to kidnap Tia. I buck the man off me again, this time far enough so that he falls into the wall and down on his ass. I quickly get my feet under me and try to rush the man holding Tia. Suddenly, a large bang diverts my attention.

I turn and see a smoking gun in the hands of the man who had just raped Lisbeth. Her head is nearly split in two from the force of the bullet. Blood and pink brain matter splatter against the light beige carpet mixing in with the crayons she'd told Tia to pick up. My stride falters as I try to process what just happened, and at that moment, the man holding Tia manages to tie her hands together before pressing his gun to her little head. "Another step and she dies."

"No, please." Even to my own ears, I sound pitiful. I fall to my knees, begging for my child's life.

"If it makes you feel any better, it's not something you did. It's just something that needed to be done." The guy who kept me on the floor comes up behind me and presses the gun under my chin while he holds my head by my hair so that I focus on Tia. "Now, say bye-bye to the little one."

Tia's eyes open wide, and I do my best to smile at her one last time to tell her it's OK. However, the force of the gunshot has other plans. Liquid heat slices through my jaw and up through my head as I watch my daughter being tossed over the man's shoulder. Every second feels like an eternity as I watch her small, tied hands reach out for me, and tears roll down her cheeks. My body slumps forward, and my head hits the soft carpet with a thud—blackness inches into my vision. My gaze locks on Tia as she moves farther and farther away from me.

They say death is peaceful.

They lied. Death is agonizing.

For me, death is only the beginning of my pain.

Chapter 2

I wish someone would turn the fucking lights off. I must have drunk an entire damn bottle of Henny last night because it feels like someone is playing a goddamn hockey match in my head.

I turn to call out for Lisbeth, but something in my throat stops me.

What the fuck?

My eyes pop open, or at least one of them does. The other is covered with something. My vision is blurry, and instead of the intense light I expect to see or the wicker ceiling fan above my bed, all I see is white ceiling tile.

"Mmmph!" I try to call out again, but whatever is in my throat is keeping me from talking. I raise my hand. The motion causes pulses of pain to shoot through my sides. I grope at my face, trying to figure out what the fuck is going on. Immediately, I get a grip on something plastic and try to pull it out. Whatever the fuck it is, it's uncomfortable.

Now, I hear heavy footsteps racing in my direction. Lisbeth. Fucking finally. I hope she can tell me what the hell is going on. A figure appears over my head and grabs my hand from the tube.

"Hey, now, you can't take that out. I know you're confused, but just settle down a little, OK, sugar?" An older woman speaks, and I can hear her clearly, but it's like my mind can't understand the words that are coming out of her mouth. I reach my hand up again to pull the tube out of my throat.

"Stop. You have to stop, or we're going to tie your arms down. Stop." She speaks again, this time with a bit more force in her voice.

The only word I can readily identify is the word stop. I drop my hand and try to speak again, forgetting this fucking thing is stopping me.

"Do you know where you are?" she asks. "Blink once for yes, twice for no." Slowly my mind begins to put the words together that she is saying.

Blink once for yes? Why the hell would I do that? I can move my head, at least.

I try to shake my head, but something has it braced in place, and even the tiny motion is enough to make me feel like the hockey match in my head has just gone into sudden death. I squeeze my eyes shut and try to wait out the height of the pain. When I open my eyes again, I still see the same woman standing over me, a clear look of pity etched on her tired, slightly wrinkled face.

"Do you know where you are?" she asks again.

I blink purposefully twice.

"OK, well, you're in Handcraft Memorial Hospital. You were involved in a horrific incident and have been here for quite some time."

She speaks slowly, and my mind does its best to keep up.

Hospital? What fucking incident? Where the fuck is Lisbeth? Tia?

I try to move my head from side to side again, not give a flying fuck about the pain it causes me. I need to get to my family. *Where are they?*

"Calm down. I'm going to get the doctor in here so we can help you. Just hold on, sugar." She pats my hand softly before I hear her rushing out of the room.

I feel her absence immediately. I don't remember a time I've ever felt so alone. *What am I doing here? I just want someone here with me. What the fuck is going on?* My heart beats inside my chest like a jackhammer, and my hands grip the sheets like they're my only tether to the human world.

I don't know why it feels like it takes forever for someone to come back into the room, but as I lay there in complete mental disarray, I do my best to focus on what is in front of me. After a few seconds, my eyesight returns to normal. At least the one eye I can see out of. Another round of heavy footsteps comes in my direction, but this time, instead of the one woman, there are two—this second one is younger and wears what seems to be a doctor's coat.

"Mr. Heavy, I'm so very pleased to see you awake. I know it must be a bit jarring right now, but I would like to ask you to remain calm, and I will try to explain as much as I can to you. Before I do, is there anyone that you would like us to call to be with you?"

I blink once for yes.

"Can you move your fingers?"

The doctor looks down at my hands, and I wiggle them. I feel my fingertips drumming against the starched sheet.

"Great. That's a very good job." She praises me like a toddler who just took his first shit on the big boy potty. "Here, try to write out who you would like us to reach out to." She pulls out a small pad from the chest pocket of her medical coat and a pen and arranges it in my hand.

I can't move my head to look down, so she holds the pad in a way that the pen won't slide off. I write as clearly as I can the word "*Wife.*"

She pulls the pad out from under the pen and reads it. Her gaze changes from intense to soft.

"I'm so sorry, Mr. Heavy. Your wife will not be able to join us." She lets out a sigh and places the pad under my hand again. "Is there anyone else?"

What the hell is she talking about? My wife won't be able to join us? Where the hell is she? What the hell is going on?

I take the pen, and this time, instead of trying to tell her who else I want her to get in contact with, I just scribble a question mark. There is no one else. I have no one else in my life.

"OK, I understand. I will give you as much information as possible, but you will need to speak with some detectives for more details. A member of my staff has already put a call out to get one of them to come over. If it becomes too much, I will give you something to help you rest. It's quite upsetting, and I don't want you to harm yourself."

She eyes me carefully as if she's telling me if I act up, there will be consequences. I can be good. I am practically a fucking master at keeping my emotions in check.

"I know my nurse has already explained that you are in Handcraft Memorial Hospital. You have been here for just over seventeen days. During this time, you have been either heavily sedated or unconscious. More?" she asks, and I blink my eyes once.

I was in a fucking coma?

She nods and continues talking. "You were brought in with a gunshot wound to the head. You are fortunate to be alive. In fact, it's a miracle you're alive. The bullet passed through under your chin, through your tongue, before it veered off to the side. It cracked your mandible and lodged into your occipital bone. Your eye suffered some damage, but your vision should return to you. More?"

If I could move my jaw, it would be on the fucking floor. *I was shot? Me?* I work as a fucking account specialist in a business firm. It isn't the best job, but it's reliable and safe, and the pay is good. *How the fuck did I get shot?*

The questions run rampant through my mind as I try to force myself to remember what the fuck happened.

Heat and pain.

I remember something exploding in my head. It felt like someone stuck a hot poker through my mouth and into my skull. Dim memories begin to flood my subconscious. I can see blood on the light beige carpet. Tattoos on someone's knuckles, a box with two lines in it? *What the hell is that?*

I focus back on the doctor and blink my eyes once. I need to know more.

"Unfortunately, you were the victim of a home invasion. From what the detectives told me, you were found bound. There was nothing you could have done." She stops and peers into my eye for a second, biting down hesitantly on her bottom lip. I keep her gaze. There's more. "Your wife was found murdered at the scene."

I press my head back into the pillow as hard as I can. The physical pain does nothing to stifle the agony rolling through me.

Dead? Lisbeth is dead?

More memories flood through me. This time, I can barely hear my wife screaming for me. Instead, I can see a man hovering over her—the man with the knuckle tattoos. Her body moves back and forth as her mouth opens and her eyes find me.

Help me.

Please, stop.

"Mmmph." I slam my head back again as the floodgates open, and now more of that night comes crashing back to me. They raped her. They raped her right in front of me, and I could do nothing to help her. *Oh God. How the fuck could this shit happen?* The tube in my throat does nothing to stop the feeling of my throat starting to close with emotions. Tears cloud my one good eye, and I sob for Lisbeth . . . the pain I saw on her face. The brutality of the attack and my own fucking helplessness. *How could I allow something like that to happen to the mother of my child?*

My child . . . Tia . . .

I focus immediately and grab hold of the doctor's hand. Hard. She winces slightly but then puts the pad back under my fingers.

I write in big letters, *Tia*.

"Tia?" Her head cocks to the side as if she were unsure what the word signifies. My frustration with not being able to talk reaches its peak.

I let go of her hand, and as best I can, bring my arms up to my midsection and mime holding a baby. Tia isn't a baby anymore. At 3, she is more a little lady than anything else.

"Baby?" the doctor asks again before her eyes open wide in recognition. "Oh, your daughter."

I blink once, so she knows that's what I'm trying to say.

"I'm sorry, we don't have the name on file." Another sigh, and this time she steps away from me slightly, out of arm's reach. She doesn't want me to grab her again.

Fuck no. Please, God, don't do this to me.

"I'm so sorry to tell you this, but when the police got there, your daughter was gone. They believe she was kidnapped. The assailants . . ."

I can't hear another word after "kidnapped." A deep moaning sound fills my ears now. They kidnapped my kid. Flashes of Tia over a man's shoulder assault my mind. Now, I wish I didn't remember. My chest feels like it's on fire. I take a breath to douse the flame inside, only for the moaning to stop. I bring my hands up to my head and claw down my face. I can barely feel it. I would do anything to stop this. Do anything to wake up from this fucking nightmare. When I open my eyes again, the doctor is hovering over me, and the nurse is trying to force my arms down. I swing back and forth. I have to get up. I have to find Tia.

A moment later, a bright light flashes in the corner, and three large men in uniform come in and hold me down. Security. I still can't hear what they're saying. My brain is stuck replaying the sound of my baby screaming and crying for me to help her.

A sharp pinch in my arm, and I slowly feel my body stop fighting, and a deep need to sleep overtakes me. The doctor is knocking me out.

I blink my eyes at her twice over and over, trying to communicate.

Doesn't she see that I need to find my daughter? Tia is out there in the grips of some madman, and the doctor is forcing me to go back to sleep.

Even my dreams won't be able to stop this pain.

Chapter 3

"Tia!" my voice croaks, and I squint to open my eyes.

Every time I wake up, I pray it's all a nightmare . . . only to see those same white ceiling boards, letting me know that I'm still in the goddamn hospital.

"Mr. Heavy, are you OK? Do you need assistance?" One of the night nurses, I think her name is Willa, sticks her head in. It's been almost a week since they removed the breathing tube, and she has been here every evening.

I close my eyes and try to compose myself. I know if I get too angry, they will give me drugs to knock me out. I don't want to sleep anymore. "No." I can't open my mouth all the way as the surgeons had to wire my jaws shut after they pulled out the bullet fragments. They had managed to repair my tongue and palate, but there will always be a scar to remind me of that horrible night. Willa nods her head and leaves me in peace. The staff I've come in contact with here at the hospital all know once they give me my medications and draw whatever blood they need, I want to be left alone. I don't need their words clouding my mind. I need to focus on getting better, not making friends.

The police came a day or so after I first woke up to ask me as many questions as they could. I did the best I could to answer them using only a pen and paper. I described what I remembered about the men breaking in and the assault, but it wasn't much more than they knew already. The only bright spot in meeting them was that they informed me they could identify and arrest the man who raped my wife. The sick motherfucker didn't use a condom, and they could use his semen to run his DNA through the system.

That's the only good news the police brought in all the time that I've been here. They have yet to come back to let me know what they have discovered about my daughter. Lisbeth is dead, and I will mourn her for as long as I live, but it is my daughter who is now in danger. I need to find her; *they* need to find her. Like I do every time I wake up, I try to will my body out of bed, but I am still healing from the beating those bastards gave me. I work hard every day to get better. I believe the police are doing everything they can to find my baby girl, but I hate this feeling of helplessness. I should be out there scouring the town as well.

Someone knocks on the door, and Willa sticks her head in, a slight smile on her face. “Darius, I know you just woke up, but you have a visitor.”

My eyebrows squeeze in. *A visitor? Who the hell could be visiting me?* A few of the folks from my job stopped by, but I don’t know them well enough for them to come again. I only just got that job. At 23 and fresh out of college, it’s amazing I got the job in the first place. So, I haven’t really made long lasting connections yet.

“Can I show him in?”

I wonder who it is, but if they are here to see me, I’m not going to turn them away. I will say hello, ignore them while they speak, and then turn them away. “Yeah, whatever,” I reply slowly through my teeth.

The nurse walks away, and a large shadow fills the doorway. Behind it walks in a man I never thought I’d ever lay eyes on again in my life.

“What the fuck?” I glare at him, sure my eyes are playing tricks on me. There is no fucking way he has the fucking balls to come here right now.

“Is that any way to greet your old man?”

“Fuck you. Get out,” I spit at him through the wire in my mouth.

“Now, now, don’t be like that kid. You are still my son. Don’t you think I have the right to make sure you’re all right?”

I want to laugh for the first time in weeks. "Are you fucking kidding me? You haven't checked on me in more than six years, and now you show up here expecting me to be fucking grateful that you decided to grace me with your presence?" The ache in my jaw is more than just a little annoying at this point, but I refuse to let him stand there and think I'm happy to see him.

No, I hate Marcus Heavy. He's everything I never want to fucking be. He was barely around when I was a kid. When he wasn't locked up or shacking up with whatever slut he was cheating on my mother with, he was over at his fucking motorcycle club. He never had any time in his life for his son. I remember clearly the times he would come home from wherever he was and beat my mother, how he tormented her and put her down. Part of me always wondered why the hell she didn't just leave him. I never saw the fucking appeal. When I was old enough to understand what was happening was wrong, the only thing she could say was that I needed a father. Well, some father he had turned out to be. I guess the only good thing I took from Marcus is the need to stay in my child's life. I never want Tia to hate me as I hate him.

Just the thought of her causes me to cringe in pain.

"Just leave." I let my head drop back. I don't want to fight with anyone right now.

"Darius, honestly, I just came to see how you're doing. I know we don't get along and probably never will, but you came out of my sack, boy. I just want to lay eyes on you and tell you how bad I feel about your little family."

I don't say anything in response. His pity means shit to me.

He walks over to the large windows that show me the outside. "Well, what are you going to about it?" he asks with his back turned to me.

My head snaps in his direction. *Did he just fucking ask me what I'm going to do about it? Does it look like I can do anything in my present conditio*n? "What the hell can I do? I'm stuck here."

He turns around to face me. "Yeah, you're fucked up right now, but you're not always going to be laid up in this bed. What you going to do about it when you get out?"

"I'm going to find Tia. The detective already put the bastard who hurt Lisbeth in jail. They'll find Tia soon." I speak as clearly as I can.

Marcus laughs and pushes himself away from the window. "Your mother sure did a number on you, didn't she? Fucking weak. You really think these motherfucking police give a fuck about you or your family? You're nothing but another statistic. If you want something done, you have to do it yourself, and that means you're going to have to find Tia the hard way."

"Then I fucking will." I grip the edge of the bed hard, the only area where I can exert some strength. *Who the fuck is he to tell me what I need to do?* The police have a job to do, and I know they'll do it, but that doesn't mean that I won't be able to help when they let me out of here.

"You say that now, but tell me, Darius, how the fuck are you going to do that?" he moves closer to my bedside and lowers his voice so no one besides the two of us can hear. "You ready to blow some people's heads off? You ready to do to them what they did to you?"

I pull away from him. I should've fucking known that's where his mind would go. The bastard never did anything the way it was supposed to be done. Always the easy fucking way out. He would rather see me get locked up than watch me trust the cops to do their job.

"I'm not going to kill anyone. I'll find them, and they'll go to jail. That's what's going to happen. They deserve to suffer, not get let off easy." *Death for them would be too simple.*

Marcus shakes his head in disagreement, "They won't go to jail. You and I both know that. You know what you need to do. You need to take all those motherfuckers out, and I can help you. You know my crew is more than equipped to handle shit like this. You only need to join—"

I raise my hand and push him away before he can say another word. "Fuck away from me. I'm not joining your damn club. I'll take care of my business on my own."

Marcus's eyes stay glued to the place on his chest I just shoved as if he expects to see my handprint still there. I'm sure it's been awhile since anyone laid a hand on him. But I'm not everyone. Sure, I can't stand the bastard, but I know one thing for sure. . . He won't kill me. I'm the last of his bloodline. The only thing that matters to him is that I stay alive and join his fucking motorcycle club.

"I see your head is still fucked up from that beating you got. I'll let you be. Know this, though . . . You *will* have to come to me for help, and when you do, you will only get it on *my* fucking terms. Get better, son." He turns and walks out of the room without letting me reply.

He is out of his mind if he thinks I'm going to join his club. The Heavy Sinners MC was one of the most feared MCs in the state, but there was always another club or gang gunning for them. I'm just not interested in that life. I don't need fucking guns to get shit done, much to my father's disappointment.

The last time I saw my father before this visit was on my seventeenth birthday. He showed up out of the blue with a fucking Harley. No apology for missing out on large chunks of my life, no help for my ailing mother. He said it was time for me to join the crew, that, as his son, it was my birthright. He even went on about how I wouldn't have to go through a "prospect trial" and how I should appreciate that he would make that exception for me. It was like the fucking *Twilight Zone*.

That was the day I told him in no uncertain terms, no matter how much money he threw at me, how much expensive shit he bought, or whatever gift he decided to shove in my face, that I would never join his fucking club. He was pissed and beat the shit out of me that very same day. Then he left, and I haven't heard from him since.

The bike, he left, and though my mother told me that she didn't like it, I used to sneak around and ride it sometimes. It was scary as fuck but exhilarating at the same time. The ride is the only part of his world that I will ever accept into mine.

I lay back and close my eyes, waiting for the anger at my father's audacity to fade, but it never does. I stay angry until my body forces me to go to sleep, not only because he showed up but also because a very small part of me thinks what he said could be true. *What if I need to pick up a gun and start killing people to get Tia back? What if I need to go against everything I pride myself on to make sure she comes home? What if my father's way is the only way? Will I be able to forsake it all and do some shit like that?*

Even as sleep takes over, I know the answer.

With no hesitation.

Chapter 4

It's been over a month since my life had imploded, and still, the worst of it hasn't subsided. The police still have no idea where Tia is. Detective Pearson is the man in charge of my case. He comes every few days to see if I remember anything new about that night but never gives me any updated news. It feels as if he's only following up because it's what he's expected to do. Like there is a specific number of times he must see me before he can take the file and bury it at the bottom of his desk.

Along with the scarring I got from the gunshot wound, I have recurring migraines. The doctor says they may lessen as time goes on, but there is a chance that they won't go away completely. Besides that and my jaw, my body is pretty much all healed. They're talking about letting me leave the hospital in a matter of days. I'm excited about that, not only because I'm fucking tired of being here, but also because that means I can finally start looking for any clues about where my daughter is. I'd be able to beat the streets myself, knock on every goddamn door. I don't care if I have to give up everything I own to find her. I would.

I sit in one of the chairs by the window, my eyes scanning the street below. Every once in a while, I catch myself thinking I see Tia. That maybe she somehow made it out herself and is on her way to me. I know the chances of something like that happening are nonexistent, but it's nice to hope.

A knock on the door startles me out of my daydream. "Mr. Heavy, you have a visitor."

Alma, the day nurse, is the one I saw the first time I opened my eyes and probably one of the only people in this place that I can stand anymore. Something about her just soothes me, even if it's just for a little while. "Who is it?"

"He said his name was Lark Thompson, but I'll be honest with you, sugar. Something about him just screams of 'bad vibes.' I don't think you're going to get good news." She shrugs and walks out.

I turn in my chair and wait for Lark to come in. Lark is my boss. I haven't seen him since I've been here, but I didn't expect to. I'm a small fish in the corporation. I don't think he even really knows who I am. When he walks in, he's flanked by two other men in suits, neither of whom I know.

"Mr. Heavy, it's nice to see you up and about." Lark walks over to me and puts his hand out for me to shake. I do, but don't take my eyes off his face. Alma is right. Something is off here.

"Thanks."

I sit back and wait for him to tell me whatever it is that brings him here. When I don't continue with the usual pleasantries, he sighs and gets right to business. "Mr. Heavy, as you know, our company takes the safety and reputation of our employees very seriously. We pride ourselves on keeping a safe workplace." He stops for a breath.

"Of course, but what does that have to do with me?" I ask, speaking slowly. I've had speech therapy every day, and luckily, the surgeons did a remarkable job on my tongue, though every once in a while, I slip over some words, or they would come out wrong. My tongue and the fact I still have the wires on my jaw mean I had to keep my speech slow if I don't want to mess up the words.

"Well, I'm so sorry you were the victim of such a heinous crime, but in the interest of safety, I've had my personal investigation team do some digging into the matter. We were unaware when we hired you that you had known connections with one Marcus Heavy."

My stomach drops to my feet. They're going to hold who my father is against me.

"I don't have any connection to him," I snap, no longer caring if they don't understand me.

"He *is* your father, is he not?" one of the men in a suit asks.

"Yes, but since when does that mean I have to have a connection with him? Do you know how many children grow up without a father in this state alone? The only thing I share in common with that man is the last name." I try not to let my anger get the best of me, but I'm quickly losing the battle.

"I don't believe that to be—"

I cut the man off. I don't know him or what his connection to my boss is, but I know I no longer want to hear the words coming out of his mouth. "Mr. Thompson, can you just tell me why you are here today?"

"Of course. Well, unfortunately, we are not going to be able to keep you on staff. This incident seems to be gang related, and we just can't have something like that associated with our company." He gives me a pitiful smile and places a manila folder on the bed.

I look at it but don't make any move to go toward it.

"This here is a very generous severance package. We understand that you are still very ill, so we won't take you off the health plan for another six months."

"Are you kidding me? A severance package? I lost my wife, my daughter is missing, and you think giving me a severance package will be enough to clear your conscience? You know more than anyone I have nothing on my file that would indicate I have any affiliation with any gang members." I raise my voice and hear metal popping as I scream at the man in front of me. Quickly, I grab my jaw to ease some of the pain.

"I'm sorry for all that's happened to you, but this is the best that we can do for you. We will have your personal items delivered to your house. Any paperwork that will require your signature will be brought to you." With that, they walk out of the room, my boss turning to me right as he reaches the doorway. "Darius, I'm truly sorry for your loss. I wouldn't wish this on anyone."

I roll my eyes and look away. "Eat a dick, Lark." I don't have anything else to say to him. It's true I have only been at the company for a short time, but I worked my ass off in that time. I'm so fucking tired of the stereotypes. They take one look at who my father is and just assume I'm a gangbanger. It doesn't matter how far away I pull myself from him or how hard I work to keep my grades up. Even how fucking hard I work to pay for that schooling—none of it matters. All it takes is one look into my file to label me a fucking bad apple.

I reach over to the bed and pick up the manila folder. A check falls out for two months' pay and a letter indicating I am no longer employed. I chuckle before I fling the folder across the room. All this hard work for nothing. I roar through my teeth and put my hands under the thin mattress of my hospital bed. I flip it with very little effort. Not enough mayhem, though. I feel like I can fucking kill someone right now. I grab the rolling tray table and fling it toward the other side of the room. The worn, light brown hideaway trays pop out of the table and crash to the ground. Next up is the IV pole. I pick it up and swing it as hard as I can at the small generic lamp on the side table. The fixture breaks immediately, and just that tiny bit of destruction makes me feel better. I don't want to stop. Sweat pours from my head, and I feel pain in my ribs and head building to an unbearable level.

"Oh my God, Darius, what are you doing? Stop it . . . Right now, stop," Alma screams from the door. I swing the IV pole against the bed, and a large section of the bed's arm rail breaks off and flies at the wall in her direction. She screams and ducks her head before anything hits her. I hesitate for a second to make sure nothing actually hits her. I am pissed off but not at her. My destructive pause only lasts a second, and then I'm back to swinging the long piece of metal at everything I think will break to pieces. Everything I think that would break in the same way that I'm breaking inside.

Alma runs out, and a few seconds later, four large security men rush into the room. I hold the IV pole out like a fucking spear. Memories of the men breaking into my home and beating me down flash in my head. I will never let anyone get that kind of a jump on me again.

"Fuck off," I scream and then cringe in pain.

"Mr. Heavy, you have to calm down. Just be calm, and we can get all this fixed up. Take it easy," one of the security guards says and moves in slowly.

"No," I yell back and swing my weapon at him. "Leave me alone."

One of the other security guards darts out to the side, and I swing in that direction, but the pole gets caught on the steel frame of the bed. I yank at it to free it, but as I'm doing that, the guards have already converged to jump on top of me.

More flashes of men in all black stomping on me, tying my hands behind my back, spring to the forefront of my mind.

"Daddy, help me!"

I cry out as I fight with all I have to get to Tia. "No, Tia, no." I feel something pull in my mouth and a spurt of blood fills the cavity. Something hard and pointy presses into my cheek. I ripped out my own tooth.

"For fuck's sake, man, just stop. We're not trying to hurt you. Calm down," the guard screams at me.

"Jesus, come on, Darius. Stop fighting. Come on, sugar, please," Alma yells from somewhere on the other side of the room. I turn my head sideways and spit out as much of the blood as I can before I feel a pinch in my arm. My ability to swing lessens by the second.

Tears run with the blood that's pooling beneath my face now. I go to sleep again, praying that this is all just a nightmare.

Chapter 5

Seven weeks in the hospital is more than enough for me. After my outburst from being fired, I managed to dislocate my jaw. They reset it for another week and a half before the doctor felt it had healed enough to take the wires out. Eating solid food after all that time is strange but a necessary step for them to let me out of the hospital. The first thing I do when the doctor gives me my discharge slip is pick up the phone to call Lisbeth, forgetting for a second that she isn't home. She will never be home again. The doctor is confident I will make a full recovery and tells me I should continue with speech therapy. She feels that my youth plays a large factor in my speedy recovery. I guess 23 is the right age to get shot in the head.

The cab ride home is long, and when I get out in front of the housing complex where my condo is, everything seems different. The white of the doors is just a little bit dirtier. The light in the walkway is a little dimmer. It almost feels like the man I was died the second that gun was pressed to my chin. I walk up the stairs, my eyes darting from side to side, making sure no one is following me or waiting for me around the corner. I don't think I've ever been this paranoid in my life.

I turn the corner to my landing and see yellow tape crisscrossed over my door.

"Are you fucking serious?" I say to myself. I walk a little faster, thinking that this must just be the remnants of when the officers were here before getting evidence. As I make my way to the door, I have to laugh at my luck. How the fuck can this shit get any damn worse? A padlock is on my door, and a notice states my home is part of an ongoing investigation, and no one can enter.

A door whips open behind me, and I spin around fast. My brain immediately lets me know that moving quickly is a bad idea. The very beginnings of a headache bloom as I try to stave off the dizziness.

"Oh my God, Darius. I didn't expect to see you. I'm so happy you're OK."

Mrs. Baxter, my neighbor, stands in her doorway with a housecoat on and her hair in rollers. She's a widow and usually keeps to herself. How she knows I'm out here is beyond me.

Where the fuck were you when I was screaming for help?

I shake the thought out of my head. It's not her fault I was attacked. I'm not going to go down the road of blaming everyone for something that a select few did to me.

"I'm alive," I reply.

Her face falls to sadness. Her hand twitches in my direction as if she wants to touch me, but she must see by the look on my face that I'm balking at that idea. "I can't tell you how sorry I am about everything that happened. You and Lisbeth were a lovely couple."

Now, I know she's a fucking liar. She's left several notes under our door complaining about the arguing. Lisbeth was my wife and mother of my daughter, but we were *far* from a lovely couple.

"Yeah, she was a good woman." I instantly feel bad that I can't even force myself to lie and say we were a good couple.

"I know this is all happening fast, and everything hurts right now, but you're a young man. You have so much life left to live. Soon, you'll be able to put this behind you and find someone else to love. Things will go back to normal." She nods her head and tilts it to the side.

"Normal?" I ask fucking shocked that she would even think to use that word in my presence.

"I mean, not normal. I mean . . . you know, better." She backtracks, and her light tan skin flushes red.

"I don't know what the fuck you heard or what information your nosy ass is out here digging for, but my wife was brutally murdered, and my daughter ripped from my life. Nothing will get *normal*. Shit like this *doesn't* get better." I sneer at her and watch her mouth gape like a fish.

"I . . . I . . ." she tries to say something else, but I don't have the patience for it. I turn from her and walk away from what used to be my home and the neighbor who thinks my life will become something that resembles normal.

I make my way over to the police station to talk to Detective Pearson, but he's already gone for the day. I try to get some information from another detective that I've seen working the case with him, but like always, he doesn't have shit to tell me. It's lucky that I go to the station, though. Apparently, while I was still in and out of consciousness in the hospital, my wife was cremated. The urn had been brought up from the county coroner's office for the detective to deliver to me. That delivery had never happened. He promises me that he will talk to Detective Pearson in the morning about getting my condo reopened, but until then, there is nothing more for him to do. I turn away again with no answers, but this time with an urn of my dead wife's ashes hidden in a small bag that he had in the office. It seems so fucking pitiful.

I manage to find a hotel room a few miles away from the police station. I don't have my car key, so I can't drive. I could have called an Uber, but the walk helps me cool off. I know I should feel bad for going off on Mrs. Baxter, but I don't. In fact, the only thing that I feel bad about is not caring that I don't feel bad. The Royal Inn on Palm Beach Road isn't anything special, just a place for me to lay my head for the night until I can get the detective to open up my home again.

The mundane process of checking in and getting the single key from the completely indifferent front-desk worker seems to pass by in a fog. I just want to get in bed. After climbing up the flight of stairs to the outside entrance of my room, I open the door and am pleased to see that everything is in order with the room—clean sheets, TV, no fucked-up smells. Exactly how it should be. I drop everything I have onto one of the side tables and plop on the bed, not even bothering to pull off my light jacket.

The quiet is what does me in.

At least at the hospital, people were walking around at all hours of the night. Nurses and doctors came in to check on me and give me medication. Here, it's just nothing. Every time I close my eyes, I see Tia or Lisbeth. I roll up in bed and squeeze my head in my hands. I don't know how to do this. This can't be what living will be like for me. After about twenty minutes of sitting in the room in silence, hearing nothing but my dead wife cry and my daughter scream for me, I've had enough. I grab my wallet and run to the small dive bar across the street. I need something to take the edge off.

The pain in my head dulls to a slight ache after about the seventh drink. I pound back my eighth shot and buy a bottle of Corona to end the night. I shouldn't even be wasting my funds in the bar, to be honest. As of right now, I only have about four months of savings. Who knows when I'll be able to get another job.

"Bro, you can't go outside with that." The bouncer tries to stop me from leaving the bar with the open bottle of beer.

The world sways slightly. It's soothing. I do my best to focus on his face. He's big but doesn't look like he's interested in any problems.

"I'm not driving," I slur hard. My tongue is really fighting against me in my inebriated state.

"Nah, man. You don't even sound like you should be standing, let alone walking out of the bar with alcohol in your hand." He crosses his arms and plants himself directly in my path now.

"Sss, not the beer. Shhhot in ma head." I let my head flop back to show him the still healing scar under my chin.

"Oh shit. Damn, bro, that shit looks fresh." He leans in closer to get a better look at the wound. "You must've been touched by God to survive some shit like that."

I let my head fall back down and almost fall straight on my face. He catches me before I do. I right myself and point at the motel visible from the front door. "I sleeping right there."

He turns, checking the area as if he would get a visual cue from someone that I have indeed rented a room at the motel. When he turns back in my direction, I can see the pity. I'm beginning to hate that fucking look.

"All right, man. It seems as if you need that beer. Make sure you get the hell off the street, though. You hear me?"

I nod, and he moves so I can get by. I take my sweet time crossing the street. There is very little traffic, but it would be my fucking luck that a speeding car would come right now when I barely have any of my mental faculties.

The cool night air seems to make me even drunker than I already was in the bar, and I have to crawl on my hands and knees up the stairs. One look over the side railing makes me feel like I'm about to drop to my death. I stand up when I get to the landing where my room is. A sudden rush of soberness smacks into me as I stop a few feet away from my room to see that it's cracked open.

Did they fucking come back? Maybe they found out I didn't die? Is Tia in there?

The last thought is the only thing to spur me forward. I open the door quickly, not bothering to make sure that it was safe first.

Marcus.

"Motherfucker, what the fuck are you doing in my goddamn room?" That is what I said in my head, but in reality, it came out in one long string of disconnected consonants.

"Boy, what?" He has the nerve to laugh. "Bring your drunk ass in here before you get arrested or some shit."

I focus hard to compose myself. "What. Are. You. Doing. Here?" I enunciate every word so that he doesn't get it confused.

"I heard that you got out of the hospital today. I'm just making sure you have everything you need."

"You heard?" I ask as I walk into the room and drop down on the bed. I hear a rush from the faucet in the bathroom and jump right back up. "Who the fuck . . . Who's that?" I look around the room for a weapon.

"Relax, Darius. Just a little company. I can't imagine you're having a good day," Marcus says from behind me.

Slowly, a short woman with a weave flowing down to the crack of her ass comes strolling out of the bathroom. When she sees me standing, her eyes light up, and she walks in my direction. She keeps eye contact with me every step of the way, but instead of stopping in front of me, she goes around and cuddles up next to my father.

"How the hell did you know where I was anyway? I didn't tell anyone I was coming here."

"After our little reunion, I had one of the prospects sit out front to keep an eye on you. When you left the hospital, he followed you. Tailed you until you lost yourself in that bar across the street. You really need to learn how to watch your fucking back better."

He's not wrong about that. The woman next to my father flips her long hair over her shoulder, capturing my attention again. It's been a long time since I paid attention to anyone looking at me that way. I've always been faithful to Lisbeth. Even in our worst times, I didn't stray.

I look from her to my father and then back to her. "Look, I don't have time for your shit right now. Just leave." I pull off my jacket and toss it on the floor.

"Awe, come on. Don't be like that. I brought her here for you. Come now, take a look." He pushes her forward and grabs her hand to spin her around slowly.

My eyes flit over to her as she shows off all her assets. She's wearing a cutoff shirt and jeans that look like they're painted on. Her tits sit up high, bouncing slightly with each movement. When she gets to her backside, she bends forward slightly, accentuating her overly plump ass. I don't know if she's had work done, but if she has, it was a good fucking job.

"I don't know if you forgot, but I just lost my wife, you heartless bastard." I walk to the bed and lie down.

"Darius, who the fuck are you bullshitting? Everyone fucking knows you only married that woman because you knocked her up. It's fucked up that she's gone, but she is. You ain't."

I pop up from the bed into a sitting position, my head and my gut swirling from the motion. "Are you saying I should just *forget* about her? That I should fucking pretend she didn't matter?"

"Not at all. I'm saying you let Missy here take the edge off. She's clean and open to whatever you want to do."

I toss my hands up in exasperation. The man isn't even fucking listening to me. I drop my head into my hands, trying to get the world to stop spinning for just a moment.

A soft hand caresses my shoulder, and the bed behind me dips slowly as Missy kneels behind me. She wraps her arms around my midsection and starts to pull up my T-shirt over my stomach. Her hand lightly trails down the center of my abs, and they contract from the sensation. She flips her head to the other side, her long hair tickling my exposed skin. I feel the first press of her soft lips on my cheek, and instead of being disgusted, my body reacts. I have to clamp my hands down on my skull to keep from turning around, throwing her on the bed, and taking what she's offering. She moves her lips down farther, angling her head so she can kiss my neck. It feels so fucking good I have to grit my teeth to keep from moaning. Her other hand follows the first one, but instead of just stopping at my abs, her exploration continues until her palm is lying heavily on my cock. The bulge of it presses hard against my jeans.

"That's right, baby. Let me help you forget." She whispers in my ear, and it suddenly feels like someone tossed a lake of cold water on my head.

Forget.

"Get the fuck off of me." When she doesn't move fast enough, I grab her wrist and forcefully pull her from behind me. "You think anything you can do will make me forget?" I yell at her. Then I switch my attention to my father. She's just doing what she's told. This is really on him. He's the one trying to force my hand, take advantage of me in this fucked-up state.

"You think I *want* to forget? There is *nothing* that's going to make me forget Lisbeth. My wife—the mother of my child—my only fucking family. I don't give a damn what slut you try to shove in my face. Nothing is going to make me forget. Now, I'm not going to ask you again. Take your bitch and get the fuck outta my room." My eyes are focused, words clearer than they've been in the last three hours, and my fists are balled at my sides, ready to knock this bastard the hell out if he decides to ignore me.

Marcus glanced down at my hands and takes a quick step in my direction before stopping. I don't flinch. He steps back and starts to laugh. "You're one crazy motherfucker giving up a prime piece of pussy like this. That's OK, though. I get it. I just was trying to help out."

"Do me a favor and stop that shit. I already told you I don't want your fucking help," I snarl at him.

He puts his hand out, and Missy runs over to where he is. "And I told you already, if you want to make shit right, you'll need it." He points to a small paper bag on the table. "Shit to get by and the address to the clubhouse. Don't keep me waiting too long, son." He opens the door and walks out with the girl in tow, not even bothering to close the door behind him. I quickly walk over and slam it shut. The fucking nerve of that man.

At first glance, I just want to throw the bag in the garbage. If I know my father, it's probably fucking drugs or some shit like that. I've never been into hard-core shit. Yeah, I'd blow down some Kush now and again, but even that's on rare occasions. The bag is heavier than I would have assumed when I pick it up. I take a chance and peek into the bag and see four tightly rolled wads of cash and a card. I empty it quickly.

At least five grand is in it. The man inside me who hates my father's guts wants to light this shit on fire, but the man who just lost his fucking job knows that the cash will come in handy. The card has an address on it. The clubhouse is out near Belle Glade. There isn't much out there but farms and open land for the most part, so it makes sense for him to set up there.

I flick the card away and shove the money into my pocket. I may not want it, but I *will* use it.

Momma didn't raise no fool.

Chapter 6

I've tried to talk myself out of walking into this building at least a dozen times. Not one fucking reason I can come up with is stronger than my need to get some fucking answers. I feel like I'm going crazy. Like Tia is just around every damn corner. That she is just inside that door. I am consumed with the need to find her when I'm awake and haunted by her absence when I sleep. In the week that I've been out of the hospital, I've spent fifteen-hour days walking up and down different neighborhoods, knocking on doors, sticking up flyers, calling hospitals, asking questions, even calling news stations to see if they will run a notice about a missing child. At every turn . . . another dead end.

Now I walk up the stairs and into the police station. I stand at the front desk for a few seconds as the woman sitting does her best to ignore that I'm standing there. Quietly, I take a few deep breaths.

Don't act a fool. You need them to help you, so don't act a fool.

I repeat that over and over to myself until I can't take it anymore. "Hello," I say louder than I need to.

The woman cuts her eyes at me and puts her finger up, telling me to wait again. Luckily, I only have to wait a few moments before she finally addresses me.

"How may I help you?"

"I need to speak with Detective Pearson."

"In regard to?"

"My missing kid."

She eyes me for a second before she picks up the phone on the desk and calls someone explaining that there is someone up front to see the detective.

"The detective's office is in the back, to the right."

I nod and try to rush in that direction, but another officer steps in the way and directs me to a board where I need to sign in and give my information. I'm almost bouncing with nerves. I just want someone to tell me something. Finally, I make my way to the detective's office, and as I walk to the door, I can hear laughter. They are laughing while my little girl is MIA and in danger. The world should stop until she's back home.

I knock on the door slightly open, and someone tells me to enter.

"Yes, may I help you?"

My mouth drops open. If I didn't know better, I would think this motherfucker didn't even remember who the hell I am. "I'm here for an update on Tia."

"Tia?"

"What the fuck?" I fist my hands before I shove them in my pockets. "Yes. Tia. Tia Heavy. My daughter who has been missing for months." My voice is louder than it should be in a police station, but at this point, I couldn't care less.

"Sir, you can't come in here with this level of hostility," the other officer who is in the room with him warns me as he gets up out of his chair, clearly ready to diffuse the situation.

"Lenny, it's good. I need to speak with Mr. Heavy anyway," Detective Pearson says.

"You sure?"

He nods his head, and the second officer makes his way out of the small office.

"Can you shut that door, please? I apologize for not recalling your little girl's name earlier. It's been a busy week." He sits behind his desk and gestures for me to sit in the empty chair in front of him.

"Yeah. Sure." I sit down in the chair as he suggests. "I haven't heard anything, no one has reached out to me, I don't see anyone canvassing the neighborhoods, so what the hell is happening with the search?"

The detective puts his hands up to get me to slow down. "We are still searching, but there is still quite a bit of information we are missing.

Until we have it all, it's unlikely we will have much more luck than what we have right now. You don't remember any new information, correct? I mean, I'm sure your main priority is getting Tia back." The detective leans back in his chair and steeples his fingers in front of his face.

"Of course, that's my main priority."

"Good good good. So, you don't mind if I ask you a few more questions, do you?"

Everything in me wants to tell him to fuck off. "If it will help you find my daughter, no, I don't mind."

"Did you know the men who came to your house?"

"I already told you they wore masks. I didn't see anyone's face. Only the tattoos. I thought you said that you already arrested the man who killed my wife."

He picks up a pen from his desk and flicks it back and forth between his fingers, fidgeting as if this conversation isn't something to keep his attention.

"We did. Shade Wills. We even secured the murder weapon at his place."

I shoot forward in my chair. "Then what's the holdup? Why haven't you pressed him to find out where my daughter is or at least who the other bastards are? One of them has to know something."

"Oh, I'm sure they do, but you know how these bangers are . . ." Detective Pearson lets his voice trail off.

Is he fucking insinuating *I'm* a goddamn gang-banger? "No, I don't know how they are," I spit back at him.

"Dumb and loyal. They know if they snitch on one of their own, the second they are out of custody, either in prison or back out on the street, they're going to get taken out. They'd rather take the years than the death sentence."

"This is bullshit."

The man shrugs before he leans forward in his chair. "Did you let them in your house?"

"What?" I'm so shocked by the question that I don't answer right away.

"There was no forced entry. Did you let them in?"

The fuck? "I told you already that I was walking out when they were walking in."

"Maybe they were waiting for you to leave? Maybe they were supposed to hit your house while you were out on this walk?"

"Now, wait a fucking minute. What the hell are you saying right now?"

He tosses the pen on the desk. "Oh, don't play stupid now, Mr. Heavy. I'm a fucking detective. It's my job to find shit out. How fucking coincidental is it that the son of the notorious Marcus Heavy is the victim of a home invasion? One where his wife is murdered. Your neighbors have given countless reports about how volatile your marriage was. A home invasion where the only thing taken is your kid . . . Tell me, is this some type of turf war involving your father? You trying to take over or something?"

Red clouds my vision, and I jump out of my chair much too abruptly. I bring my fist down hard on his desk. Pens and papers fly to the floor. Immediately, his hand drops to his side, where his gun is holstered.

"I don't care what the fuck you looked up in my background or who the fuck my father is fighting with. *I* have nothing to do with that shit. You said *you* are a detective, so then do your motherfucking job and find my daughter." My voice bounces around the small office, and my head throbs from stretching my jaw.

"You might want to settle down, Mr. Heavy. I'm sure you don't want me to drop you into a holding cell. Then I'd have to divert my attention to you instead of doing my job, as you say."

I shake my head at the man. I'd put my faith in the system, so fucking sure they were invested in finding my daughter, but I was so fucking wrong. I'm not going to get any help from this man or any of the police. My poor baby has spent the last two months waiting for someone to save her—waiting for these men to break down the door and bring her to me. It will never fucking happen. All he's concerned about, like everyone else in my life, it seems, is my fucking father.

"Find my daughter. That's all I want. I had nothing to do with this. I have no fucking hand to play. I'm just a civilian and a victim of a horrible crime. All I want is for you to make it right." I calm my voice down.

"I wonder how many people were victims of your father? You going to make *those* right?" He grabs another pen and continues to twirl it in his hand.

I feel like I can see into his soul, and that shit is dirty as fuck. I shake my head and turn to leave before I do something I'll regret and end up catching a case.

"Mr. Heavy, despite what you may think, I *am* looking for your little girl. I just want you to be as forthcoming as you can so we can get her back as fast as possible. Even if you have nothing to do with your father's life, you might want to realize that his problems have a way of trickling down to anyone in his reach. As his son, you are definitely a target." He stares at me for a second before he leans over and picks up one of the folders I knocked on the floor.

Nothing.

No one has any answers or explanations except that this happened because I am Marcus Heavy's son. That they came for me because of my bloodline. If all the questions I get are about my relationship with Marcus Heavy, I wonder what answers I could get from the man himself.

I've gone through every channel I can, begged, and pleaded with every official I could reach for help. I've stayed away from my father because I never wanted to be associated with his type of evil.

Now, I have no choice. They've taken away my every option. They've made me desperate, and desperation breeds monsters.

Chapter 7

"Man, are you sure you want me to drop you off here? There's a lot of fucked-up people in these parts." The Uber driver turns in his seat and glances at me. Belle Glade may be full of sugarcane farms, but there's nothing sweet about the area. Most of it is run-down and in need of a serious restoration. There's a small community, but it's mostly farmland and abandoned buildings on the outskirts of the town.

Right along with all that is the enormous Heavy Sinners' compound. It's like its own little fucking gated community dropped down right in the middle of nowhere. It's right for the driver to be scared to leave me here. Most people who come here either leave fucked up or don't leave at all. Lucky for me, I know the owner.

"Yeah, man. This is the place." I nod my head to him in thanks as I get out of the car and walk toward the entrance. The gates are open, and what looks like dozens of bikes line the small dirt lot. The music blares through the night, and the closer I get to the door, the more I know I will be ending this night with a hell of a fucking migraine. There's a party going on. It's the only explanation for the shit I'm seeing. For fuck's sake, one guy has his woman bent down, her hands to the ground, as he fucks her from behind. Neither one of them cares that they are in full view of anyone outside.

The door to the compound is black metal with the words *Heavy's House* etched into it. I've never been here in my life—never even thought to find out where this place is. So even reaching out to open the door hurts my pride. But my daughter is worth more than my pride.

The music, along with the thick fog of both cigarette and weed smoke, is suffocating. I do my best to locate my father, but there are so many people here, it seems more like a fucking dance club than a motorcycle club. My eyes scan the men looking for their vests, indicating who they are and their rank in the club. If I can find a patched member, I can get them to tell me where my father is, and then I can get the fuck out of here.

"Oh fuck, baby. I've never seen you before. Tell me you're here to have fun." A woman boldly stops right in front of me and pushes me back against the door.

"I'm not here for this shit," I yell over the music.

"What you mean? This is a fucking party. If you not here to have fun, then what the fuck you come for?" she screams back.

When I just glare at her, she shrugs her shoulders and walks off, finding another man on her way. Is it really that fucking easy? I hate this shit. At least make me work for the pussy.

I push my way through the crowd, making sure to keep a hand on my wallet. I am down to about $3,000 of the money that Marcus gave me. My savings account is getting smaller by the day. The bill collectors don't care that you lose everything. As long as you are breathing, they are coming for their money. There is no way I can afford to get pick-pocketed.

A horseshoe-shaped stage is set up in the center of the clubhouse, and women dance on some of the poles scattered about. They flip their hair, roll their hips, and pop their asses to lure the men in attendance. Crowds of guys line the stage with money in their hands and lust in their eyes. I barely bother to look up.

A full bar stands on the left side of the clubhouse, fully stocked, with three bartenders behind the counter. I'm sure one of them can tell me where Marcus is. I put my hand up when I get there to grab the attention of one of the fast-moving barmaids.

"What can I get ya?" she asks before she even fully gets in front of me.

"I need Marcus," I yell back at her.

She chuckles and says, "If Marcus wants to see you, he'll find you. I don't keep up with that man's whereabouts." She turns and tries to go to the next customer. I grab her arm before she can move farther away. "What the fuck is your problem?" She snatches her arm away.

"I don't have time to explain this shit to you. Just have someone get him or do whatever you have to, but I need to see him," I shout over the music.

She looks over my shoulder and picks up her hand. Thirty seconds later, two men walk up behind me. "You messing with my bartender here? This the type of fucking problems you want?"

I turn and get a good look at the two men behind me. My eyes quickly drop from their faces to their chests to see if they are members. They wear the signature leather kutte, the vests that members of motorcycle clubs wear. Both of them are patched members but have no rank. Trim is the taller of the two, but he is slimmer and looks to be Hispanic. Next to him is a man named Gambit, according to his patch. He is dark, not a scar on his face, has a toothpick in his mouth, and has a cocky smirk on his face.

"Nah, I don't want any problems. I want to talk to your president," I repeat my request.

"Our president is busy. We don't interrupt him while he is entertaining guests. Maybe you want to come back another time," Gambit says as he switches the toothpick from side to side in his mouth.

"I'm not leaving. He's expecting me."

Trim looks me over once, then looks at his partner, probably trying to assess if I'm a threat. "Who is he expecting?"

"Darius."

"Darius, who?" Trim asks forcefully.

"Darius Heavy."

Both of their eyes pop open in surprise. I'm sure they must know who I am, but I doubt that they'd ever think that they would see me in the flesh. Neither one of them move from in front of me. Instead, Gambit pulls out his phone and swipes the screen a few times, sending Marcus a message, I guess. I turn back to the bar and get the bartender's attention again. "Let me get a Hennessy, please."

She grabs a tumbler and pours about a knuckle's worth of the brown liquor into it. I quickly pick it up and down it before turning around to face the two members who have become my personal guards. A double door opens on the other side of the compound, and even through the crowd, I can see Marcus step out. I don't wait for the two men in front of me to move. I simply push my way through them and make a beeline straight for Marcus.

Before my fourth step, a large forearm wraps around my neck, and I'm being pulled back into someone's chest. "Who the fuck said you could go anywhere?" Gambit shouts in my ear. I try to push him off, but he has a firm grip on my neck.

"Gambit," Marcus's loud voice booms across the room, over the people talking and the music. "Get the fuck off him."

Gambit lets me go instantly. I don't turn to retaliate but instead continue on my way toward my father.

"What the fuck is he doing here?" A patched member that I do recognize, Apollo, asks as I walk by him.

By the time I get to Marcus, I can feel a lot of eyes trained on me. "We need to talk," I shout at him.

He smiles at me, not because he's happy to see me, but because he's right. At least in my mind, that's what it feels like. Marcus turns briefly into the room he just walked out of. "Get the fuck out." Three naked women scurry out of the bedroom before he even has the chance to turn back in my direction. I figure he kicked them out so that we could talk in the room, but when I take a step forward, he puts a hand on my chest to stop me from entering.

"Over here."

I follow behind him as he pulls open a large barn house-style sliding door.

"Heavy? You calling church?" another man calls from the side, and a few members rush toward the open doors.

"Nah, keep partying. I got business to handle."

When I look back at the men that were just denied entry, I can see disbelief and anger on their faces. Obviously, I am fucking with their routine. It doesn't bother me none, though. I'm already here to talk to a man I want nothing to do with. Them being angry with me is the last fucking thing I'm concerned about.

The second Marcus slides the door closed, the room becomes almost deathly silent. It must have some sort of soundproofing.

"I knew you would show eventually."

"Are you just going to fucking gloat about how I have nowhere else to go? If so, then you don't have the help that I need either."

He turns away from me and slowly walks to a large leather sofa pushed against the side wall. The room is large, with hardwood floors, high-steepled ceilings, and random pieces of framed art on the wall . . . mostly of naked women. In the center of the room is a large triangular-shaped dark wood table. One end has an extreme point, while the other two ends have a rounded curve. I've never seen a table like it, but it only takes me a few seconds to understand why my father chose that one. He wants to be at the point, the pinnacle . . . the king. Since he's the president and founder of this club, I would assume he's as close to a king as any.

He sits on the couch and pulls out a blunt from his pocket, lights it up, and takes a long pull. "You going to sit the fuck down or not?"

I do what he asks and sit on the couch, making sure to keep my back to the armrest and my eyes directly on him.

"You said you wanted to talk, so fucking talk." He takes another pull before he blows a big cloud of smoke directly into my face.

"I need to find my daughter."

"What happened to the police you were so sure would find your kid?" Another smirk crosses his face.

"They seem to be more interested in what I know about you than finding Tia."

The joy on his face falls away as he trains a death glare on me. "And what the fuck did you tell them about me?"

"What the fuck do I *know* about you? Nothing. Just because you and I share the same fucking blood doesn't mean I know you. I tried to explain *that* to them, but they didn't seem to want to listen." I stare right back at him until he averts his eyes.

"That's a fucking shame. We lost a lot of time, it would seem."

I stare at the side of his face and wait for him to laugh. He can't be serious. "Lost a lot of time? What fucking planet are you on, Marcus? We didn't lose shit. You threw away any time we could have had chasing after these fast women and a quick buck. Don't start acting like you regret not having a relationship with me now. That was *your* fucking choice."

"Darius, you sound bitter. Like a bitch. Is *that* what the problem is? You want me to cry and tell you how fucking sorry I am that I didn't stay with your momma? You want me to make up for all the fucking birthdays I missed? I'm *not* sorry for a damn thing. I was given nothing, and I made a fucking empire for myself. The only part I regret is the fact that you turned out just like your bitch-ass mother."

My fist flies toward his face before I can process the words that come out of his mouth.

"You piece of shit. Don't you ever fucking talk about my mother." I punch again, and just like the first time, I make contact with his jaw. Unfortunately, that's all I'll get. I swing my other hand, but he blocks that attack and sends his elbow directly into my face. I may be quicker than him, but at the age of 40, my father isn't exactly an easy target. Blood trickles down my throat, and I watch him draw his arm back to hit me again. I duck and roll to the ground but use my momentum to turn and jump back up. When I stand, Marcus already has a gun pointed at my head. The sight is enough to draw me up short.

"You've got some fucking balls to think that you can lay your fucking hands on me. You think you're special because you got my last name?" he snarls at me, and I have to laugh.

"Not special, but I know I'm your only option. That's the problem with being a fucking slut and sticking your dick in everything that walks. STDs are everywhere. My momma told me how you had chlamydia for so long that it killed off your ability to have kids. You not going to kill me. Even I know that shit."

I take a step toward him, the gun pressing hard against the top right of my chest. "You know, even on her deathbed, my mother defended your sorry ass. Through all the chemo and pain, she never spoke badly about you. When she knew it was her time to go, she tried to get me to open up and start a relationship with you. That woman gave her life to make sure I was good with no help from you, and you have the nerve to say you regret that I turned out like her? You probably wish you had at least one person in your life who is even half as loyal as my mother was. If you don't, you're a fucking fool."

He doesn't respond. Instead, he drops the gun from my chest, walks back to the couch, and then sits down. "What do you want, Darius? Why are you here? I have guests to attend to."

"I already told you. I want to find my daughter."

"Who took her?"

"If I fucking knew that shit, do you think I would be standing here in front of you?" I roll my eyes in frustration.

"Fine. I'll help you get your little girl. But what are you going to do for me?"

I let out a sigh and close my eyes tightly. Of course, I knew this shit was coming. Marcus Heavy never does favors for free. "What do you want? I don't have anything to offer you."

"You do, and you know it. I told you before. I want you as part of my club. I didn't start this shit so I could hand it off to some random motherfucker. Heavy Sinners MC should always be led by a Heavy." He leans forward in his seat, his hands folded in front of him.

"So, what? You saying you're going to step down?"

He laughs heartily at that. "Boy, are you out of your fucking mind? No, I ain't stepping down. No time soon. I'm leading this club to the motherfucking top. Why would I give it up for you? Nah, I'm not going anywhere, but I want you in the club. I want that patch on your back. You need backup on this, and we are just the ones to give it."

I shake my head. Every part of my logic fights against even the thought of me joining this MC. "I'm not a fucking killer, Marcus. I don't do the shit that your people are known for doing."

He stands from the couch abruptly. "We're all motherfucking killers, especially when we have something we will kill for. Would you kill to get your daughter back, Darius? Or was that all just fucking talk?"

I would. I knew I would. "Maybe I—"

He cuts me off before I can even get any type of compromise out of my mouth. "Look, this is the only choice I'm giving, and it's a generous one at that. Either you join the club, or you can go back to pasting her photo on the side of milk cartons. Hurry the fuck up and make your decision."

Momma would be so disappointed. "Fine. I'll join." The second the words come out of my mouth, it feels like I signed my soul over to the devil, and from the way his lips curled up into that sinister smirk, I think I'm right.

"That's the smartest fucking decision you have ever made in your life. There's a lot of shit that you're going to have to learn—and quick. This club and the members are like our own fucking government, and I'm the fucking king. If it seems like you're trying to go against me in any way, I will make sure you fucking regret it. My word is law. Don't snitch on anyone and do as you're told. You'll figure out the rest as you go along." A wide smile crosses Marcus's face. He is absolutely giddy that he's gotten his way.

"What about Tia? When do we go find her?" I ask, trying to get the focus back on the real problem at hand.

"We'll start right away, but that doesn't mean it's going to be an easy fix. You've already wasted months with those dumb-ass police. She could be fucking anywhere by now. This club is into other shit too. Do your part there, and we'll make sure finding your kid is a priority. You with that?" He puts a hand out and waits for me to shake it.

Am I with it? Fuck, no. I don't *want* to be OK with this shit, but I don't have a choice. I raise my hand and shake his. "Yeah, I'm with it."

"Good. Now, let me introduce you to your new family."

Chapter 8

Marcus sticks his head out the door. The sounds of the party and the good times being had by all flood into the room the second he pushes the door open. Maybe this won't be so bad. I say anything to myself now, trying to feel better about what I just did.

"Shut it down," Marcus yells loudly over the music.

"What?"

I hear someone answer. Whoever it is must be close to the door.

"I said, shut it down. The party is fucking over. We got shit to handle right now. I want everyone the fuck off my property in the next five minutes and all the Sinners in church." Marcus walks back in but leaves the door propped open. It's like a well-trained machine. I watch as everyone stops what they're doing and files out of the clubhouse. No one causes a ruckus. No one cries about how they just got here. The music is cut off, lights up to the brightest setting, and people just go about their day as if they aren't watching women strip like it's the only profession in the world.

It's impressive.

Five minutes later, ten men, all members of the Heavy Sinners MC, walk into the "church" and wait for Marcus to speak. Most of them do not even acknowledge my presence, and those looking my way aren't exactly waving me over with their friendly faces.

"Something going down?" the man named Apollo speaks up.

"Yeah, you could say that. Something *is* going down."

Marcus makes his way over to the tip of the triangle table before he continues talking. "It's a wonderful day for us Sinners. My son, Darius Heavy, has decided that he will be joining his old man in this life."

"Your son? The same one who said he wanted nothing to do with you or this club? *That* son?" Apollo speaks up again. That VP patch on his chest must be making him a little braver than the rest of the crew in attendance.

"Yeah, that same one, motherfucker. Anything else you have to say on the subject?" Marcus leans in Apollo's direction, daring him to say another word, but the man just stands there and clamps his mouth shut. "Like I was saying, my son is here and will be joining our ranks. I want him as deep into this shit as possible, and with that said, I feel like there is only one way for that to happen. He needs to have a seat at the table."

"What the fuck?"

"You gotta be shitting me right now."

"He needs to prospect like the rest of us."

The uproar from the men in the room almost had me backing out of the space, but the second Marcus's eyes lock on mine, I know this is just another way for him to make sure I do what he tells me to do. I stand still and keep my mouth shut.

"He needs to be what the fuck I say he's going to be. If I want to step the fuck down right now and declare he is the next motherfucker who will run my club, then that is just what the fuck will happen." Marcus's voice roars above the chaos in the room.

"What position is he going to take?" an average height, redheaded man speaks out. That hair against his light brown skin and freckles would be jarring had it not been for the fact that he is missing fingers on both hands, and I can't look away from that. *Bill,* it said on his kutte, and his title is treasurer. It would make sense for me to take that position since it's the business I was in before I was fired.

"Apollo, give me your tags."

"What the fuck?" Even I can't stop myself from speaking up this time. Vice president? What the fuck do I know about being a VP of a motorcycle club?

"Marcus, you can't just fucking take Apollo's patch away. What the fuck did he do to deserve that shit?"

"This is bullshit."

"Fuck that. I'm not giving this little ingrate my fucking patch. I worked my ass off to get this damn patch, and you just want me to hand it over to him?" Apollo slams his hand down on the table, clearly trying to intimidate my father. Marcus simply smiles and gets up from where he's sitting at the tip of the table. He walks over to where Apollo is standing, staring him deep in the eyes.

"Did I ask for your opinion on what I should do with my club? Apollo, I think maybe you got me fucked up." Marcus pulls the largest fucking knife I have ever seen someone carry out of the sheath on the side of his pants and presses it to Apollo's cheek. "You have two motherfucking options here. Either you give up your fucking patch, or you give up your fucking life."

"Marcus—" Apollo opens his mouth to speak, and Marcus presses the long hunting knife to his face, the blade slicing off a few of the perfect hairs of the man's goatee.

"Think carefully about what you want to say to me right now because anything besides, 'Yes, Heavy,' is going to get you gutted like a fish."

Apollo cut his eyes in my direction, but I just look away. He may not realize it, but I'm just as stuck in this situation as he is right now. No matter what I do, there's nothing I can say that will get me out of doing what Marcus wants me to do.

"Now, Apollo, tell me what you were going to say about my son taking over as VP. You think that's a good idea, don't you?"

"Yeah, Heavy."

"Good, man. *That's* what I want to hear. Now, let me help you out a bit with that." Marcus pulls the knife down from Apollo's face. He grabs the edge of the vice president's patch and begins to cut the thread that keeps it attached to the leather. Every second he saws at that small patch, I can feel the rest of the club members trying to figure out ways to kick my ass. I disrupted the natural order of shit by showing up, and I'm sure none of them are going to let me live it down. Finally, when the patch is detached, Marcus walks over to me and slaps the small piece of cloth into my hand.

"Welcome, son. Our new VP." He claps me once on the back, but no one laughs or congratulates me along with him. No one wants this—not even me.

"What of Apollo? He just gets kicked to the bottom of the totem pole?" A man with a tag that says "Creeper" speaks up.

"Nah, brother, you know I wouldn't do something like that to him." Marcus digs into his pocket, takes out his wallet, and pulls out a folded-up patch. He tosses it to Apollo, who looks at it but doesn't say a word. I hope he didn't make him a prospect or something like that, because from what I can remember, that's the worst of all. "Now, Apollo, Exit, Grizzly, take your new VP up to his space. Make him feel like he's at home." Marcus turns and looks at me. "Darius, don't worry about anything tonight. I'll get you all set up tomorrow. You still ride, don't you?"

"This motherfucker can't even ride? What the fuck?"

"I don't have my bike anymore. I sold it."

"That's all right. We'll get you a new one. Get some shut-eye. Dismissed." Marcus turns his back on everyone here, and part of me is surprised he'd do some shit like that. With all the blood he just spilled, I would think one of the club members would be out to get him, but there is no fear in that man's heart. There's nothing but entitlement and evilness.

Everyone files out, and I follow behind, suddenly aware I'm pretty much locked in with a bunch of killing motherfuckers who don't like me.

"It's this way," Grizzly says.

I check my surroundings before I follow him. The last thing that I need is for anyone to be behind me with a weapon. I make my way to the far side of the clubhouse and behind a door is a staircase. It's a small fit, as if it were built here as an afterthought. Before the door behind me can slam shut, both Exit and Apollo line up behind me. Neither of them says a word. They just follow the orders of their president.

I follow Grizzly up the stairs, where there is a row of doors apartment style. He stops in front of the second door on the left, pushes it open, and I can instantly smell the musty odor as if no one had used this room in years. "This will be where you live."

I step inside and look around. This shit looks like a full-fledged apartment. Sure, it's small, and it's only one open space, but the house I stayed in as a child was smaller than this shit. The day after my father caught up with me at the motel, the detective had the no-enter order for my condo evoked, but the second I stepped a foot inside, I knew I couldn't stay there. Even from the door, all I could hear was Lisbeth and Tia screaming for me. I stayed in the small hallway by the main door for an hour before knowing I would never live there again.

"Damn, this is nice," I say under my breath. I don't want them to realize how much of a godsend this really is, even if it isn't under the best conditions.

"What the fuck ever." Grizzly walks by, bumping me on the way to the wall. "You can press this here to look over the main area. It's a two-way mirror. You can see down, but they can't see in here." He presses a button on the wall, and sure enough, the opaque windows quickly turn transparent. "If you need anything else, speak with one of the prospects, and they'll get it for you."

"Who are the prospects?"

"Figure it the fuck out yourself," the one behind me says.

I may be outnumbered, but I'm not used to people just talking to me any type of way. "What the fuck you think I'm trying to do? Why the fuck do you think I asked?" I snap right back.

"Motherfucker, you think someone here is going to fucking *help* you?" Apollo pushes his way to where I'm standing, his hands balled into tight fists. "This is *our* motherfucking family, and you think because your daddy is the leader of all of this shit, it means we will just take you in as one of us? Nah, man, that's not how this shit goes down. Not now, not ever. You want to be part of this world, then you need to bleed like the rest of us have. Until then, don't expect shit from any of us. In fact, I have it on good authority that you won't make it a week as a Sinner."

Now, it's my turn to step into his face. "Are you threatening me? Because if that's the case, then we don't need to wait for the week. We can handle this shit right the fuck now."

Apollo has the nerve to step back and laugh. "You are as dumb as you look. If I took you the fuck out now, your pops would know I killed his little boy. I'm not stupid enough to do some shit like that. No, what I'm going to do is let your demons and the motherfuckers who are after you do it for me. What you don't fucking understand is this isn't like a fucking gang you can just jump into. If you don't have any family here, you got no shot at survival. Don't know one motherfucking Sinner who is going to step between you and a bullet. VP or no VP, you on your own here. Hope you enjoy your fucking stay." Apollo turns and walks out. The other two who are supposed to be helping me get adjusted follow behind him like puppy dogs.

If my survival or the chances of finding Tia involves these men helping me, I am as good as fucked.

Chapter 9

Three days have passed since my father pretty much signed my death warrant by forcing me to take on the VP patch. By the next day, I'm thrown into the thick of shit, having to decide whether a rival gang of ours is really trying to step in on our territory. Not only do I not know who the fuck our rival gang is, but also, I have no idea what territory is ours and what isn't. I am so out of my league. I have to defer to my father or Apollo for most shit. I feel like a fucking phony, not to mention a fucking laughingstock among the rest of the club.

They were right to say that I don't belong with them. When I'm not doing my best to figure out what the fuck they're talking about in the club, I'm out on my own again looking for my kid. When I'm not doing that, I'm back in the clubhouse drinking myself stupid. I went back to the motel, picked up the urn the detective gave me with Lisbeth's ashes and the one photo I have of Tia to put in my room. It's all I have left of them that's not tainted with the memory of what happened that night. The only ones in the place that I can talk to.

The bottle of Hennessey I'm nursing is empty, but I'm far from drunk. When I look out the window to the main area, I see that Marcus has just come in. Two young girls are on his arm. They seem more like his kids than someone he should be entertaining.

I make my way out of my room and down to the main area. The music is blaring just as it does every day.

"Oh, Darius, come here. I was looking for you earlier. I got something for you." Marcus pushes the two women away as he makes his way in my direction.

"You have a lead on where Tia is?" I ask, my voice slurring heavily. I guess I must be drunker than I realize.

"Nah, soon, though, I promise." Marcus puts a hand on my shoulder and pushes me toward the back entrance of the club with a large smile on his face like he's so proud of whatever it is he's done. I let him lead me to the back of the building. A few of the club members are out there as well. "Check this shit out. This is the same one I bought for you years ago, just a different color. I know you liked that one before. Now, you have no excuse not to ride out with us." He presses a set of keys into my hand.

Maybe it's the drink, or the fact that this man who has never done anything for me in all my life is acting like him buying me another bike is like him giving me the pony I always fucking wanted. *What the fuck does a bike have to do with finding my daughter?*

"I don't fucking want a motorcycle. I want my daughter. What about this don't you understand?" I try to give him back the keys, but he pushes them back into my chest, hard.

"Don't be so fucking dramatic. I told you we're going to find your damn kid. Be fucking appreciative for once in your goddamn life." He pushes by me, making his way back into the clubhouse, and the rest of the guys outside are laughing at me.

"Aww, did Daddy make you cry?" Trim mimes a crying baby, and the rest of the guys step in my way as I try to enter the clubhouse.

"It's a fucking shame he would waste his money on a beauty like this for you. You don't know what the fuck to do with a monster like that. It's a fucking waste." Apollo leans against the door, and a woman rubbing on him has the nerve to laugh along with him.

I'm tired of them getting on my ass. I'm nothing to them but a fucking joke. I walk into the clubhouse, grab another bottle of Hennessey, and go straight up to my space. I don't fucking belong here. It feels like a fucking school yard all over again, and I'm the new fucking punching bag.

"Daddy, Daddy."

"Tia!"

I wake up with sweat pouring down my face and my head pounding from me grinding my teeth. I look around the dark room and take a few moments to figure out that I'm not back at home. I lean to the side and look down at the empty bottle of Hennessey. I can't sleep like this. I stumble out of bed and make my way downstairs.

Of course, there is a group of people down there. It's like these motherfuckers don't fucking sleep. I walk around most of them, not wanting to piss them off in any way. It feels like being in a fucking jail in this place. Like if I say the wrong fucking thing, I need to be on the lookout for one of them coming at me with a fucking shank.

I walk over to the bar and reach for a bottle of Hennessey, but in its usual place is a big empty space. That shit is impossible. When I got one yesterday, there were at least three bottles left. There's no way unless there's a party that someone can go through three of those bottles.

"You look a little thirsty."

I turn my head to see who's speaking. Exit, the club road captain, leans against the other side of the bar with a full bottle of Hennessey pressed to his lips.

I swallow back my disgust. How fucking old are we to be doing shit like this? I'm doing my best to make sure I don't mess with anyone here, but they keep fucking testing me. They keep pushing me to do some shit I don't want to do, pushing me to go off on them. "Are there any more bottles in the back?" I ask him.

"What the fuck does he look like? Your fucking waitress? Get off your sloppy ass and check for yourself," Apollo spits out from where he is, another bottle of the mind-numbing liquid in his hands.

I let out a sigh. "Fine. Where can I find the rest of our supplies?"

"Figure it out yourself, VP. I'm sure you can do something as simple as that. I mean, you're supposed to be our fucking leader, are you not?" Apollo speaks again, jabbing at me with his words.

"Whatever. I don't have time to play these fucking games with you motherfuckers. I'll have something else to drink." I reach over and pull up a bottle of Jack Daniels. Gambit quickly walks by and pulls it out of my hand. "Sorry, VP, this one here is mine. Maybe you need to go back there and fetch another."

I look down at my hand. This motherfucker just played me in front of everyone standing here. All of them laugh like they realize it. I didn't come here to fight any of them. I didn't come here to lead them or take anyone's fucking position. I came here to beg for help from Satan. This is the price I have to pay to get it. They just can't understand that I don't want this position as much as they don't want me to have this position. I am more than happy never walking into this building ever again.

I open my mouth to say something but decide against it. There are too many of these motherfuckers for me to be arguing with right now, and even with just looking at Gambit, my vision is swaying back and forth. "Whatever," I say under my breath and turn to go back to my space. I would wait until they leave, or I can find a different way around.

"That's exactly what I thought. Go hide in your room, pussy," Creeper barks out from behind me, and the rest of the crowd starts to laugh.

My hands ball into fists, and it takes everything in me not to turn around and just charge the motherfucker. I know that I don't belong here with all the fucking criminals and killers, but I'm a fucking man, and my pride can take only so much of this shit. I look to my left and see that Apollo is walking by me with a huge smirk on his face. Just as I'm about to pass him, the immature fuck sticks his foot out, and I go flying to the floor. I try to stop myself, but I'm so fucking drunk I have no hope of staying upright.

"Oh, poor baby. Let me help you up."

I don't see him, but I feel it as he pulls back his foot and kicks me square in the fucking ribs. The air explodes out of my mouth, and the memories of being pressed up against the wall and the group of motherfuckers stomping me out flash to the front of my mind.

Anger like I've never felt before flushes through my body, and I push myself up to my feet. In that same instance, I rush Apollo. A clear look of surprise registers on his smug face as I wrap my arms around his midsection and power drive him into the floor. A loud thud sounds as the hard wood and his solid body make contact. Now, it's *his* turn to have his breath forced out of his body.

I hear a round of "Oh shit" behind me. Clearly, no one thought I would be the one to fight back. Apparently, no one told them the story about the frightened animal in the corner. I know I'm outnumbered, and I know I'm probably not stronger than Apollo, but I also know that these backward bastards truly believe that my father is the end all be all, so I know none of them will think of killing me.

Apollo tries to flip me over and swings his fist twice into my side in the process. My body recognizes the pain, but it does nothing to stop me from my goal. I can see nothing but the fuckers who stole my little girl. I do my own damage this time around. I pull my hand back and punch Apollo with all my force over and over in his face. He puts his hands up to block some of my attacks, but when I no longer feel the softness of his face, I lean back and drive my forearm into his chest. He gags hard and drops his hands from his face—my shot to hit him again. I feel people pulling on my arms, trying to wrench me off him, but I lock one of my free hands onto his shirt. I briefly catch a glimpse of Apollo's eyes as I pull my hand back to swing on him again. Fear is plastered on his features.

Since I've been here, I've kept to myself, and they all know I don't want to be part of this club, and that has made them think that I am nothing more than a pussy. . . . Someone who would sit back and just let anyone do whatever the fuck they want to me. But I have my father's blood in my veins. I may never have killed before, but that was always at my own choosing. The same crazy they feared my father for having is the same crazy that flows through me.

I see something silver glinting from Apollo's waist, and I reach down for it.

"Darius, get the fuck off." I can finally hear the rest of the club trying to get me off Apollo, but when I rise with Apollo's gun firmly in my hand, they all drop back. I press the gun hard against Apollo's forehead, and even he knows not to move.

"Darius, you better fucking—" Apollo starts to order me to do something, but I'm done taking shit from this man. I pull my hand back and hit him upside his head with the butt of his own gun.

"I better do shit. I'm going to say this shit one fucking time, so make sure you listen good. You may not fucking like this shit. I don't like it either, but I'm the new VP of this fucking club. I let you play your little game for as long as I'm going to allow it. Either you respect the fucking patch, or you can get your head blown off. *That's* your choice."

I remove the gun from Apollo's head and point it in the direction of those who have crowded around us. "The same goes for every one of you. I've lost too fucking much. I'm not afraid to die. If you're feeling extra brave and want to test me again, I dare you to try your hand. Anyone got something to add?" I scan the crowd. No one moves. I see anger on every face—fear on a couple of them, and lastly, confusion on very few. I'm pretty sure none of them were expecting me to do something like this.

Then I see movement out of the corner of my eye near my father's room, and I catch sight of him leaning up against his door with the biggest fucking smile I've ever seen on his face. Like I'd just scored the game-winning goal. Marcus being proud of me digs into me like a thorn. I hate it. I don't want him to be proud of me—ever. For him to be proud of me means I did something so fucked up that he's happy about it.

I shake off my anger and look down at Apollo, who is still on the ground bleeding from his nose and head. I drop the gun to my side, put my free hand out, and offer it to him. I'd be pissed if I were in his place too if I had worked all my life to get to a level of status, only to have it ripped away from me because I didn't have the right last name. It's a fucked-up situation. He takes my hand, and I pull him up.

I stare at him for a second, trying to measure if that disrespect is still lingering just beneath the surface. I don't see acceptance, but he doesn't seem to be as smug as he once was. I flip the gun, so the grip is facing him and wait for him to take it. He does without so much as a peep. Then I make my way through the crowd, stopping where Trim is standing with a full bottle of Hennessey. I put my hand out, and he places the bottle in my palm. I nod once and continue on my way. Then I make my way back up to my space and try to drink my demons away.

Chapter 10

A knock on the door jars me out of my sleep. It takes a few seconds for me to recognize that I'm in the clubhouse.

"Yeah?"

"Darius, it's Grizzly. I have something to show you."

I pull on a pair of lounge pants and stumble over to the door. My head hurts from the hangover I'm sporting to residual everyday pain from my jaw. "Hold up. I'm coming." I pull out a bottle of water from the mini-fridge and make my way to the door.

I open it up to see the large man standing in the doorway with a manila envelope in his hand. When he doesn't say a word, I stand back and motion him inside. "You can come in if you want."

"Thanks." He runs a hand through his hair before he turns back in my direction. "Look, I didn't even fucking think that maybe you were forced into this position. Most of us thought you came in here demanding to have it. That's on us for assuming. This club is our family, and it feels like an outsider just forced his way in. It's true that this club is your birthright. Heavy has always told us that he wanted to keep it in his family, so whatever position you choose to take up shouldn't be fucking questioned."

"I understand, truly I do." Part of me wants to let him know that my father demanded that I join and accept the role of VP. That if I go against Marcus in any way, they wouldn't help me find my daughter, but the last thing that I want right now is for that to be seen as me going against Marcus. "What you got in the folder?"

"Oh yeah. I was going over the information you dropped off a few days ago about what happened with your family. It's hard to get any real information, but the word on the street is the man who went in for murdering your wife is part of the Eleven-Quad gang."

"What the fuck is that? Another MC?" I ask, walking over to the small sitting table and taking a seat.

"Nah, they strictly bangers. Little dumb motherfuckers who like to work as hired guns. None of them loyal to anyone but the people with the biggest wallets. I just wanted to show you a few photos of some of their identifying marks. Maybe we can figure out which set took your little girl." Grizzly quickly opens the folder and spreads out a few different photos for me to see.

I stare at the amount of material he has here. This is more than the police have ever shown me in the two months they had so-called been working the case. I flip through some of the photos, most of them profile pictures of men I don't know. Nothing on them seems significant to me, but there's one photo that's close enough that I can see the side of his neck. The man in the photo has an entire arm and neck of tattoos, but there is one larger, clearer piece. It is the same one I saw on the knuckles of the man who raped Lisbeth. My eyes squeeze shut, and I will myself not to spiral out of control. I don't have a chance of making it through the day sober if I go down this rabbit hole.

"What is it? Do you see someone you know?" Grizzly angles the photos so that he can see the ones I'm looking at.

"Nah, I don't know him but that tattoo. I know that tattoo." I point to it, and his eyes squint for a second.

"Yeah, all of Eleven-Quad have that tattoo." He slams his hand down on the table in excitement, "Wait a minute. Where did you see the tattoo? Most of the crews only get the tattoo in a certain place. We might be able to find out which crew is responsible for fucking with you."

Why hadn't the police thought of that? No one ever told me that they could find out which crew was responsible by the tattoo placement. "It was on his knuckles."

"Ugh, motherfucking brawlers." Grizzly rolls his eyes and closes the folder on the desk.

"What? Is that wrong or something?"

"Nah, I guess I should have fucking figured it would be them. The fucking bane of our existence.

There are four separate crews with marks on their knuckles. Separate people run each crew, but they all work together like a governing board or some shit like that. So it'll be hard to find out which one of the brawlers was responsible, especially if we can't get in to talk to the bastard they locked up. We can work on it, though." Grizzly stands up from the chair and rubs his hand over his face. "You ready to get your hands a little dirty?"

"Whatever it fucking takes," I answer right away.

"We've been keeping tabs on a safe house where some of the brawlers of the Eleven-Quad crew work from. Mostly drugs and money coming in and out of the doors, but that doesn't mean they won't know something about your little girl. We can question them."

"You mean by questioning them, shoot them in the face until someone tells us something that we want to know?" I say what Grizzly really means.

"Yeah, Dare, that's what we do here. Like it or not, our business is killing. You want answers, and sometimes we gotta kill to get them."

I nod my head. I already knew it would come down to this. I just hoped it wouldn't happen so fast. "Dare?" I ask when I realize what he called me.

"Yeah, after last night. I'm sure no one here is going to dare mess with you." He chuckles heartily and walks out of my space in stitches over his joke.

I couldn't help but laugh right along with him. If I have to become Dare to fix this wrong, then so be it.

I take the bike my father gave me and ride out to one of the many malls down by Palm Beach. The kutte my father had made for me with my VP patch is displayed proudly on my chest. When I first put it on, it felt heavy. I must admit now that I've asserted some dominance in the club, I'm getting used to the feel of it.

"Aye, papi. Let me ride with you." A woman with a honey complexion, fake boobs, long blond braids, and wearing a bikini top blew a kiss at me as I pull my lid off my head and park my bike near the store. Her friend pulls her along as I train my eyes on them. What is it about bikes that make girls go crazy? I could be a fucking killer for all she knows.

I secure the bike and walk into the store. I always bring the bare minimum out of the condo, only going there from time to time to see if there are any leads on Tia and to collect my mail. I drove my small Honda to the clubhouse, but I will probably give it up to the scrap yard. Too many memories. Tia's car seat is still in the back, her cup still holding a little bit of whatever juice was last in it. I brought some clothes, the urn, a picture, and a few important documents like my passport and shit like that, but nothing else. Hell, I didn't even have my bank cards for most of the time that I've been at the clubhouse.

I walk into the small store and pick up a few pairs of sweats, a pack of black tees, and some toiletries. There's more than enough booze at the clubhouse, so I don't need to worry about that. I get to the register, and just like the woman outside, the woman at the counter seems to be fucking mesmerized by me.

"Is this all that you need?" she asks, her voice soft and breathy.

"Yeah, I'm straight."

"OK, if you need anything else, let me know." Her eyes run down my body, and when I lean forward near the register, her breath catches in her throat, and she wrongly scans one of the pairs of sweats I brought to the counter.

"Take your time. There's no rush," I say and am surprised to hear that my voice is low. I'm flirting with her. I've never been one to fight for a woman's attention, but I never paid anyone any mind since I've been with Lisbeth. It's different to find myself entertaining anyone who's not my wife. The thought's a hard slap right to the face. I back up and move away from the space while the woman finishes up what she needs to do to get me out of here. Moments later, I'm throwing some money down on the counter, grabbing the bag, and rushing out of the area.

"Would you look at what we have here?"

I whip around at the sound of the detective's voice behind me.

His face is set in a scowl as he glares at me.

"Detective," I say, trying to keep the surprise out of my voice. Has he been fucking following me?

"You know, for someone who swore up and down that he has nothing to do with his father and his gang, I find it a little amazing that you are now running around with a kutte on." He walks over to where I'm standing and fingers the VP patch on my chest. "And the vice president at that."

"Yeah, well, it's all about who you know," I smirk and take a step back from him. I'm not dumb enough to hit an officer, but I'm not going to let him stay in my space either. "Besides, I'm just taking you up on your advice anyway. Weren't you the one who told me that if I wanted to find my daughter, I needed to speak with my father? Well, I did. Happy to report that we are working just as hard as you, I'm assuming, to get Tia back."

The scowl on his face deepens, and he takes another step in my direction. "Mr. Heavy, I don't know what the fuck you are trying to prove by doing whatever the fuck you think you are doing, but I suggest that you leave this investigation up to the professionals. You want justice? You're not going to get it running behind Marcus Heavy."

"That's all I fucking want. Justice. I want justice for my wife and daughter, but you seem to be dragging your feet on it. I'm tired of being fucking patient. I like my punishment swift and absolute. If you don't want anything drastic to happen, then maybe you and the rest of the department need to hurry the fuck up and find my kid. I'm tired of being fucking patient. Tired of waiting for y'all to deem this case a fucking priority. It's *my* priority, and I'm going to do whatever the fuck I can to make sure that everyone else does too."

I take another step back. "Now, is there anything that you would like to add? Maybe an update on the case?" I put my best professional voice on and wait for him to say anything that would make me believe that he's taking me seriously.

"Make sure you stay out of trouble, Darius. I would hate to have to lock you away before we even have a chance to get your kid back."

I shake my head and walk away from the man. Doesn't he realize that threatening me now will do nothing? If I don't have Tia, I have nothing to live for.

It's a bit of a ride back to the clubhouse, but it gives me a chance to cool down.

The door opens right away, and my father is in my face before I have a chance to understand what is going on.

"Why the fuck did you not answer the fucking phone?"

"What?" I try to move by him, but instead of getting out of my way, he pushes my chest, making me fall into the wall.

"When I fucking call, you answer. I don't care if you're balls deep in the best pussy you've ever had in your life. Answer the fucking phone," he roars at me before he turns around and storms into the clubhouse.

I dig my phone out of my pocket and see that I have three missed calls from my father and two from numbers I don't know.

"Fuck."

"Yeah, that's a big thing. We need to be able to get in contact with you at all times. You never know what the fuck is going down here or somewhere else," Gambit says as I walk in the door. He must have been standing there waiting for me to come in.

"I didn't even realize that it was ringing. I rode down to the beach to do some shopping."

"You don't have a Bluetooth?"

"Nah, I've never needed it," I answered.

"Come on. Let's fix that shit right now." Apollo is over near one of the couches. How he hears what Gambit and I are talking about, I have no idea.

I follow behind Apollo as he walks over to a walk-in closet. Inside is a whole cache of small electronics. Chargers. Hard drives. Headsets. Everything someone would find at a small electronic store.

"What kind of phone do you have?" Apollo puts his hand out, and I show him my old iPhone. It's a 5, but it's done what I need it to do. I'm not one of those people that needs to get a new phone every time one drops.

"Bro, what the hell is this? You need to upgrade—seriously."

Bro? Did he call me bro? Last night, he was trying to kick my ass, and now, he's calling me bro?

"One day. It still works, and that's all that matters right now," I reply.

Apollo opens up a new Bluetooth headset and syncs it with my phone. He quickly shows me how to use it and then enters all the important numbers I need for the club.

"Thanks," I say when he hands it back to me.

"Yeah." He walks off, and I have to run to catch up with him. I feel like shit that I put a gun to his head. I know what the fuck that feels like, and I know I never want to feel that shit again. But if this is supposed to be a group of people that I will be spending most of my time with, I don't want them to think I would do some shit like that to them without a good cause. Last night was a good cause, but I can at least try to make nice with them now.

"Apollo, hold up for a minute."

He turns quickly in my direction. His jaws are clenched tight, but obedience is evident on his face. "VP?"

I should have known that it's the cause of his change of heart. He is finally starting to adhere to the rules. As his VP, there is a certain respect that comes along with the title. I only have to answer to one motherfucker in this club, and that's my father.

"Look, man, that shit that went down last night was fucked up. I'd do it again in a heartbeat, but I don't want it to be like that if we can help it. I promise I'm not here to mess up anything."

"Then leave," he spits out immediately, his true feelings inching out.

"Apollo, I can't do that. I hope that you can get past that. I'd hate for us to be going at each other's throats for the rest of our lives. As the SAA, I'm supposed to be able to depend on you, ain't that right?" I ask him. Marcus has already pretty much explained what each member of the club is around for. When he stripped Apollo of the vice president patch, he made him the sergeant at arms. He's the man who's supposed to make sure everyone abides by the rules. The bodyguard. If he is supposed to be the one I depend on, us fighting each other isn't going to work, and I'd never trust him. I don't want to suggest that someone else take his place, but I will certainly bring it up to my father if we can't get on the same page.

"Yeah, you can depend on me."

"Can I?" I look pointedly at his hands which are balled into fists, one of the only outward signs of his agitation.

"Yeah, man." He shakes his hands loose and stands up straighter.

"All right, so tell me what the problem is. Something must be going down if Marcus was trying to get in contact with me so badly."

"Yeah. We're about to run through a safe house of the Eleven-Quad boys. According to Grizzly, one of the brawler crew has been trying to set up shop in our territory, and he may have some information about your kid."

"Marcus wants to go because he thinks they have some information about Tia?" I ask in surprise.

"I can't call it, brother. I will say that he didn't really seem that hard up until Grizzly told him he'd already told you about the information. Part of me thinks your pops believes you are going to go out on your own and try to take down that entire gang."

I think about that option. It doesn't seem like it's such a bad idea.

"Do us all a favor." Apollo breaks through my daydream. "Don't run off and do something hasty on your own. You may not think that your father gives a shit about what happens to you. But I know for sure that if you get into some shit that you can't handle, it'll be all of us who will have to rush in and save your ass. I say that with all the fucking respect in the world."

I simply nod at him. I can promise him for now that I won't go up against an army on my own, but if I'm without my daughter for much longer, all bets are off.

Chapter 11

I am shitting bricks.

Marcus told me to stay with Gambit and Grizzly. They are supposed to watch my back as we raid the underground safe house of one faction of the Eleven-Quad gang. I have no idea what the fuck to expect, but the fact that they make sure I have at least three guns fully loaded on my person *and* a blade make me think that we aren't just going to go in there to parley with them. This is a kill mission.

"Dare, you good?" Grizzly said through the in-helmet earpiece that they'd set me up with.

"What the fuck is Dare?" someone else says out loud.

"Dare is the motherfucker who waved a gun in all of our faces and told us to jump." Grizzly chuckles through the line, and a few others join in.

"Yeah, I can get down with that shit," someone else replies.

"Dare, you straight?" Grizzly asks again, and this time, I nod.

"A'ight. This is what's about to go down. I know that there is a shipment of powder being delivered today. It should already be there, and they should be in the process of either cutting it or paying the distributor. If there is anything there that we can keep, take the shit. We do what we need to do, get in, and get out," Marcus says over the mic.

I don't want to show them how scared I am, but I'm sure that they would know if I were to speak right now.

"Park up here and make sure you have everything that you need," Trim directs and pulls into an abandoned lot about three blocks away from where we're supposed to be. I follow behind Grim, and Apollo is only a few steps behind me. It's already night. The area isn't very well lit, so we don't worry about anyone catching us. We rush into a tall, decrepit-looking building. The walls are still erect, but that is the best I can say about the structure. Vermin and what looks to be homeless people are in every corner.

"What the hell is this?" I whisper to Gambit, who is walking next to me.

"Decoy. The shit is downstairs."

I can't believe that there is anything of use downstairs, especially from the way the place smelled, but I follow behind and make sure to keep my eyes open for anything that might jump out at me—rat or human.

I take another deep breath and try to steady myself. It isn't that I'm scared to die. If today is my day to go, then fuck it. I just have to die. But something about wading into a gunfight where other people are depending on you to have their backs, where one shot would be enough to end someone else's life regardless of whether they deserved it, it's a ncrve-racking feeling.

The second that Marcus kicks in the door, complete fucking mayhem erupts. We aren't into the hidden drug den before the bullets fly.

"Motherfucker! Who the fuck are you?" a man with short dreads calls out as he dives behind a desk and starts firing shots in every direction.

Apollo grabs me by my kutte and pushes me behind a large metal container. A few bullets whiz in the air above me.

"What the fuck are you doing in our territory?" Marcus screams back but doesn't wait for an answer. Instead, he shoves a rolling table in the direction of the man hiding behind the desk. The man pops his head up for only the smallest of seconds before a shot from the side crashes into his skull.

I lean up and look in that direction to see Gambit sure and focused with his gun aimed at the man.

The rest of my club pushes farther into the space, but I'm still behind the metal container where Apollo left me. I hear guns firing and bodies falling to the ground. People are screaming, and product's being thrown. The one thing I don't hear is anyone asking about Tia. If they kill everyone, how can we find out who took her?

"Fuck." I do my best to focus as I force myself up from my hiding spot. Dead bodies lie everywhere, and flashes of a dead Lisbeth try to cloud my mind, but I can't think about that right now. I need to start getting answers, and this is the closest I've been to get them in months.

I hear a loud thump to my left and see Bill in a side room fighting with someone. He's on the ground, and it looks like he's lost his weapon because the other man is leaning over him with a blade inching closer and closer to Bill's chest. I pull my gun up and fire twice at the man. One shot hits him in the neck while the other drills him directly in the head.

Bill startles at the sudden death of the man who was just trying to kill him. "You good?" I call out to him, making sure to keep my head down and out of the line of any incoming fire. My brain's already looking for my next target. I thought it would have been hard for me to get over killing the first time, but it's freeing. These motherfuckers are standing in the way of me getting information about my kid. They have to go.

"Yeah, good looking out." Bill gets off the floor, but I don't wait for him to get himself together. I need to find out where everyone else is.

I rush over to the side and see Apollo popping two shots into another man's chest. There aren't as many people here as we thought. Apparently, there is a long-standing truce between the Heavy Sinners and the Eleven-Quad gang, but the fact that they spilled blood first by coming after my family meant they were free to be killed.

The bullets stop flying, and when I make it to the back room, I hear Marcus and Apollo giving the rest of the club directives about what to do with the drugs and money they found in the rooms.

"What the hell is this?"

"What the fuck does it look like, boy? They were dealing on our turf. They're dead now, so their shit belongs to us."

I shake my head in annoyance. "That's not what the hell I'm talking about. How the fuck are we supposed to question them about where my kid is if all of them are dead? You think maybe one of them left a fucking note?" My tone is harsh and bordering on insubordination. Everyone in the room stops what they are doing and now look between Marcus and me. It's a new dynamic. One they aren't used to.

I glance at our audience. I need to keep my cool. I need to make sure they all think that Marcus and I are on the same page. "Marcus, I was just expecting there to be someone here that I could get some answers from."

"Nah, all these motherfuckers are low level. Tweakers and wannabe gangsters. They wouldn't know anything besides where their next hit is coming from." He shrugs and goes back to gathering up the drugs in the room.

I let out a sigh and stand back. I don't feel like doing any of the cleanup. Then to the right of me, I hear a very soft sound, like someone's shuddering breath.

"What the fuck?" I whisper to myself and do my best to drown out any other sounds from the room so that I can focus on what I just heard. A second later, I hear a creak of metal.

"Has this room been checked completely?" I say loudly.

"What the fuck, bro? You're standing in the room, aren't you?" Exit says. "Of course, we cleared the room."

I hear another soft sound and pull my gun out. "I don't fucking think so." I slowly walk toward a large metal cabinet at the side of the room. It looks to be one of those lockers people store sports equipment. "Grizzly," I say out loud.

"I got your back," he replies, and I feel him moving behind me.

Quickly, I pull open the door, and some women start screaming and throwing things at us.

"What the fuck? Kill those bitches," Marcus screams out just as he ducks to get away from an incoming shoe.

Five of them dart out, all of them screaming and trying to get away. "Wait," I call out and am thankful that I don't hear any gunshots. "Hold them."

"Please, please, I'll do whatever you want. We were just here to get some blow. Don't kill me," a woman with short brown hair begs me as Trim holds her.

"You're not going to get any blow here today. You work for Eleven-Quad?"

"No, we don't work for them," another woman answers, this one shorter and thicker than the other. "This bitch, *she's* the one that works for them." She points to a short woman at the back of the crowd. She doesn't look like the typical junkie. Her copper skin is clear, and her light brown eyes are focused.

"You work for them?"

"I'm not telling you shit," she bites out.

"Bitch, you need some incentive? When I'm through with you, you'll wish you had something more to tell me." Creeper steps forward. Her eyes dart to him, but she doesn't balk. Instead, she pulls her shoulders back and lifts her chin. Strong.

"Nah, I'll take care of this one." I pull Creeper back and reach for the woman.

She rips her arm out of my grasp. "Don't you fucking touch me," she hisses.

"What? You need a hit or something?"

"No, asshole. I'm not tweaking out. I don't use. I just don't want your filthy hands on me."

I smirk and grab her. "Sweetheart, you're lucky it's only my hands on you; now, move your ass." I push her toward the front door.

"Looks like you got yourself a new pet," Marcus jokes as I make my way out of the back room. I don't respond to him. I have no idea what the fuck I'm going to be able to get out of her, but if she knows anything, I have to try.

The problem is, I feel like I'm about to go through a twelve-round bout before I get anything out of this woman.

Chapter 12

Dharia

"What the fuck is taking you so long, Dharia? Damn, bitch, I thought you was smart as fuck. I can count faster than you."

I bite the inside of my cheek to ignore him. Clip constantly screams at me about something or other. He thinks that I'm not worth my weight in shit. Fortunately for me, before I came on, the cash count has always been off. Since I started my sentence, I've never made a mistake. It would make sense that they would use me to make sure their money is straight. I mean, when I was an accountant, all I did was make sure that money was straight.

When I started working for this degree, I did it because I wanted a stable job that would pay my bills. Nothing extravagant. I never thought that I would be helping some of the worst fucking scum on earth make sure their books were balanced.

"We all can, daddy. Y'all need to just turn her out like the rest of us. I mean, I bet she'll make you all a good penny. I can show her the ropes." One of the women there to cut up the coke speaks up clearly, trying to get on Clip's good side.

"I should. I bet your pussy is tight as shit." He grabs the back of my head and pulls it back. I drop the stack of money in my hand and grab his arm.

"Get the fuck off me," I growl out.

"Why should I? Hmm? You think you better than me?" He leans down, his sour breath churning my stomach.

"If I get this count wrong and tell your boss that it was you who distracted me, who do you think is going to be the one he comes after? I'm sure it won't be me."

"Are you threatening me, bitch?"

"No, just telling you the truth. Let me do my job."

"Your job should be sucking my cock." He rubs himself on my thigh, and I cringe.

"It's not. You have all of these other women here for that. You're making me late," I reply through my clenched jaws.

He lets go of my head and pushes me back against the cash locker. There is a big metal closet at every one of the locations where all the product and cash go until it's time for me to check it. Clip is the only one with those keys, so if the count comes up wrong, both of us will end up dead. He knows better than to fuck with me when I'm in the middle of a count.

"Hurry the fuck up. I got shit to do," he says as he walks over to one of the women. He sticks his long pinky nail into the coke she's packing up and snorts it. He does it again, but this time offers it to her. She giggles and snorts it up herself.

I never understood the allure of drugs. Why take something that fucks with your skin, costs you more than you would ever make, and makes you act like a dumb ass, all at the same time. Yeah, just not worth it.

"What the fuck are you looking at, bitch?" the girl asks me, but as always, I ignore her. I pick up another pack of fifties and begin my count.

"Clip, something going on upstairs," Geo, one of the other members responsible for the drop, comes running into the room.

"What the fuck are you talking about?" Clip wipes his face and looks around.

"Octavia says she sees a group of men upstairs."

Clip rolls his eyes and goes back to what he was doing. "Of course, she sees a group of men upstairs. Everyone is always looking for a little pussy. Tell her to shut up and get those legs open. I want all that money." He laughs and sticks his pinky back into the coke for another bump.

The woman in front of him pouts when he doesn't offer her more.

How the fuck did I get here? Well, that's not a fair question. I know *exactly* how I got here, and I will stay here as long as it takes to make sure my brother is safe.

A loud crash startles me, followed by screams and bullets flying.

"Motherfucker, who the fuck are you?" I hear someone screaming from the front.

"I fucking told you. They trying to stick us up." Geo pulls his gun out, and I back away from the table. I want to run and scream like the other women in the room, but I know there is no way out. That shit isn't going to do nothing for me but make me a target.

Geo and Clip rush past us, not caring if the women in the room are safe or not. I grab one of the women running by and shove her in the metal closet. It's the only place to hide and big enough for the five of us.

"Come on, come here." I wave the other three girls over, and they all stuff themselves into the closet. I jump in and try to close the door. It doesn't lock. "Fuck. Nobody move," I order them.

The gunshots get louder. Finally, they're in the room with us. I have to cover one of the girls' mouths to keep her from screaming.

I hear Clip and Geo yelling and the sound of heavy feet rushing around the room. The cabinet has three slits where I can see out. I don't recognize any of the people in the room. When the bullets stop flying, all that's left are the guys wearing the kuttes that read *Heavy Sinners*.

I watch them stuffing the money in their bags. I'm going to die today. Either by their hand or by Breach's. It is my job to make sure the money's right. He doesn't care what the circumstances are. I am going to die, and so is my brother.

Another man walks into the room.

He immediately starts arguing with someone he calls Marcus. Apparently, he'd wanted to talk to someone. He couldn't since everyone is dead. Everyone but us, that is.

One of the girls to my left whimpers, and I turn my head to glare at her. She takes in a deep breath, but she doesn't make another sound. Then, right on cue, the girl to my right lets out a soft sneeze. She presses her hands to her face hard, but it's too late. The sound is loud enough to get attention.

"Has this room been checked completely?"

I look through the tiny slit in the door, and a man with cocoa-colored skin walks slowly toward the closet. His almond-shaped eyes are dark, filled with danger and something that looks like despair. If he weren't about to find me in here and kill me, he would be just my type of man. Fit, neat beard, and low fade. He has an angry-looking scar on the side of his face under his ear, but it does nothing to take away from his appeal. In fact, it only adds to it. Tall, dark, and sexy. Sexy and fucking dangerous.

He opens the door, and all the women start to scream. One of them takes her shoe off and throws it at him.

"Kill those bitches."

"No, wait." The man standing in front of me stops everyone from shooting.

Fuck, how the hell am I going to get out of this?

The rest of the girls all begin to beg for their lives, but I don't. There's no use. Either they're going to kill me, or they aren't. Letting them use and abuse me isn't going to get nothing but them to feel good, and then they'll kill me after. No. If it's my time to go, then so fucking be it. I only pray that Shaquan can protect himself.

"You work for Eleven-Quad?"

"No, we don't work for them," the girl that sneezed answers. "This bitch, *she's* the one that works for them." She points at me. So much for girl code. Fucking bitch.

"You work for them?"

"I'm not telling you shit," I say through my teeth. I can't. I don't know much.

"Bitch, you need some incentive? When I'm through with you, you'll wish you have something more to tell me." A tall man with dark skin takes a step toward me. He has scars running down his face. I can tell by how he's glaring down at me that he's used to intimidating people. That's the problem with going after people who have nothing to lose . . . hard to scare.

"Nah, I'll take care of this one." The man with the scar under his ear reaches out his hand to grab me. I pull my arm back out of his grasp.

"Don't you fucking touch me."

"What, you need a hit or something?" He squints at me. Of course, he would think I'm a junkie.

"No, asshole. I'm not tweaking out. I don't use. I just don't want your filthy hands on me."

The bastard had the nerve to smirk at me. "Sweetheart, you're lucky it's only my hands on you; now, move your ass."

"Looks like you got yourself a new pet."

Pet? Oh, he's going to figure out—and soon—that I'm no one's fucking pet.

Chapter 13

Dare

The rest of the boys decide the four remaining women would make good playmates instead of killing them. The women don't seem to mind. If the options are either die or entertain a bunch of rowdy bikers, I guess the latter is the lesser of two evils.

I have to ride with the woman on the bike that I pulled out of that closet. She fights me every fucking step of the way. I'm sure that if I put her on the back of my bike, she'd try to jump off.

I can hear the laughter coming through the headset from the rest of the club. Apparently, the drugs they picked up were quite a score, not to mention the stacks of cash there. Marcus is happier than a pig in shit that he could get the product before it was sold off. This would just add to the Heavy Sinners' bottom line. I don't care about any of that. The only thing I care about is the woman sitting in front of me on my bike and any information she might have for me.

When we pull into the clubhouse, I secure my bike and hop off. “Let’s go.”

“Fuck you. I’m not going anywhere.”

I am so tired of fighting with women. “What the fuck do you think you’re going to do? Sit here in the parking lot all day? You think you’re going to run away? Maybe you think your people are going to come for you? Let me tell you a secret. There’s absolutely *no way* you’ll get out of here alive. If you want to try your luck, then, by all means, have at it.” I step away from her and wait for her to make her choice.

Her eyes drill into mine for a second before she turns and looks around the compound. The heavy gate is closed and locked. Through the bars, the only landscape visible is endless fields of dirt or sugarcane. Even if she tries to run, she’d never make it far. Finally, she hops off the bike and storms in the direction of the clubhouse.

“Mmm, when you done with that one, send her to my room. I got something for her.” Creeper blows a kiss in her direction.

I roll my eyes and follow behind her. The other women that we’d pulled out from the closet are all hanging on someone from the club as if they’re so grateful to be there. I guess the promise of drugs and a good time can make anyone forget that they were just about to be killed.

"Creeper, make sure you and some of the prospects go back and get that placed cleaned up. I don't want to see this shit on the nine o'clock news," Marcus orders and then turns toward Bill. "Bill, get this shit in the safe and divvy up the cash." Finally, he looks in my direction. "Dare, good shit for not dying. Whatever you plan on doing with *that* one," he points over my shoulder, "make it known. Women tend to end up in different beds if there's no claim on her." Marcus walks off, following Bill to the back room with the saddlebags filled with drugs and money.

When I turn back around, I can see the woman is cringing and holding on to herself. She's fresh meat in a room full of animals.

"Let's go." I reach for her arm, and just like before, she rips it away. Part of me just wants to grab her and throw her over my shoulder. I don't have the patience that I need to keep fighting with her. She must have known that I'm close to being at my wits' end because she finally walks in the direction I was trying to get her to go without any more fuss.

I open the door that leads to the stairs that go up to the apartments, and she trudges up. I do my best not to focus on the swing of her ass, but it's right in my face. I wonder if she's an escort or something. I honestly don't believe that she's a druggie.

"Which one?" she asks when she gets to the hallway. Her voice bounces around the empty space. It's the softest I've heard from her since I met her.

"Second door on the left."

She nods and opens the door. I walk in behind her and close the door. I wait for her to move in farther, but she just stands in the corner by the door with her arms crossed over her chest.

"You going to sit down or what?"

"No. I don't want to sit down. I'm not a whore. I don't know what you want from me, but I don't fuck for money or whatever you're thinking."

I smirk and walk around her, "Fine. Suit yourself. If you want to stand there all day, then stand there. I don't need to pay for pussy, by the way."

She rolls her eyes and leans her weight into her hip. "Of course, you don't. You probably just take it."

I shake my head at her judgmental remark and get a bottle of water. I pick one up for her as well and walk it back over to her. I put it out for her to take. She does, but her eyes narrow at the gesture. "You don't know nothing about me. You're lucky it was me that grabbed you and not one of the others."

"Yeah, real fucking lucky." She takes a step around me and makes her way to the couch. "I don't know anything."

"I haven't even asked you a question yet."

"If you didn't bring me here to fuck, and you haven't killed me, then it means that you want something from me. I don't have anything for you." She opens the bottle of water and takes a swig.

"Well, I hope for your sake that's not true. I would hate for you to be of no use to me." I lean against the wall and stare at her, making sure she realizes that I'm serious.

A knock on the door cuts the tension in the room.

"Yeah?" I answer.

"Dare, Heavy needs us for a second," Apollo says through the door.

"On my way." I focus my attention back on her. "You're free to lie down or eat whatever I have in here, but I would advise you not to do anything stupid. I don't want to have to kill you."

She doesn't reply; just sits on the couch with her eyes locked on the floor. She could play badass all she wants, but behind the death glares and the attitude, I can see a slight twinge of fear. That's all I'll need to get what I want.

Chapter 14

"Oh yes, fuck me harder." The second I make my way down the stairs, I hear a woman screaming and flesh pounding against flesh.

"What the fuck?" I don't bother to look around the main area because, honestly, I have no interest in seeing anyone else fuck.

"We just had a big win. The boys want to let loose a bit. Especially since those sluts were more than willing to work off whatever debt they had with the Eleven-Quad gang with us, so most of the club will be having their fun with them." Apollo shrugs but doesn't stop walking.

"A win? You call killing all those people to not find out any information a big win?"

"I call any day that we don't end up in the fucking ground a big win."

He had me there. Life is way too fucking short to not appreciate being alive. "Y'all not concerned about those girls running around? I mean, they junkies, right?"

"Yeah, but that's why Trim and them have them in the Spank Room. They'll fuck them until those girls are all used up, give them a couple of grams of bitch, and send them on their way. None of them will snitch. They all know better."

This life is so much different than what I'm used to. I don't understand how anyone can be interested in anyone who would decimate their bodies so completely. Those women look one snort away from death. "To each their own, I guess. So what does Marcus want with us now?"

"The top members of the club get their share first. You before me," Apollo says, and even though his voice is still even, I see his shoulders tense up. This is going to be a problem for him for a long time.

I walk into church and see large stacks of money. My father fans his face with a large wad of bills and a Cheshire grin on his face. "Take your cut, Darius." He points to the first mountain of bills.

"What's my cut?" I don't know what the breakdown is to understand what I'm supposed to take.

"That pile there," Apollo says from behind me.

Pile? There had to be well over $20,000 here.

"What?"

"The spoils of being a Sinner. Bet this is better than any bonus you would have gotten at that shit job."

I lean over and grab the pile of cash, doing my best to put it into my pocket.

"Your club dues," Marcus barks at me.

"What? What are you talking about?"

Apollo reaches around and pulls out $4,000 from the stack of cash in my hand and puts it back on the table. "You need to pay your dues whenever we get cash in. It goes to the clubhouse to make sure shit runs the way it's supposed to."

It amazes me how smooth this clubhouse runs, especially for a bunch of degenerates and killers.

Marcus picks up the cash that Apollo drops on the table and puts it in the safe behind him. He doesn't say another word to me, but I still have more questions. "So, what did we learn?"

"Say what?"

"We went there to find out about Tia, so I'm assuming that we found out some information." Then I stand back and wait for him to tell me something.

"What? When did we say that?" Apollo asks.

"Apollo, step out." Marcus sits in his chair.

"Is there—" Apollo tries to speak, but Marcus bangs his hand on the table to cut him off.

"I said, get the fuck out," Marcus roars.

Apollo snaps his mouth shut and walks out of the room. The minute the door closes, Marcus trains his eyes back on me.

"Didn't we already go over this shit? No one needs to fucking know what you and I have discussed. I don't need anyone on my fucking crew thinking you are going against me."

I wave my hand in the air trying to get past the intimidation bullshit that he's trying to spew. "Look, what did you find out?"

"I didn't find out shit. There was nothing there for me to find out." He shrugs.

"Marcus, I didn't sign up just because I wanted to be a part of the fucking team. You said you would help me find Tia. I could have run through there and killed those motherfuckers on my own if that's all I wanted to do." My anger is on the rise. This feels like the fucking police department all over again. More fucking dead ends.

"What the fuck did you think was going to happen? We would walk in on the first group of motherfuckers, and your kid would just magically appear? This shit takes time. Let me do what I do best."

"I'm going to need you to speed up the process of what you do best because right now, all I see is you worrying about your fucking drugs and territory. That crap means shit to me."

"Darius, I'm going to give you this fucking warning one more time because you are my only fucking seed. Don't think you can come in here and start telling me how to run shit. You're a patched-in member now. There is no way out of this club for you besides death. Even if we never find your little girl, you're not getting out. I suggest you think about how pissed you want to get me and how that will affect both of our lives. Now, why don't you go upstairs and have fun with that fine piece of ass you got hiding in your room."

I want to retort, but I know he's right. I'm depending on him and his connections to help me get Tia. If he doesn't come through, I have no cards left to play. This is my last resort. "Just keep me fucking updated." I turn, but I don't leave. I'm starting to pick up on all the rules of the clubhouse. Once I'm in church, the president is the one who would have to dismiss me.

"Go on, Darius. We're having a party tonight. So I'm sure that pretty little thing will fit right in."

I'm not interested in any party or in extending an invitation to the woman stuck up in my room. I need information from her. I'm not here to show her a good time.

I open the door toward the main area of the clubhouse, and the loud scream of a woman assaults my ears.

What the fuck . . .

I rush out to see the woman that was supposed to be sitting in my room fighting off Exit and Mali as the rest of them look on, laughing.

"What in the fuck is this?" I run over to the area and pull Mali off her.

"Bro, what the hell?" Mali's eyes are glazed over as he tries to focus on me.

"What do you mean what the hell? What are you doing to her?" I look over to Exit, who lets her go, and she falls to the ground clutching at her legs.

"We having fun with her. She came down here looking for us," Exit replies.

"That's bullshit. I didn't come looking for nothing," the woman screams at Exit.

"Bitch, who the fuck are you talking to?" Exit pulls his hand back as if to smack her across the face.

"I fucking dare you to do it. Lay one fucking finger on her, and Bill is going to have more digits than you." I glare at him and wait for him to make his decision. I don't know jack shit about this woman, but I know she doesn't need to be beaten.

Exit puts his hand down and glances over at Apollo.

"Apollo can't do nothing to stop me, so I'm not sure why the fuck you looking at him. Get the fuck away from her."

"Dare, that's not how shit goes around here. No disrespect, but we all used to doing things a certain way. If she's not claimed, then she's fair game for everyone. Exit and Mali didn't do anything wrong besides acting like a dick," Gambit says from the side of me.

They told me before we got in the clubhouse to make it known what I was doing with her. "Fine, this one is off-limits."

"There's a party tonight. You might want to make sure she stays in your room," Apollo informs me before he walks away from the crowd.

Everyone backs away from her, and I put my hand out to help her up. She doesn't grab it.

"I don't have time for your bullshit. Let's go," I say through my clenched jaws.

Then she grabs my hand, and I heave her up. She lets go of me the second she's on her feet. She wraps her arms around her midsection and speed walks back to the stairwell up to the apartments.

I catch up to her and turn her around before we make it up the stairs. "What the hell were you down there trying to do? I already told you that you're not going to make it out of here. Did you think I was fucking lying?" I slam a hand against the wall by her head, but she doesn't flinch.

"What did you expect me to do? Just sit there and stare at the walls? I came out to see where the fuck I am. How the hell could I know that a bunch of savages would attack me?"

"You're in a fucking lions' den. What did you think would happen? They'd just let you walk around?"

"I thought they would be civil." Her hazel eyes lock on mine. Fire and anger blaze in those beautiful orbs. Her breaths are fast, and I can see her pulse pounding away in her neck.

"What's your name?"

“Dharia, and who are you?”

“Dare. You need to learn when to quit. All this fighting that you’re doing isn’t going to end well for you.”

“Quit? I don’t even know what the fuck that looks like.” She raises her chin and steps farther into my space. Her small frame tenses and waits for the next attack.

I’ve never been someone who looks for a particular type of woman. Tall, short, thin, thick . . . If you are beautiful, you are beautiful. But as I stand here staring at Dharia, I can see that I was wrong. I do have a type. Every woman that I have ever been attracted to all have that same fucking fire. That fire in her eyes is going to get me in trouble.

Chapter 15

"Take your ass back to the room and don't come out. I don't want to have to do this again." I back away from her so that she could go up the stairs. I need to put a bit of distance between us . . . need to make sure that my head is on straight before I question her. Besides, I have questions for someone else first.

I walk back downstairs and out into the main area. The prospects that were there and a few hang-arounds have already started getting the club ready for the party that is supposed to take place tonight. It's fucking amazing how quickly they can turn the space from a regular clubhouse into what looks like a damn strip club. I have no interest in helping, though. Instead, I look around the area and quickly spot the man that I'm searching for. At six foot seven and built like a fucking oak tree, it's almost impossible to miss him.

"Grizzly," I call out for him.

"VP?"

"Let me chat with you for a minute." I wave him over and wait for him to join me on the staircase.

"What's up, Dare?"

"Did my father give any directives to search for information on my daughter? Something I missed?" I wait for him to answer. I haven't been part of this club for very long, but Grizzly and Gambit were the only ones I would think of as associates.

"Yeah, he told us that he had reason to believe that they were behind what happened to you and your family. So he said that we were supposed to take them all out and take whatever they had. He said we were taking over any turf Eleven-Quad had as retribution for what they did to you."

I shake my head in disbelief. "What the fuck does that have to do with us finding Tia?"

"Honestly, I don't know. Maybe he's trying to draw them out? I can't call it." Grizzly shrugs his broad shoulders and waits for me to continue.

"All right, man, thanks for keeping it straight with me."

"You got it, Dare." He steps down, but before he opens the door to the main area, he turns to ask me a question. "I'm not trying to step out of line or anything like that, but that little spitfire you got in your room may be just what you need to help you out."

"Yeah, that's what I'm hoping. Maybe she knows something about who has—"

"Nah, man, that's not what I'm talking about. Granted, if someone took my kid, I would be doing the same shit as you, probably completely out of my mind by now. Dare, from what I know, you've been going hard since you left the hospital. You lost your wife and your kid. The only reprieve I ever see you take is when you are drowning at the bottom of a bottle of Hennessey. I'm not saying you should stop the search or give up or no shit like that, but maybe she could help take your mind off the shit that's going wrong in your life. You're going to go crazy if you don't find a way to release some of this fucking tension."

"I don't need to be jumping in bed with some random chick we found in a damn drug den. I just lost my wife." I dismiss the idea.

"Yeah, I don't know about the rest of the guys, but even I can see she's no druggy. Besides, your wife is gone." He throws his hands up in surrender when I take a step in his direction. "I mean no offense, but it's the truth. From what I've heard Heavy say, it didn't seem like the two of you were a match made in heaven or no shit like that. I get you want to keep her memory alive, but you are going to burn yourself out, and then you'll be no good to anyone, let alone your little girl like that."

I rub my hand down my face. The stubbornness in me just wants to say no, that he's wrong, but I know he's not. I'm back and forth between the fucking police department, trying to figure out how to navigate the fucking club, and drinking my liver into submission. I need to find a way to let go.

"That woman don't want to be anywhere near me. She's here solely for information. I don't think I'll be losing myself with her anytime soon."

"Well, there's a party tonight. We always have plenty of entertainment. I'm sure you can find someone that tickles your fancy." He slaps a hand on my shoulder before he turns and walks out the doorway.

I think about it for a second, and the same dull ache of guilt wraps around my chest. I don't know what the proper fucking time frame of mourning is when you're 23. Are a few months good enough? Even before she died, Lisbeth and I were on shaky grounds. I loved her, but I had long ago fallen out of love with her. I shake my head and walk up the stairs and into my apartment. I could fight against my baser needs another time.

"What do you want from me?" Dharia is sitting on the couch and speaks the second I walk into the door.

"I want to know everything you know about your employers."

She scoffs and leans back against the couch. "I don't have employers."

"That's strange because I could have sworn we just plucked you out of a drug house owned by Eleven-Quad."

"You did, but that doesn't mean I know anything about them." She sighs and runs her hand through her hair. "I can't tell you something I don't know."

"I think we both will be surprised at the shit you know with a little persuasion. Tell me, you need a hit or something? You look like you're fading."

Her head is pressed against the back of the couch, and her eyes are barely open.

"I already told you, I don't use. I don't know how many times I'm going to have to say it. I'm exhausted. I've been up for longer than twenty-four hours now." She tries to sit up but quickly falls back down.

I'm not going to get anything out of her right now, and my mind seems to be fixated on the party getting ready to start downstairs. I want to get a drink. I want to get out of these fucking clothes that still have droplets of blood on them. I just want to put today out of my head.

"You sleep there." I point at the couch that she's on. "I've already put my claim on you, so no one is going to come in here and mess with you."

"Your *claim?* I'm *no one's* property." Her eyes open wide at that.

"I didn't say you were. I just let them all know that you're not to be fucked with. For fuck's sake, stop making everything so damn hard." I blow out a breath before I continue. "There will be a party going on downstairs in a bit. I've only been around for one other, but from what I know, they can get pretty out of hand. I don't want you to come down, and someone does something to you. Just stay here."

She leans her head to the side like she's trying to understand what I'm telling her. "You don't want someone to do something to me? Why the fuck do you even care? You're the VP of this shit show. The second in command. Shouldn't you be telling your boys to come up here and run through me? Ain't that what all you people are about?"

"Dharia, you don't know the first thing about me."

A slight smile crosses her lips, and suddenly, all I can think about is what those lips would feel like wrapped around my cock. "No, I don't, but something tells me that before I'm out of here, you intend to show me." Her head falls back down against the couch.

I can't say that she's wrong. One way or another, she *is* going to find out about me.

I walk over to the area where my bed and dresser are, grab a towel and some clothes, and head for the bathroom. I quickly turn on the shower, strip out of everything I'm wearing, and jump into the spray of warm water. The events of the day flash through my mind, but I'm surprisingly at ease with all of it—except for the fact that it feels like my father is trying to pull the fucking wool over my eyes. I think back to what he'd said in church about me not going against him. I don't get why me looking for my kid would be something that he's against. It seems like I'm going to have to use his connections on my own. I can't trust him to give any help on his own.

I wonder what role Dharia plays in all this. If she isn't a druggy and doesn't work for Eleven-Quad, what the hell was she doing there? A quick flash of her face erupts in my mind. Then like a projected movie image after image of her rolls through my head, a deep pull at the base of my gut brings my attention back to the present. When I look down at my midsection, I realize my dick is as hard as a rock. I step farther into the water and let the stream pelt down on me. I do my best to ignore it and think of anything else, but every time I close my eyes, Dharia's angry, beautiful face pops into my head. I grab some of my body wash and squirt it in my palm. It's been awhile since I've taken care of myself, and I've had fantasies about other women besides my wife even when she was still alive. What makes this one so different? There's no reason for me to feel guilty about this. I wrap my hand around my cock and slowly begin to pump back and forth. Every stroke brings another image of Dharia.

"Fuck." I lean my head back, and the shower splashes hard against my chest and midsection. My hand moves faster as my fantasy morphs from just her face into replays of the way her breasts heave up and down when she's breathing hard. How her ass perfectly fills out the jeans she's wearing. Even the way her mouth moves when she says my name. "Goddammit," I growl as I stroke faster, and my cock gets harder as my body coils up, ready to explode. I'm going to come hard. I can feel the intensity building to an unbearable peak. I brace myself with my free hand on the shower wall as my balls contract up into my body and my thighs shake from the tension. Then I suck in a deep breath as small explosions from the top of my head down to the soles of my feet erupt. "Oh shit." I slam my hand down on the wall as pulse after pulse rocks through me. When I finally stop coming, I open my eyes, and everything seems a bit brighter suddenly. That was the best orgasm I've had in years. I thought this would be a normal fantasy, but this is more than a fucking fantasy. This shit feels like heaven.

Chapter 16

Within the twenty minutes that I was up in my small apartment, the clubhouse had already begun to fill with hang-arounds and women who were clamoring to party with Heavy and his boys. The music hasn't even been turned on yet, but the booze is flowing freely. I walk over to the bar and pull a bottle of Hennessey from underneath the bar top.

"That shit's going to kill you," Bill says as he drops a case of beer on the ground behind the bar.

"Yeah, and so will a bullet to the brain. At least this way makes me feel all warm and fuzzy on the inside." I turn away from him, but I can feel him staring at me. I look over my shoulder. "What?"

"I can't get a fucking read on you. All this time, you've had the chance to join your father, to reap the benefits of being a Heavy, but you never wanted it. And now, you're here acting like you were made for this life."

"What makes you think it's an act? I've tried the everyday, nine-to-five, good-boy routine that got me nowhere. So I figured I would give this lifestyle a try. Maybe my other lifestyle was the act, and this is who I'm meant to be all along." I shrug my shoulders.

"It seems like it. I've been around some hardened killers in my day, but I rarely see someone who can just switch off like you do. There was no hesitation. You pulled that trigger like you've been blowing motherfucking heads off your entire life."

"I have good reason to kill," I reply. My justification is solid in my head as I remind myself that this is all for Tia.

"Yeah, I heard about that. I guess that is as good a reason as any to become a murderer."

I bristle at the term. *I'm a fucking murderer?*

Yes, I am.

I release the breath that I'm holding as I come to grips with the fact that what Bill's saying is true. I am a murderer. Nothing will ever change that, and I'll never be able to take it back. I open the bottle I'm holding in my hand and take a long swig. Then I push away from the bar and watch as the hang-arounds assemble the horseshoe stage and stripper poles. I see Gambit coming from the stairs. He has changed what he was wearing. He now has on light grey jeans with a light blue checkered button-down shirt and is wearing a huge gold watch and long chain. The man is the epitome of a pretty boy.

"What's up, Dare? You ready to party?" He catches up to my stride.

I'm still trying to figure out the entire clubhouse, so I tend to follow people around just to see where they're going. Right now, I want to see where the hang-arounds are getting the stage from. I didn't think we had a large enough area in the clubhouse to hold it even in its broken-down state.

"I guess. I'd be lying if I said that I was looking forward to it, though someone recently told me that I need to loosen up a bit."

He chuckles at that. "I couldn't agree more. We already deal with a bunch of heavy shit. If that is all you're focused on, you're going to burn out and end up dead before you need to be."

"I hear that." I walk out the back door and watch where the men are going. There's a whole garage in the back that I hadn't noticed. It's a bit away from the main compound but still within walking distance. I was going to follow behind them, but I notice that Gambit doesn't take a step out with me.

"What's wrong?"

"You think I'm going to step out in the dirt with these shoes on?" He points down to a pair of fresh white Nikes. "Nah, I didn't get this pretty to walk around in the dirt."

"You fucking wuss."

"Yeah, I might be high maintenance, but I bet you I'll be the one getting all the pussy tonight. The ladies love a man that takes care of himself." He systematically pushes his sleeves up, his tattoos covering all the available space from his elbow to his wrist.

"I'm not looking for no pussy."

"Boy, please. We Sinners. We don't need to look for pussy. That shit just falls into our laps." He laughs and claps me on the back before he walks back into the clubhouse, leaving me standing at the back door watching the hang-arounds drag another piece of the stage in my direction.

It couldn't be that easy.

The music is blaring, and my head feels as if it weighs a million pounds. The pain in my jaws vibrates with every pump of the bass. Luckily, I have my bottle of Hennessey to keep me company.

"Daddy, you look like you need someone to help you tonight." A woman with bright pink lingerie saunters up to me and brazenly palms my dick through my pants.

"Only if you share." Another woman I can't see comes up behind me and wraps her hands around my midsection, letting her nails drag down my chest and over my abs.

I've heard people say you have to beat them off with a stick, but fuck . . . That's exactly what I felt like I had to do. Gambit was telling the absolute truth when he said that pussy just comes to us. Since the party started, I haven't been on my own, and the women see that I'm a patched member of the Heavy Sinners MC.

"Ladies, maybe some other time." I pull myself away from them and walk through the crowd, but before I can get far, another woman grabs my kutte and presses her ass to my pelvis. When she starts dancing and grinding with the beat, I follow along. She bends over and lets the music drive her motion. Her ass is big, and I have to stop myself from pulling my hand back and smacking it just to see how it'll jiggle.

Right as the song ends, I'm out of breath and now horny as fuck. I reach down and grab hold of her shoulders, lifting her, so her back is to my front. I wrap my hand lightly around her neck and move her head to the side so that I can kiss her there. When I look down, I see a dark red mark on her skin—a hickey. Someone has already been here, and I would guess it happened tonight from the darkness of the spot. Talk about a fucking turn-off.

I let go and, without any explanation, walk away. My eyes scan the crowd, and I see Grizzly hunched over, dancing with a small woman. When he picks her up and starts walking toward the Spank Room, I feel a bit sorry for the woman. She is all of five feet tall and a little more with those high heels she's wearing. Grizzly is a fucking behemoth of a man. I hope she knows what she's getting into. Grizzly catches me looking at him and winks at me as he speed walks to the back room.

I find an empty lounge chair in front of one of the strippers. Dollars fly from every direction at her, but she focuses solely on me the moment I sit down. She has dark hair with bangs, dark brown eyes, and the puffiest lips I have ever fucking seen outside of Megan Goode. She rolls her hips with the music and then climbs the pole that she's working and flips herself upside down in an amazing show of agility. Next, she slides down the pole, holding on with nothing but her legs. She holds her arms held out, and her eyes focus on me. When she makes it down to the floor, she rolls slightly in the cash before she pops up to her hands and knees. Now, she arches her back deep so that her ass is sticking up in the air.

I hold on to the chair and remind myself that I'm in public and can't just whip my dick out and start jerking off. This woman has sex appeal down.

As she makes her way to the end of the stage, she still focuses solely on me, and now, some of the men have diverted their attention to someone who isn't ignoring them. The stripper doesn't seem to mind. She sits up on her knees and lets her head fall back so that her long hair brushes against the curve of her ass. She palms her breasts through her purple bikini top before she slowly trails one of her fingers up her cleavage and into her mouth, sucking hard on the digit.

"Fuck this." I jump up from my chair and grab her off the stage. She laughs as she latches on to my neck. I wait for half a second for someone to tell me that I can't do that, but *I'm* the fucking VP. I can do whatever the fuck I want.

Several spank rooms are on the bottom level of the clubhouse. I open one only to see Trim's skinny ass railing into one of the women we picked up from the drug den earlier. I close it quickly, internally trying to erase the memory from my mind.

I quickly open the door to another room, and this one is free. I pull her into the room and close the door behind me. Then I push her up against the hardwood surface. My hands are on her body in an instant. Fuck, I need this.

"Easy, papi, I'm not going anywhere." Her voice is deep yet breathy like a fucking phone sexy operator. She licks her lips slowly before she presses those soft pillows against mine. I kiss her back, but it's not what I'm looking for. Not the release I need.

"What's your name?"

"Star."

I shake my head. I don't want to know her stage name. "What's your real name?"

"That's the only name you need to know, papi." She smirks in defiance.

Fine. If she doesn't want to tell me, I won't push it. Everyone has their secrets.

"You're Dare?" She runs a hand along the new patch on my kutte that displays my name.

"Yeah. What are you here for tonight? Just dancing?" I don't care what I'm involved with. I'm never going to force a woman to do anything sexually that they don't want to do with me.

"Fuck that shit. I need that dick." She pulls me back so that she can kiss me, but this time, she runs her hands over my dick at the same time. That shit feels so good.

I press harder into her palm.

I don't remember the last time someone touched me like this.

Lisbeth.

"Fuck." I rip my mouth from hers and try to do a mental purge of my deceased wife. Right now is not the time that I should be thinking about her.

"What's wrong? Did you finish? We can get you going again." She grabs for me once more.

"Get that ass on the bed."

She smiles brightly as she kicks off her shoes and rushes over to the barely made queen-size bed. The room has a generic bed frame, a small side table, a love seat, and a coatrack. Nothing else in the room and nothing else that I could want. I open the drawer hoping to find what I need, and sure enough, it's filled with lube, condoms, dental dams, and even fucking wet wipes. I don't know who stocked these rooms, but they thought of everything. I put my bottle of liquid courage on the small table and begin getting undressed. Star does the same. I dim the lights in the room and go to hang my kutte on the coatrack.

"I'm so fucking wet for you, papi," she says as my back is turned to her. When I turn back around, she is already out of her purple outfit, and her legs are splayed open for me to see her cunt. She's right. Even in the dim light, I can see how wet her fingers are as she pulls them back and forth out of her pussy. I take a second to admire the sight and focus on the small hoop that she has pierced through her clit. I wonder what the fuck that will feel like in my mouth. I'm not going to be eating her out, though. That's not what I'm here for. I'm here for the release.

"Keep finger fucking that pussy. That shit better be dripping by the time I get inside of you."

"Oh fuck, yes, papi." She moves her hand faster and uses her other hand to play with her nipple. I kick off my boots and pull my pants and underwear off. I'm aroused, but I'm not as hard as I thought I would be. Maybe that one thought of Lisbeth was enough to put a clamp on my libido.

I stroke my cock a few times before I open the condom and roll it down my length.

"Oh, big boy." She licks her lips and stares at my dick. I roll my eyes. I hate this porn star routine. I know I'm nothing to fucking laugh at, but it's like she has a fucking script.

"Shut up," I growl out to her as I make my way over to the bed and get into position over her. I drop my face down so that I can kiss her again. I suck on her lips and kiss down her jaw. Then I suck on her neck for a second before the nasty, unsavory taste of body spray coats my tongue. I want to spit it out, but I don't want to be a complete ass to her. I use my free hand to massage her breasts, and to my surprise, they feel real.

"Fuck me, papi. Mmm, you feel so good already." She pulls her nails down my arms. I look into her face for a second, and like a fucking scary movie, her features slightly transform to Lisbeth's. I close my eyes and reach down to my cock. I have nothing to feel guilty about. I'm a single, 23-year-old man—a widower. I'm not cheating or breaking any vows. I am living life.

I press myself into Star's slick folds, and the heat instantly sucks me in. Her walls are tight around my dick, and I let out a sigh at the feeling. I pick up a steady pace and watch her face as she rolls her hips so she can meet me thrust for thrust. She sucks her lips into her mouth and moans loudly as I pump into her.

"Oh fuck, this shit is so good," she whimpers, and I continue the motion. I move faster and wait for the ride to start for me. Her pussy feels good, but nothing more than a soft cloth rubbing against me. There's no fire, no intense need: nothing but the mechanics of it. Something is off. I reach down between us and flick that ring in her clit. She squeals, and her hands drop down to the bed. She grips the sheets, and I continue to play with that impressive piece of jewelry. When she comes on my cock, even the squeezing of her cunt and her screaming my name does nothing to get me any closer to my own climax.

"Fuck—what the fuck?" I close my eyes and try to focus, but nothing I think about helps. I don't remember ever having this problem before. Finally, I pull out of her abruptly, grab her by her legs, and flip her over. Then I smack her ass hard once. "Ass up."

She giggles and quickly pops up, so her ass is level with my dick. I push her back so that her chest and head are on the bed before I grab both of her hips and slam into her. I look down at the scene in front of me. I watch as my cock disappears into her slit, and her ass ripples with the force of my thrusts. She screams out at the new punishing pace I picked up. She bangs her hand down on the bed and digs her nails into the sheet to get some traction. I fuck her until it feels like my heart is about to pump out of my chest—but still no dice.

"Oh fuck, you going to make this pussy come again. Oh fuck." She moans, and just like she said, her pussy clamps down hard on my dick as she rides out another orgasm while I'm still desperate to find my first one. I fuck until I can feel my legs beginning to cramp up. What the fuck? I want to be fucking done with this shit already. When the hell has fucking become a chore?

I push her off my cock, and she lies on the bed, almost lifeless.

"Get up. I want to see my cock shoved into the back of your throat." She looks over her shoulder at me, and a slight smile crosses her lips. She's spent but still game.

I lie back on the bed and feel her crawling into position. She pulls the condom off and begins sucking me off. Just like before, it feels good but not mind-blowing. It's nothing like I'd felt earlier today.

A sharp zing of electricity shoots through my body, and I look down at what Star is doing. She's sloppy, spit running down the side of my dick, and her head bobs quickly up and down. I reach down and press her head down until I hear her gagging on my dick. I push farther since so much of my shaft is still out of her mouth. Feels good but not great. I let my head fall back against the pillow and resign myself to the fact that I'm going to come tonight. I should have just gone back upstairs and jerked off to Dharia again. That same spark pulses through me. I fucking love that feeling. I close my eyes and think back to the woman who is in my small apartment upstairs . . . her honey-colored eyes, that phat ass.

"Oh fuck." I reach out for Star's head and pump up into her mouth hard, vivid images of Dharia taking up all the space I have in my mind. Star gags harder and tries to push off. I let go for a second so she could breathe, but then I'm thrusting back into her mouth. My body tenses up hard, and I can finally feel myself getting ready to bust my load. "I'm coming. Fuck, I'm going to nut down your throat." I groan loudly as I fantasize about Dharia sucking my cock. Bright lights flash behind my eyelids as spurt after spurt of my cum splashes against the back of Star's throat. My eyes roll back slightly; it feels so fucking good.

Once I'm finished, Star pulls off my dick with a pop.

"Damn, I need more of that. Every day." She wipes my cum from the sides of her mouth and pulls herself up to lie next to me.

I'm so damn uncomfortable. "Nah, Star. I'm not here to cuddle. Get cleaned up." I reach over to the side table and pulled out the pack of wet wipes. I take a few for myself, then hand the pack to her. She doesn't say anything, but the smile on her face falters slightly. She nods once before she walks over to the corner and begins to wipe herself down. I grab the bottle of Hennessy from the table and take a swig. I clean myself off and toss the used wipes into the small trash can. I'm already pulling on my underwear and pants by the time Star turns around.

"You done for the night, or you have another set?" I ask her, wondering if she is about to start following me around like a little puppy dog. I don't want to entertain anyone today. Finally, I got what I wanted, what everyone thinks I so desperately need. Problem is, it only adds to the fucking issues I have rattling around in my head.

"I can dance whenever I want to. There are no set time frames. The longer I dance, the more money I make," she answers. "You really haven't been here very long, huh?" She pulls on her bikini top and ties it, followed by her bottoms.

I smirk at her. "Yeah, Star, you could say I'm a newbie."

"A newbie with a VP patch? That shit a lie? Or how did that happen?"

The jokes going back and forth between us stop at that very moment. "Don't question my patch or my place. Do it again, and I'll make sure you never fucking dance here again."

Her eyes open wide, and she tries to backtrack her statement. "No, papi, I wasn't questioning you. I just never seen anything like that happen before. I know who the boss is here." She walks over to where I am and tries to wrap her arms around me. By now, though, I'm completely through trying to play nice.

"Go on back out there. Someone else might want some of your time."

"Hmm, how do I get more of *your* time?" she asks with a whisper.

"You know where I'm at. I'm sure I'll see you around at other parties."

"You know it." She walks around me, and I watch her stroll to the door. "I'm going to be thinking about that beast between your legs all night." She shoots me a wink and walks out the door.

I look down at the "beast" between my legs after the first piece of new pussy we've gotten in years, and he's not happy with it. All I seem to want now is the headache I left sleeping on my couch.

After another hour of mingling and drinking at the party, I'm through. Star tries to get my attention a few more times, but finally, Mali takes her off my hands. I could see the disappointment on her face the second he grabbed her hand. She wanted more of me. It's flattering.

I walk up the stairs to my space, leaving the loud music and gyrating women downstairs to play with the rest of the club members. I've had my fill. I stumble slightly into the small hallway, my bottle of Hennessy more than three-quarters empty. When I open the door to my apartment, I don't see Dharia on the couch. "Motherfucker, where is she?" I hear myself slurring. I turn again, the motion causing me to stumble over my own feet.

I hear a door open and do my best to turn in that direction, but my brain is still trying to catch up from the previous turn I did. I stumble into the wall, and the bottle of liquor falls from my hand. "Dammit. I wanted that."

"You don't fucking need it."

I turn slowly so that I don't fall and bust my ass in the direction of the voice. Dharia is standing by the door to the bathroom.

"You're so sloppy." She shakes her head and takes a step toward me.

"What were you doing? Where did you go?" Logically, I know what people do in the bathroom, but I just feel the need for her to tell me what she was doing. Maybe she was trying to find a vent to crawl through.

I suddenly start to laugh at the thought of her crawling through a small ventilation shaft like a fucking *Mission Impossible* movie.

She squints her eyes at me, and the corner of her lip jumps slightly. "What the hell is so funny?"

"Nothing." I do my best to compose myself and try to push off the wall. My upper body is moving faster than my lower body, though. I end up pitching forward and falling to my knees. "Fuck," I moan out, and just as I'm about to give up and roll on my back to sleep on the floor, I feel small hands tugging underneath my arms.

"This is ridiculous. Why the hell would you drink this much, Dare? What the hell are you trying to prove?" She scolds me as she does her best to pick my almost-dead-weight off the ground.

"I got a lot to drink about."

"You and me both, but you don't see me stumbling around like a fucking idiot."

I focus my eyes on her. "Watch your mouth."

"Or what? Honestly, you need to know when to threaten, and right now, you wouldn't be able to do anything to me besides throw up on me. You're useless like this."

I don't say another word. She's right. Right about me being useless, right about me being a fucking idiot, and right about me needing to throw up.

I clench my jaws to keep myself from vomiting, but my mouth is already starting to water.

"Move," I warn her through clenched teeth.

"What?"

My stomach lurches up once. Then, quickly, I push her back and slap a hand to my mouth.

"Oh, wait, wait!" she yells at me and runs to the other side of the room and picks up a small wastebasket. She gets it under my mouth right before all the liquor I forced into my system comes out of my mouth.

I get down to my knees and take the bucket with me. I hurl over and over until it feels like I've vomited a few organs into the bucket. She doesn't hover over me, but once I'm finished, she hands me a bottle of water.

"Ridiculous," she mutters.

"No shit. Don't you think I know that this shit is ridiculous? I can learn my own fucking lessons without someone reminding me every goddamn second, Lisbeth," I yell at her.

Her eyes blink a few times, and I sigh out in defeat when I realize what I've done.

"Who's Lisbeth?"

"Don't worry about it. I'm going to sleep." I try to lift myself off the ground again, but I don't have the strength to do it just like the first time. Dharia comes over and helps me up to my feet. She doesn't say another word, just pushes me down on the bed. She pulls my boots off and tries to pick up my heavy legs to put onto the bed.

"Fuck. How much do you weigh? It's like moving a fucking tree." She complains under her breath, and I can't help but laugh. She's comical. She gets my leg halfway on the bed, and then it just falls back down. I should really help her. Any second. I'll help any second. I feel the bed move and see her crawl on the other side of me. She grabs my jeans and tugs. Finally, one of my legs is on the bed, and then she does the same motion with the other one. My body decides now is the right time to help. I roll fully onto the bed, trapping her under me.

"Oh fuck, Dare. Get the hell off me." She tries to push my weight off her, but I don't move.

"Shush," I grumble at her ear.

"Shush my ass. You weigh a ton."

I turn my head and feel her hair rubbing against my face, her heart pounding in her chest. I move off her slightly, I think, but I wrap my arm around her waist so she can't move.

"I already told you that I'm not a prostitute. I'm *not* doing this."

"Don't want nothing, can't do nothing. Just sleep."

She huffs out a deep breath, and I can feel her tense up, but she doesn't say another word. That brief lull of silence is more than I need. I'm asleep seconds later.

Chapter 17

My eyes feel like they are lined with sandpaper, and my mouth is so fucking dry, I might start a fire if I grind my teeth together. My head pounds with every breath. I have been drinking heavily since my life went to shit, but last night was extreme, even for me. I feel something soft under me and groan at the thought. Star must have found her way back into my bed. I lean up slightly, not wanting to wake her up if it is her, but instead of the long-haired stripper that I expected to see under me, I see Dharia lying on her side, a small pout on her mouth as she sleeps heavily.

"What the fuck?" I whisper and push myself up. What the hell did I do last night? How the fuck did she end up in my bed, and why am I holding her like she is the best thing since sliced bread?

I have yet even to question her, and somehow, I managed to get her underneath me. I look down and see that I'm still fully clothed. I even still have on my kutte. I try to think back on what happened last night, but I draw nothing but blanks every time I do.

A sour, pungent smell wafts up my nose as I inhale. I cup my hand against my face to stop the assaulting odor. "What the hell is that?" I move off the bed and try to find where the smell is coming from. I see a bucket half full of dark brown vomit. Mine, I have no doubt. I must have been really fucked-up last night.

I pick up the garbage pail and walk over to the bathroom and dump the disgusting body fluid into the toilet, then leave the bucket in the shower with some water in it. I look in the mirror and rub my hand down my face. I look as bad as I feel right now. I need to get something to take the edge off.

I find my boots at the side of the bed and tug them on, then grab my gun from the side table and slide it into my pants at the small of my back. I don't ever remember taking this off. If Dharia did it for me, she had every opportunity to kill me, yet she didn't. In fact, after the first few minutes of her being stuck in the apartment, she seemed to be quite comfortable here. I have to get rid of her quickly. The last thing I need right now is someone playing girlfriend.

I do my best to move as quietly as possible so that I don't wake her up. I know we didn't have sex last night. At least, I *think* we didn't have sex last night, but I was so fucked up that I'm sure she dealt with some shit she shouldn't have.

I hold on to the railing as I walk down the stairs to the main area. This has to be the worst fucking hangover of my life.

"Ah, he lives," Gambit says.

"Shut the fuck up," I mumble as I shuffle my feet toward the bar.

He just laughs and walks behind the bar to get me a beer.

"Seems like you had a good time last night."

"Yeah, better than I should have. I'm paying for that shit now."

"I would think so. You were tossing them back last night."

"I remember having a bottle," I say, trying to think about the last thing that I remember.

"A bottle? You had two."

"Fuck, how the hell am I still alive?" I should have died from fucking alcohol poisoning.

"I was about to go up to your place and make sure you were still breathing. I know I told you to live a little, but I didn't think you would take me *that* seriously." Gambit laughs at me as he pulls a beer out for himself.

"Yeah, I didn't think I would either."

"So, word around the club is Star is sweet on you."

I roll my eyes and shrug. "That's her problem."

"Oh shit." He lets his head fall back and laughs again. "Fucking savage. Yeah, we try to make sure that we keep the entertainment at arm's length, or all of them would be up in here trying to be our ol' ladies. The only one who's snatched up is Creeper."

"For real? I would have never thought. Where the hell is she? I've never seen her." In all the time I've been here, I've never even noticed a woman around here besides those who come to dance or serve.

"Yeah, you have. You grabbed her arm the first night you showed up. She's one of the bartenders."

Fuck, that couldn't have gone over well with Creeper. "Damn, thanks for letting me know."

"What's up with the sweet thing you got hiding in your room?"

"Dharia? She's still up there. I'm actually surprised she hasn't tried to make a run for it. She seems quite comfortable. I haven't even been able to ask her anything yet, though she keeps saying that she doesn't know anything. I'm going to find out for sure and then cut her loose. I got no use for her." My cock throbs once to remind me that there's at least *one* use for her.

Someone knocks at the door, and it feels like it echoes in my head. "Shit. Who the hell is that?" I look down at my phone to see it's only eight in the morning.

Wick, one of the club prospects, opens the door and talks to whoever is there. I turn my head away—the sun is too fucking bright.

When I turn back, Wick is patting down the man and pointing in the direction of one of the spank rooms. He must have left something last night. I keep an eye on him because he seems very tense even though he is moving in the right direction. I guess I would be tense too if I were walking in a club full of killers.

"Before you let her go, make sure you find out her full deal."

"Yeah." I'm barely paying attention to Gambit, though. Now my attention is focused on the man with the large grey hoodie. His eyes dart from side to side, like he's waiting for someone to jump out at him. Something is definitely off.

I get off the stool I'm sitting on and slowly walk in his direction, making sure I'm out of his line of sight. I want to see what he's going to do.

"Dare?" I hear Gambit call from behind me. I really should let someone know what's going on, but I don't fully understand what's going on right now. I could just be stuck in a drunken stupor, and he could just be a hang-around looking for something he left.

A pool table stands to the right of where he's going, and I lean against it feeling silly that I followed him around in the first place. The man walks right into one of the spank rooms and walks back out with a jacket hanging over his arm after a second.

Dread starts to creep up my spine when, instead of walking straight back out of the club like he should have, he turns in the wrong direction. His pace quickens slightly, and I see him rooting around for something inside his jacket.

Don't jump to conclusions, don't jump to conclusions, I chant in my mind over and over, but my hand goes to the gun at my back. The massive hangover that I had before is gone while my heart thunders away in my chest. My eyes look in the area that the stranger is walking toward. Nothing is over there besides Apollo talking to one of the strippers from last night. He's leaning against the wall, and she's enjoying the attention that he's giving her.

My eyes swing back to the man, and I watch him pull something long and shiny out of his jacket.

"Apollo," I scream out. It only takes a fraction of a second, but it feels like everything is happening in slow motion.

The man cuts his eyes at me, realizing that I know what he's going to do. Apollo stands straight and turns his head in my direction, a deep look of confusion on his face, and I pull my gun from behind my back. The man rushes Apollo, who is still oblivious to what's going on, with the large blade drawn and pointed directly at him. I pull the trigger three times. The first shot hits him in the leg, the second misses completely, and the third catches him right in the head.

It's dead silent as the large machete-like blade flies out of his hand and drops right at Apollo's feet with a heavy metal ring.

"Holy shit," Gambit calls out from where he's standing.

Within seconds, the entire clubhouse erupts in confusion. There are hang-arounds all over the place and a few strippers.

"Gambit, get everyone out of here. If they're not patched, get them the fuck out," I yell and rush over to Apollo. His eyes are enormous, and his jaw is slightly slack. He was seconds away from death. "You good?" I ask him. I didn't see the man with another weapon, but I have to make sure. He nods his head but doesn't speak.

"What the fuck is going on?" Grizzly comes bursting out of the stairwell that leads up to the apartments. "I thought I saw a fucking gunshot flash."

"You did." I kick over the man who had the nerve to try to take out Apollo just to make sure he's truly dead. A large chunk of his head is missing, but I've been shot in the head before, and I'm still walking around.

Once I verify that he's dead, I start looking in his pockets. I need to know who the fuck has the nerve to come here and try to take out one of us. I hear whimpering, and when I look up, the woman Apollo was just talking to is still pressed hard against the wall shaking in fear. “Apollo, take care of her.”

He quickly turns and pulls her away from where I am. There is nothing in the dead man’s pockets, but when I grab his hand, something gritty rubs off. I use his shirt to wipe off more of whatever is caked on his hands, and slowly, tattoos begin to show. It’s fucking makeup.

“Who is it? Do we know?” Grizzly asks me.

“Motherfuckers, it’s—” I stop talking as the sound of what I think are engines revving float through the air. I get up and race to the door. If he was with his crew, that could be them trying to make a run for it now.

I push Wick out of the way and look out the door. Sure enough, to the left in the sugarcane field is a large cloud of smoke.

“Fuck.” We can’t let them get away. I pull my head back into the clubhouse to see who’s around. “Apollo, Grizzly, Gambit, we on the move.”

Creeper slowly walks out of the stairwell, wiping the sleep out of his eyes. He has no idea what’s going on.

“Creeper, move your ass,” I call out to him.

His head pops up, and when he sees Gambit and Apollo running to me, he follows suit.

Grizzly reaches behind the bar and pulls out two guns as he makes his way over. I rush to my bike and start her up before anyone can even figure out what the fuck is going on. I hear four other bikes start up quickly right behind me. I peel off in the direction I saw the large cloud of dust. They are far ahead, but there is only one way for them to go. I push my bike to the limit as I try to catch up to the cars hightailing away from the compound. I get close enough to read the license plate when someone in the car leans out the window and fires a shot. A high-pitch whistle rushes past my head.

I duck down to get out of the line of fire and pull my own gun out. I shoot twice but don't hit anything. Grizzly races up to the side of me and gets closer to the car. He pulls out the shotgun he keeps behind the bar. He shoots once directly at the back wheel of the speeding car before he brakes and falls back to where we all are. The car fishtails from side to side on the small dirt road before it finally pitches far to the right and begins flipping side over side through the sugarcane field. Finally, the car slams to a stop, and a giant ball of fire erupts from it.

"Shit." We slowed down when the car flipped, and the other vehicles were able to get away. I hop off my bike and race to the crash site, hopeful that maybe someone is still alive. The rest of the guys follow right behind me.

"We got a live one," Gambit says as we walk up on the scene. One man who looks to have crawled out of the window of the car is still breathing, but he's bloody and badly burned.

"Grab him," I say, and Creeper and Apollo jump right into action.

They pull him away a safe distance from the burning car. I look over at Grizzly. "What has to happen to get that shit under control? I don't want this whole crop to burn down."

Grizzly has his phone to his ear. "Already on it."

I go back to the man that Apollo and Creeper had pulled from the crash site. "You stupid fuck, did you think we wouldn't catch you? Did you think you could come into our clubhouse and fuck shit up and just walk out?"

"Let me fucking kill him." Apollo stares down at the man, his gun pointed at the man's head. I put my hand out to stop him. Not yet.

"You traitor. Dumb cocksuckers," the man wheezes out. "You went back on your word."

"What the fuck are you talking about? You were the ones to spill the first blood." I got as close as I could. "It was your gang that killed my woman and took my kid." I grab him by his shirt and lift him slightly off the ground by his collar. "Where the fuck is my kid?"

He closes his eyes without saying a word, but I jerk him once to get him to wake up. "Hey, asshole, where the fuck did you put Tia?" I scream out at him.

"You'll never find her . . . your leash . . . dumb mother—" His words cut off midsentence, and I shake him again.

"What the fuck are you talking about?" I keep fucking shaking him, but he doesn't speak.

Gambit comes up behind me and pulls my hands off the man. "He's gone already, brother. It's over."

They were fucking playing with me. Tia is still alive, and every time I come close to an answer, another door slams shut, and I get nothing. "Fuck, fuck!" I grab my head and scream at the top of my lungs. After a second, I gather my wits. I need to get back to the clubhouse and make sure shit is still good there. They could have circled back. "One of you fucking make sure this shit gets cleaned up." I jump on my bike without waiting for anyone to acknowledge my order.

I ride back to the clubhouse with more questions than I've ever had. *He called us traitors. How is that possible, and what does that have to do with them keeping Tia?*

Chapter 18

The second I step into the clubhouse doors, my father walks over to me. "What the fuck is this shit?"

"What you mean what the fuck is this? What does it look like? It's a dead man on the fucking floor."

"I know what he is, but who the fuck told you to kill him? We don't just go around shooting people in the club. This shit wasn't your place." He glares at me, trying to intimidate me.

"Not my place? So you're saying I should have just let your SAA die? That I should watch some-one gut Apollo like a fucking pig just because you don't want guns going off in the clubhouse?"

"He was going to kill Apollo?" His eyebrows scrunch in, and he takes a step back. Either he's genuinely concerned for Apollo, or he's confused.

"You know something about this?" I ask him.

"No. I was knocked out, and when I came out, I find a dead man in the middle of the fucking floor. What the hell was going on outside?"

"His little friends from Eleven-Quad must have been waiting on him. We chased them as far as we could down the road, but one of the cars swerved off and exploded in the sugarcane field." I take my time to explain as I walk over to the bar. I'm going to need another beer if I'm going to get through this day.

"What the shit? You just got a car burning in the field?"

"Old man, chill the fuck out. Apollo and Grizzly are out there handling that along with the bodies."

"And did you find out anything?" Marcus asks from behind me.

"Yeah, the one man that managed to stay alive long enough to speak to us told us that we were traitors. Not sure why he would say that, though. Do you know anything about that?" I pick up the beer and press the cool bottle to my lips.

"Why the fuck would I know anything about that? I don't have anything to do with the Eleven-Quad gang. They're probably referring to the bitch you have in your room."

I haven't even thought about that. We did pick her up from their drug den. Fuck, that's exactly what they were talking about. They were here to get her.

"Son of a bitch, you're right." I slam the bottle down on the counter. "You need me down here for this?" I point behind me at the dead body on the floor.

"Nah, I'll get one of the prospects to clean this shit up. Let me know if you have to kill her. They'll handle her too."

"If she has to die, I'll do it myself." I walk toward the stairs and up to my apartment to find out what kind of traitor we're dealing with.

I open the door and find her sitting in the small chair, looking at the TV. She is acting like this is her fucking home. I should have known that something was up when she didn't try to run away. Why the fuck is she just sitting here waiting for whatever I'm going to do to her?

"Is something going on downstairs?" she asks as I close and lock the door behind me.

"Yeah, something is going on downstairs. A few of your friends showed up and tried to act a fool. It's OK, though. We handled that for you." I pull the gun from the back of my jeans. "Dharia, do you think I'm a fucking idiot?"

"What the hell are you talking about? Why the fuck would I think that? I don't know shit about you."

"You're right. You don't know anything about me, but what you should know is you're in fucking hostile territory. Playing games with me isn't something that you should be doing right now." I saunter closer to where she is, making sure to keep eye contact with her the entire way.

She cringes back into the cushion slightly, but she never looks away.

When I get to where she is, I lean over her, one hand on the right side of her body while the other hand holds the gun, ready to shoot if she so much as breathes wrong. "Dharia, are you communicating with your boss or something like that? Is that how they knew you were still here?"

"What the fuck are you talking about? How the hell could I have talked to anyone? You've had me stuck up here for the past two days. The only people that I've had the chance to talk to are the people in this club."

"Yeah? So, why the fuck would a whole fucking crew of the Eleven-Quad gang show up at our doorstep? Why would one of them suddenly get the balls to try to kill one of our members under our own roof? Whatever you are to them must be important. So now, I want you to fucking tell me everything you know about your bosses, and if you do a good enough job, maybe I won't throw you out for the rest of the club and the hang-arounds to use." I raise the gun, so it's near her head, but I don't touch her with it.

She chuckles slightly before she rolls her eyes and looks away from me. "You know what? You're right. I don't think you're a fucking idiot." Her eyes dart back to mine. She isn't scared; she's annoyed. That's not something that I thought I would see right now.

"I don't know shit about the Eleven-Quad crews. I don't know anything about them coming in here. I don't know anything besides the fact that you have me stuck in this fucking apartment," she snaps at me.

"What do you do for them?"

"What?"

"What . . . what . . . what," I mock her. "You fucking deaf now? I asked what it is you do for them."

"I count their money."

"Excuse me?" I pull back from hovering over her.

"I count their money. I'm a fucking accountant." She crosses her arms over her chest and clenches her jaws.

"You mean to tell me that the only reason you were in a drug house was to count money?" I couldn't believe that shit. They could count their own fucking money. Why would they need an accountant? It's not like they had millions and millions of dollars just sitting there.

"Yes, that is *all* I'm there for. I make sure that the bills are legit and there is enough money to pay for the product. I make sure that the money is logged in the appropriate ledgers. I'm just an accountant. I don't know anything about what the hell they do or why they came here. One thing I do *know* for sure is Eleven-Quad didn't come here for me."

I take a few steps back and put away my gun. It seems like she's telling me the truth, but that still doesn't explain why the hell she's so comfortable here. Why would she rather be my captive than make a run for it?

"Why haven't you tried to leave?" I ask her.

"What makes you think that I haven't?" One eyebrow raises up on her face in defiance.

"I would have seen you leave, and if you went back downstairs, one of the members would have dragged you into their room already. You're the new toy. Everyone wants to play with you." I smirk at her and almost enjoy when I see her gulp in fear.

"Truth is, it's safer in here than it is out there." Her voice is clear, but the edge of anger that she always seems to have when she's talking to me isn't there.

"What do you mean? How could a club full of killers be safer than out there?"

"You don't have a reason to kill me. I know for sure if I go out there and get caught by . . ." Her breath catches, and she doesn't say another word. "Listen, I don't need to explain myself to you. If you want to kick me out, that's your choice. If you want to shoot me for information that I don't have, that's your choice. Either way, I'm fucked."

She's not your responsibility. You don't need to play the fucking hero. I do my best to convince myself that I don't care about whatever has her so scared—scared enough she would take her chances with the Heavy Sinners than go outside, but it doesn't work. She's too much of an enigma.

"Sit down. I'm not kicking you out. I have a feeling that you know more than you're telling me, and I think you need to stay here until we can get it out of you. I warn you that I have quite a bit of patience, but my enforcer, Creeper, does not. If I find out that you're lying about the information that I do or don't get from you, I'll make sure that he takes his time getting all the answers out of you. Be smart, Dharia." I make my way into the bathroom to take a piss when I notice the shower was used. *She took a shower? With what? My soap?* I fight back the urge to imagine her sexy body washing right there in the shower.

When I walk back out to the main area of the apartment, she's sitting in the love seat, her forehead to her knees and her shoulders shuddering up and down.

"Hey, don't do that shit in here. I don't know what the fuck your real deal is with Eleven-Quad, but you brought this shit on yourself." I walk over to the small kitchenette area and pull out a can of soup that I bought.

"You think I did this to myself?" She gets up from the love seat and storms over to me.

I turn quickly to face her. I've been in arguments with women before, and one thing they don't want to see is your back. "I think you don't end up in this life if you don't want to." I put the can on the counter and stare back at the woman who seems to want to charge me like a bull.

"I don't *want* this fucking life. I have no choice, you selfish piece of shit. You think that I want to be holed up in some drug den or running for my life with bullets flying past my head? I didn't go to school so I could count how many fifties would fit into a fucking happy meal box. I don't have a choice. You, on the other hand, do. You're the fucking VP of a well-known and feared MC, and all you're worried about are the little fucks trying to get inside. Why don't you worry about what the fuck caused them to want to get in here? Tell me, what made you think that I knew something about them? Did they call me by name? Did they try to get up here to find me? Hell, did anyone even chase after you when you took me?"

I cut in on her tirade then. "There was no one there to chase after us."

"Oh, you can't be that fucking dumb. Do you think that the only people at that drop were the ones in the fucking basement? They have lookouts on every fucking corner. They saw you come in. They saw you go out. They may not have wanted to have a shoot-out right there in the middle of the street, but they would have chased after you if I were so damn important to them."

I think back to the man in the sugarcane field and what he said right before he died. "One of them said that we were traitors. I figured he thought you had switched sides and were now with us."

"Boy, please, I'm so low level they probably don't even know my name. I'm nothing in the grand scheme of things. You got the wrong fucking idea." She drops her hands to her sides, and I see her shoulders drop down slightly. At least she isn't going to charge me anymore. Her fury has passed.

"I don't know what the fuck is going on here. I just want to find Tia. I guess we are more alike than I thought. I didn't sign up for this shit either." I turn around, open the soup can, pour it into a bowl, and pop it into the microwave.

"Who's Tia?" she asks, her voice softer than it was before.

"None of your concern." I don't need to tell her anything more than she already knows. I've never been someone to trust easily.

"Dare, really? What can I do from here? There is no one that I can call. There is no computer, no phone, nothing but the TV and you." She leans against the side of the small table and looks over at me.

"Why do you even want to know? What does it matter to you?"

"It doesn't matter to me, except I'm stuck in here with you, and I would rather find out what kind of man I'm sharing the same space with. I like to think of myself as a good judge of character. Your president, he's ruthless, coldhearted, and psychotic. I figured that out from just the few seconds

I was in his space. Some of the other members are more bad than good, but you"—she tilts her head to the side as if she were examining some great work of art—"you don't fit here."

I laugh and open the door to the microwave as it beeps that the bowl of soup is done. "You think I won't kill you if I have to?"

"I know you will kill me if you have to. But I know it's because you have to, not because you want to. I think your president would kill me because he wants to. There's a difference." A loud gurgle comes from her, and she presses her hand to her stomach. Her eyes shoot down to the floor. Her copper cheeks darken slightly in embarrassment.

Fuck, she's been here for a while, and I haven't thought about feeding her. I haven't thought about shit besides what she can do for me. I know I'm running around with a bunch of brutes, but that doesn't mean that I have to act like one.

"You hungry?" I ask, but I'm already reaching up for another can of soup. She needs to eat.

"It's OK. Don't worry about it." She walks away and hurries back to the love seat as far away from the small kitchen as she can get.

I put the second bowl of soup in the microwave and pick up the first bowl. Then I grab a spoon and walk over to her. "Here, eat this." I hand it to her, but at first, she doesn't take it. "Look, you need to eat. I don't want to have to fight you about this."

"How much is it?" She looks up at me, her eyes wide, showing her pain.

"What? What do you mean, how much is it? I'm not asking you to pay for it." I shove the bowl in her face.

"Nothing is free. You're going to want something for this." She takes the bowl from my hands, and her eyes drop to the brown liquid in it.

"I'm telling you I don't. What the hell kind of arrangement did you have with Eleven-Quad?" I shake my head in slight annoyance before I walk back to get my bowl of soup.

"The arrangement where I do what they say and my family stays alive," she whispers softly before she slurps up the first spoon of soup.

My hands stop right as I get to the microwave. Is she doing this to keep her family alive? Am I making a big fucking mistake? It sounds like she's in the same fucking position that I'm in. She's doing fucked-up shit to save her family while I'm doing fucked-up shit to get my family back. I finally pull my bowl of soup out of the microwave, take one of the folding chairs out of the corner, go to where Dharia is eating, and sit across from her. She's a mystery, for sure, and one that I am determined to figure out.

Chapter 19

"Motherfucker." I swipe the stack of papers off the desk that I'm standing in front of. It's been a week since the Eleven-Quad bastard made his way into the clubhouse to kill Apollo. We've raided two more of their drug houses, but all the members and product are gone by the time we get there. There is no one there for us to speak with—no one there to tell me where I should even start to look for my daughter.

"This is some bullshit," Creeper said from the last room that he just cleared. The whole place was empty. We knew from the surveillance that Gambit did that this place usually is busy. Apollo passed by just yesterday and saw some of the Eleven-Quad crew in the vicinity. So how the fuck is the whole place just suddenly fucking empty? This shit doesn't make any sense.

"There's nothing here," Grizzly says as he kicks the papers that I just threw on the floor as he exits the door.

The anger inside me has started to build to an intolerable level. Three months Tia's been gone. I go to the station constantly to see if they found out any new information, but there's nothing new, just like every other time. The man that killed my wife is in jail, waiting for his trial date but refuses to co-operate. It's like my daughter just upped and vanished. Like she's being erased from the world. I can't remember what her laugh sounds like.

"Fuck." I slam my hands to my head and try to push down the emotions. I can't break apart right now. I can't afford to look like I'm about to lose my shit no matter how true that shit might be. The club is finally starting to respect me. Apollo even came to ask my opinion on the best way into the complex. I can't afford to lose the ground that I've made with them. So far, the only thing my father has told me that I know to be completely accurate is that I can't do this without them. I'd still be waiting on the police to get off their asses if I did.

"Dare, you good? You want us to check somewhere else?" Exit asks. As the road captain, it's his job to make sure that we have a way out of every situation, and if there is a change in plans regarding where we go, he's the one to set that up. If I want the club to go somewhere else, he would have to scout it out first and give us the best options of a way in.

"Nah, he doesn't want us to check anywhere else," Marcus says as he lights up a cigarette and takes a long drag. "There is nowhere else for him to check today. We need to go back and regroup. I still think that bitch has something to do with why we haven't been able to find out any information."

"How? For fuck's sake, Marcus, how the hell do you suppose she's doing that shit? She's been stuck in the fucking clubhouse like a prisoner for more than a week—unless you telling me you think one of us in the club is giving her access to the equipment she needs to make these so-called moves?"

Marcus flicks his still-lit cigarette at me, and as I move out of the way, he quickly moves to grab me. He catches hold of my kutte before I can move away and swings his heavy fist twice before I can even get my hand up to protect myself. Then he lets go of me, and I fall to the ground on my ass.

"Darius, you better watch your fucking mouth. I've given you many passes because you didn't grow up around the club but don't you ever accuse me of going against my patch again. That shit is a death sentence, and if I find out it's you going against the patch, son or not, I'ma kill you."

I hadn't expected such a furious response. Marcus stares me down for a second before he backs off. "Let's get the fuck outta here. I want to be balls deep into some pussy in the next damn hour." He walks out the door alone. Everyone else stays back to help me up.

"You good, bro?" Gambit asks.

"Yeah. What did he mean by that?" I ask him, but it's Apollo that does the answering.

"It's one of our most absolute rules. If a club member is going against the patch, and there is proof, they are killed. No matter your rank. There would be no retaliation. We don't fucking tolerate that shit."

I rub my face. The metal and pins that were surgically implanted to keep my jaw in place do nothing to dull the pain of my father's punch.

"Here." Creeper pulls a bottle out of his jacket and offers it to me.

"What the fuck is this?" I look at the unmarked bottle with a few pills in it.

"Percs. I know you get migraines and shit. I'm sure that hit must have your head spinning." He smirks and waits for me to take one of the pills.

"Yeah, shit wasn't fun. Thanks." I pop one of the pills and hand the bottle back to him. "You heard him. Let's get the fuck outta here."

"We're right behind you," Grizzly says as I walk out of the door, the entire Heavy Sinners MC at my back.

By the time we make it to the clubhouse, my head feels like it's trying to crack open. I don't know if Marcus messed up some of the metal in my mouth, but not even the Percocet that Creeper gave me is enough to take away all the pain.

I walk into the small apartment and see Dharia on the couch with the TV on. I gave her a few of my basketball shorts to wear and some wife beaters. I wasn't about to spend money on her, so that is what her wardrobe consists of. Over the past few days, she's constantly saying that she doesn't know anything about Eleven-Quad. I press her about it every day, but to be honest, it is nice to have someone around that isn't always about to kill someone. She feels like a bit of my old life . . . the normal times.

"Are you OK?" she asks and puts her feet on the floor as if she's going to get up.

"Stay there. Leave me alone," I say between gritted teeth.

"No. You look like hell. What the hell happened to you?" She gets up anyway and walks over to me.

"Why don't you fucking listen? I told you to leave me alone. I don't want to be bothered." I try to sound mean, but I sound more pitiful than anything.

"Dare, I'm not trying to fucking bother you, but whatever is happening to you right now seems painful. I'm just trying to help you, though you probably want to lose yourself in another bottle of Hennessy." She takes a step back and waits for me to say something else.

A drink does sound good right now. "I have a headache. That's all."

"Do you get them a lot? Is this a worse one?"

"What the fuck—are you a doctor or something?" I slowly walk over to the bed.

"No, but my mother was one. I thought I would follow in her footsteps. I'm good with blood, and I'm good with sickness. It's the people that come along with it that I don't want to deal with."

I chuckle at that, but the simple sound amplifies in my head like I did it with a goddamn bullhorn.

"Yeah, I get them often. But this might be the worst one so far. I guess that comes with being shot in the head." I pull my kutte off and lay it on the other side of my bed. Then I kick off my shoes and try to lie down.

"Are you serious?"

When I look at her, I see that her face is frozen in a state of complete shock.

"What?"

"You were shot in the head?"

"Oh yeah." I lift my head and show her the scar under my chin, then turn my head so she can see the other scar on the side of my face near my ear. It's still pretty red, but luckily, it seems to be healing really well.

"Fuck, did the bullet miss everything?" She comes over to the bed and kneels on the floor. The fact that she's on the floor and not on the bed irritates me.

"Mostly, my tongue got some damage, but my jaw's fucked up. It was wired shut for weeks after the surgeries."

"Well, no wonder you have a damn migraine. You're about to grind your teeth to dust any second because you're so tense." She gets up from the floor, but before she moves away, she looks at me again. "Look, I know that you're making shit much easier than it needs to be for me. Easier than I've had it in a long time. I want to help you. My brother used to get migraines a lot. If you going to get belligerent, then I'll just go back over there on the couch."

I would sit back up if I didn't have to move my head from the pillow. I don't know what she's talking about, but it sounds like she is about to do something to relax me. There are only so many things that you can do to relax someone. If she were talking about fucking, though, I'm game.

"Yeah, you can help me."

"Good. Hold on. Do you have a spare hand towel?"

"Yeah, in that closet. What do you need it for?"

"Just relax."

She walks over to the closet with the very small selection of linens and pulls out a plain white hand towel. It isn't something I brought with me from home, but it looks clean from where I'm lying. She walks over to the kitchen and runs the towel under the faucet. I see steam coming up from the sink.

After a few seconds, she wrings out the towel and makes her way to me.

"I'm guessing by the wet towel in your hand this doesn't mean that we're gonna have sex?" I raise an eyebrow at her.

Her face crumbles in disgust. "Eww, what the fuck? I said I did this for my *brother* when he had his migraines. Did you think I was fucking my brother? What kind of nasty shit are you into?"

I laugh. She did tell me this was a technique she used with her brother. I should have realized. I stop laughing when the banging in my head becomes too much. "Sorry, my bad."

"Yeah, perv." She smirks slightly before she moves closer to me. "Remove your shirt and turn onto your stomach."

I do what she asks and settle in for whatever it is she's going to do. "This is going to be hot, but don't jump. It's not going to burn you." It's her only warning before she drops the wet towel on my back from my neck down to midback.

"Son of a bitch, that shit is fucking scalding."

"Oh, don't be such a fucking baby. You got shot in the head, so you should be able to take a bit of heat." She continues adjusting the towel the way she wants it.

"Ha, I guess I'm never going to live that shit down." I let the towel settle down on my skin. The heat is less intense than it was a few seconds ago.

"I'm going to sit on your bottom, OK?" she asks softly.

"Yeah."

I hear her rushing to the other side of the room, and suddenly the lights dim until they are almost off. Before I ask her what she's doing, she's back at the bed and sitting down on my lower back.

"You're so tense. If you don't relax, this migraine is going to get worse. My brother suffers from anxiety, and every time he has to do something that he knows would trigger it, he would get these crazy migraines." Her voice is so soft I barely hear anything she's saying.

Her hands softly massage my shoulders and neck through the warm towel. The warmth, the soft voice, and the pressure of her touch immediately put me at ease. "I used to feel so bad for him when he lay there basically in a ball as he battled these headaches. As his sister, of course, I wanted to find a way to help him. He always fought me, but when it got too bad, he would let me do this."

It sounds like she's whispering on purpose. I have to strain my ears to hear what she's saying.

"Once, he had to give a presentation at school, and he was all bound up about it. He paced back and forth all night because he couldn't figure out how he would get through it. He didn't eat, didn't drink anything, and by the time I woke up in the morning, he was so tense his shoulders were pulled up by his ears."

Her hands move expertly on my neck and shoulders. I let my arms hang at my sides as she places more pressure on my back. The warmth of the towel seems to have drifted into my entire body. My eyes flutter closed, and for the first time in a long while, I feel content. I lie still and listen to her soft voice and the story about her brother. I've never had any of the problems she describes concerning her brother, but I enjoy the sound of her voice anyway. It is so different from the constant hardness that I'm around all day with the rest of the guys in the club.

Her voice is the only thing I can focus on. I feel the towel move away, and her hands take its place. She swipes her hands over my shoulders two more times, pressing down.

"How are you feeling now?" She bends down by my ear.

My eyes open, and I wait for the mind-numbing pain, but I don't feel it. My jaw is loose, my arms are flexible—hell, even my legs are loose, and she never touched me below my shoulder blades. I can still feel the headache, but it's far less intense. I think a regular Excedrin would make it go away.

"Better, much better. You have magical hands." I reach behind my back and push her softly onto the bed so that I can sit up. "Thank you," I say as I get up to go to the bathroom to get the Excedrin.

"You want to talk about what's bothering you?"

"Why do you want to know what's bothering me?" I ask when I make it back to the bed to lie down. She kneels on the opposite side of me. This I like better.

"Maybe it'll help." She closes her eyes and heaves out a deep breath. "Dare, I haven't had anyone but the junkies and the people who want to kill me to talk to for the better part of a year. I just want to talk."

A year? Another part of the puzzle that is Dharia falls into place. "I feel like I'm not making any progress. That I'm sacrificing so much of who I am to get to the other side of the shit show that has been my life for the past few months, but I'm not getting anywhere," I admit to her. I don't need to tell her much. That is true, at least.

Her eyes go wide when she realizes that I'm indulging her. "What are you trying to do?"

I lean my head to the side. That is more information than I'm willing to give. She smiles tightly before she turns to get off the bed. "Where's your brother?" I ask her.

She turns back in my direction, a wistful smile on her face and her eyes filling with tears. She looks up for a second so that she doesn't cry. "He's in jail."

"Fuck, I'm sorry. I know that's hard on a family. You want to tell me what he did?"

"He was caught with a lot of drugs. He'll be in for a long time." She sighs and looks down. "You went to college?"

"Yes, do you think I'm just an uneducated savage?" I say, teasing her.

"No, I already knew you were a very smart savage. Probably smarter than all the rest of the savages in the area." She raises her face to look at me. "What did you study?"

"Business with a minor in communications."

"What the fuck?" Her mouth opens. "I would have never thought that. I figured it was something like law enforcement. Something like that."

"No, I graduated near the top of my class with my business degree and got a good job. I was living a totally different life up until about three months ago." I turn away from her, the flashes of that night trying to force their way back into my mind.

"Then the shit show began?"

"Yeah." I turn back to her. I want to clear something up before we talk about anything else. "Look, I don't know your deal, but I know I don't feel like you're telling me the whole fucking truth about Eleven-Quad—"

She cuts me off. "I don't know anything about them—nothing."

I put my hand up to stop her. I don't have the energy to fight with her. "I also don't feel right about just sending you out there on your own. I'll make you a deal. As long as you don't do nothing dumb like steal from me or lie to me, I'll let you stay here until I figure out what to do with you."

"You're going to help me?"

"I'll help you until I figure out if I have to kill you. Until then, you can eat whatever you want when you want. I'm not charging you for anything." I tell her, genuinely disgusted by the fact that she thought she had to pay for the food I had offered her earlier.

"It's the best deal I've had in a while." She wrings her hands together, anxiety clear on her face.

"Don't fuck it up because I'm the only one here who'll give you this deal. If you step out of this apartment, I can't stop what they'll do to you out there if I'm not there to protect you. I've claimed you already, but like you said, 'We're all savages here.'"

"You've claimed me? Does that mean I'm yours, Dare?" Her voice is huskier than usual, and her eyes are focused on my lips.

Oh, please don't fucking tempt me with this shit right now.

I lick my lips once, and she shakes her head as if she were coming out of a trance. "I mean, does that mean I'm your slave or something like that?"

"No, not a slave. But if you leave, you're on your own. I don't think you would be able to handle the crazy shit that they do downstairs anyway." I close my eyes.

"Hmm, shows just how much you don't know about me. Maybe one day I'll show you what *I* can do." I feel her get off the bed and walk back over to the small couch where she has spent most of her time. She turns on the TV but keeps it low. I keep my mouth shut so that I don't tell her what I'm thinking. I don't want to admit to her how badly I want to see what she *can* do.

Chapter 20

After a quick nap, a sharp knock on the door woke me up. Thankfully, the headache's gone. I slowly get up from the bed and walk over to the door. When I open it, it's the last person I expect to see.

"Dare, she said you were expecting her?" I stick my head out the door and look at Mali, who had escorted Star upstairs and is now waiting at the landing to make sure that it's OK that she's here. I nod and send him on his way. I can handle Star. I don't need any backup on this one.

"Star, what the hell are you doing here?"

"What you mean, papi? I told you I would see you at the next party. You said it was OK." She pouts, her pretty, thick lips pushing out subtly.

"Party?" I don't remember there being any party today, but I guess when Marcus wants to party, everyone does what they have to for that shit to happen.

"Look, I don't know if I'm going to be there tonight," I tell her, but she's not focused on me. Her eyes are focused over my shoulder. When I turn around to see what she's looking at, I realize that Dharia is sleeping peacefully on the small couch. I step farther out into the hall and pull the door closed behind me. "Star, I don't know what you're thinking, but we don't got nothing going on."

"Who, you and her?" she asks innocently.

"No, me and you. What happened the other night was nothing more than a quick fuck. You do understand that shit, right? I mean, I don't need to have you banned from the club for stalking, right? I don't have time for no fucking drama." It's been a long time since I had to deal with anyone's drama besides Lisbeth's, and I'm not looking forward to it.

"Oh, I know I don't want any drama either, but I'll tell you one thing. That shit was so fucking far from just a quick fuck." She moves in close to me. Her large breasts press tightly against my bare chest. She's wearing a small, cutoff shirt and tight skirt. "Dare, I've been thinking about sucking that fat cock all week. You really going to deny me, papi? Just one more time and I'll be on my way." She pulls up on her tiptoes and bites my earlobe. My cock seems to spring to life on its own. What the hell? It's not like I have to chase her down. If she wants more, I have more to give her.

"Go downstairs. Let me get dressed. I'll be down in a bit." I push her away softly. She turns in her sky-high heels and provocatively walks away from me, smacking her ass once so I can see.

"Fucking freak," I mutter, and she blows me a kiss over her shoulder before she walks down the stairs and into the party downstairs.

I open the door, and Dharia is still sound asleep. I stare at her for a few seconds. I don't know what it is about her that entices me. Sure, her demeanor is fun. She is sassy and has a slick, fucking mouth, but I'd seen others just the same. She is gorgeous, but so are the girls I assume are downstairs. The only difference between her and the women downstairs, I know from the many fucking times she has told me, is that she doesn't want to fuck me. Star, on the other hand, would fuck me on the roof if I told her to. It's the chase. It has to be. Dharia is the one I'm not supposed to want, the one that plays hard to get. That only made me want to play harder to get her. It's a dangerous game. If she turns out to be the traitor that Marcus thinks she is, *I'll* be the one to put a bullet in her head.

I shake the thoughts from my head and walk toward the bathroom. I still don't have the time to deal with that shit right now. So far, I have no proof that she's the one we need to watch out for.

I wash up quickly, then throw on some deodorant and cologne. A quick change into a short-sleeve black tee and dark jeans, my black and red 12s, and my kutte, and I'm ready to go party. The second I make it out of the stairwell, though, I regret the decision. There are more women here than I've ever seen. What the fuck are they all doing here? Marcus thought it would be better if we didn't have too many hang-arounds or any entertainment around for a while, but I guess that doesn't apply to parties. I find myself watching everyone's hands just to make sure that no one is pulling anything out of anywhere. I find Apollo, and before he realizes I'm looking at him, I notice him doing the same thing that I am—scanning the crowd. I push my way through the women to get to him. He has on a bright red shirt, so it's not like I could fucking lose him in the crowd.

"VP?" he screams over the music and stands at attention like I'm about to give him an order or something. I see why he made such a good VP before I got here. The man is always fucking ready for whatever is thrown at him.

"Chill, it's good. I just came over here to check you. You all right?" I lean up and shout near his ear. He nods once, and I turn my head slightly to let him know that I don't believe him.

He sighs before he leans back down to yell near my ear. "There's too many fucking people here. I keep watching their hands."

I knew it. He's just as fucking paranoid about this shit as I am. We have to figure out a way to clear some of these people out without making it seem like we're shutting down the party. I wouldn't go against Marcus's wishes, but I can go around them.

"Is there a mic here?" I ask.

He nods and gets Mali's attention. The prospect runs over the second he sees Apollo. I don't hear what he's saying, but I assume it's to tell him to get the microphone when Mali runs off.

Mali comes back with the microphone, and I climb up on the bar. I signal over to the DJ to cut off the music. The music stops, and everyone groans slightly, thinking that I'm about to tell them that the party's over.

"I'm not sure if you all noticed, but I'm the new VP of this club." A loud round of applause and a bunch of catcalls from the ladies in attendance erupt over the crowd. "Quiet down now. I was just over here talking to one of the other Sinners, and I feel like maybe I was slighted a good welcome party. What do you ladies say? You want to welcome me into the Heavy Sinners MC?"

The applause is louder than it was before. I have to press a finger to my ear to drown out the piercing screams of the women in attendance. I stroll slightly down the bar and stand behind Grizzly, who's laughing at my antics. "Well then, I want you to show me what you got. There's one catch, though. I only want the best of the best tonight. I want ladies who can work that pole like they were born to do it. If you can't do that, you got to go. Let us know if you're game."

I hop off the bar, and just like I anticipated, a large flock of women leave on their own. None of them will complain about what I asked. I'm sure this is tamer than anything Marcus has ever asked them to do. Still, quite a few who want to try their hand at the pole remain. I pull the mic back up to my mouth as I push through the dwindling crowd.

"DJ, make 'em dance." With that, he drops a hot mix-up of Nas and Cardi B, and all the women go crazy. "Sinners, I'm going to need your help deciding who stays," I speak through the mic again.

I see the Sinners walking through the crowd, trying to get to the horseshoe stage. Trim jumps up on the stage with a pencil in his mouth like he's really taking points for certain things. Gambit laughs loudly as some of the ladies obviously have never been on a pole before in their lives. I'm as nice as I can be and usher a few toward the door, promising that we'll have more parties soon.

"You should have made the contest about who sucks the best dick. I would have won that one," one of the women I told to hit the bricks said, and part of me wants to take her up on that idea. That would have been a much better contest.

Once the strippers got back up there, the number of people in the club was down to about 60 percent of what it once was. Still a lot of people, but it is much more bearable than before.

"Good shit." Apollo walks up behind me and claps a hand on my back. "There were way too many of them before. This shit I can deal with."

"You know it, brother," I say quickly before I clamp my mouth shut. It's normal for the guys in the club to call each other brother. After all, it's a brotherhood that we're a part of. But as an outsider, it's been hard for me to feel that way about them. I don't know if they thought of me in the same way. I came in and bulldozed through their way of life, even if it wasn't my idea.

Apollo smirks slightly, nods once, and slaps my back again. "Now, we can have some fun. Seems like someone has you in their sights, brother. Have fun." He turns me around, and I see Star hopping down from the stage after her set and staring straight at me.

I want to be excited about it. I know she will try to blow my mind, but I just don't feel it. She quickly gets to where I'm standing. "You made me wait a long time," she says into my ear.

"I have shit to do, Star. You could have had fun with anyone else in here. You didn't need to wait for me," I reply. She grabs hold of my arm and leans up again to talk into my ear.

"You know, can't no one make me scream like you can."

She is laying it on thick as fuck. "Star, get the fuck out of here with that shit. I don't know nothing. You starting to sound like a desperate bitch. I'm not with that shit. Period," I yell loudly while looking her right in the eyes. I want to see if she gets the point. If she's trying to make me her man or some shit like that, it isn't going to happen, not with me.

"I'm not desperate, papi. I just know how good we are. Come on, let me make you feel good." She tugs my arm, leading me toward the side where all the spank rooms are. I follow behind because, fuck it, why not?

When she starts to lead me to the stairs that go up to the living quarters, I yank her back hard. "Where the fuck do you think you're going?"

"Your space. Upstairs."

I almost laugh in her face. "Are you dumb? What the fuck makes you think I'd fuck you on my bed? Nah, that's where I lay my head. You don't need to be up in there."

She smiles weakly and starts walking again, this time, in the right way.

We get to one of the open rooms, and the second she gets in, she goes straight for my shirt. I like the enthusiasm, so I let her do what she wants to do. Star is really a beautiful woman, probably one I would have fantasized about at another time. If she weren't throwing up so many clingy-as-fuck flags, I would be happy just to let my guard down, but I know I can't.

"I can't wait to feel you inside me. I told you I would be thinking about this all night."

I take my shirt and kutte and hang them on the doorknob. She kisses everywhere she can reach. I push her back until her legs are touching the bed. She falls down with a cute giggle, and I start working on getting her top off.

"Let me see those pretty tits."

She pulls the small shirt over her head, and I reach down to palm them with both my hands. She quickly works underneath to get my pants off. When she yanks them down, I take a step back, but she pulls me close to her again.

"Squeeze them, papi."

I do, and she takes my cock while she angles herself back slightly. She spits into her hand and then starts stroking me off.

"Shit." I let my eyes close and try to get into it. She moves closer to me and presses her wet hands over mine. She lines up the head of my cock right against her breast, and like nature, I feel a slit I want to push in. I peel my hands away and watch as she pushes her tits as close together as possible and lets me fuck her chest. I put one foot up on the bed to get better leverage.

"Yes, I like that shit. Fuck, that's so sexy." She moans loudly, keeping eye contact with me. It's a nice visual, but it's a bit too rehearsed. I wonder if she does this with every man she fucks. I push her back. I'm done with that. I lean over to the side table and pluck out one of the condoms. I push off my jeans, making sure to kick my shoes off as well. Then I roll the condom down on my dick and crawl onto the bed in between her legs. I push up the skirt she's wearing up to her waist. She's not wearing any panties.

"Hmm, were you just waiting for me to fuck you, or were you open for business for anyone?" I quickly rub that pretty ring she has in her clit. Her body trembles in pleasure.

"Oh fuck, Dare. Shit. Oh my God. Just you. I only want you," she moans. "Don't you fucking stop."

"Come. This shit is going to be fast today," I let her know. It's almost sad that I hope for it to be over so quickly. I keep rubbing at her clit until I watch her abdomen contract hard, and she screams out my name over and over. I don't wait for her body to stop shaking before I thrust into her. She screams and puts a hand out to buffer me. Quickly, I grab it.

"If you can't handle me, don't come looking for me." I toss her hand to the side and slow my pace down. I let her get used to me when it's the last thing I want to do. I don't want to do any damage, but I don't feel like being sweet right now. I want to fuck. She came to find me because she wants to fuck. This sweet shit is for the damn birds.

"I'm good now; do it. Do it, papi." She grabs the sheets, and I pick up my pace to a punishing level. I wrap the fabric of her skirt around my hand and use it as a leash. She moans and groans. She calls out for the Almighty. All I'm worried about is what I have to do to come.

"Fuck, Dare. I'm never going to get enough. My God," she yells, and her legs begin to shake as another orgasm rolls through her body. Star two, me nil.

I pull out of her, and before she can adjust, I flip her over onto her stomach. I pull her so that her legs are off the bed. Then I stand up behind her. I push back into her and close my eyes, trying to get to my happy place. Unfortunately, I know exactly what I need to get off—Dharia.

I pull up the images that seem to be stuck in my head—the ones of her sleeping. The very few times she'd laughed. The way she'd whispered to me as she massaged my back.

"Fuck, Dharia," I moan.

"What?"

Oh shit.

I quickly recover. I smack Star on the ass, pound into her harder, and she buries her face back into the mattress. Then I go back to thinking about Dharia, this time biting my lip so that I don't mistakenly say her name out loud again.

A few seconds later, I'm exploding in Star. The condom fills up as my orgasm weakly rolls through my body. I suck in deep breaths, but I don't feel as satiated as I should. Part of me wants to gear up for another round, except I know that's not going to do anything but make Star feel like I'm more into her than I am.

"Get your stuff. Time for you to go."

"Wait. Jeez, Dare. You act like you can't stand to be near me. What have I done to you?" She sits up in the bed and crosses her arms over her chest.

I exhale, trying to get some of the annoyance out of my tone. "Nothing. Just clean up and enjoy the party. I have to make sure everything is going good." I try to lace as much charm as I can into my words. I quickly get rid of the condom, get dressed, and run out of the room. She's right, though. She didn't do anything to me. She just isn't the woman I want to be fucking.

Chapter 21

By one in the morning, the party is all but done. All the strippers have finished their sets. Star left after letting me know that she thinks that she will be here at the next party if I want to have fun with her again. I should have told her no, but I'm not one to turn down free fun. I hope she isn't getting attached. Now, as everything is starting to get cleaned up, I sit at the bar with a beer in my hand, just sipping away.

"What's going on, man?" Grizzly and Gambit sit next to me.

"Man, nothing. Same shit, you know." I shrug and take another swig of my drink.

"If I dance, will I get a tip?" Exit smirks as he walks on the bar to where we're sitting.

"Get the hell down, boy. You know better than that." Brynn, who I found out is Creeper's old lady, swipes at Exit's legs with a cloth.

"I know, I know." Exit jumps down on the other side of the bar and stands in front of the three of us. "What are you guys bitching about over here?"

"The same thing we bitch about every day, Pinky."

I laugh at the reference. I hadn't even thought about the cartoon, *Pinky and the Brain*, in years.

"I wonder what Heavy has on the agenda for tomorrow," Gambit states.

"Probably another den to hit."

"Is it normal for so many of them to be cleared out by the time we get there?" I ask.

"Fuck no. This shit has never happened before. It's like they know right beforehand that we're coming, and they clear out. It's very fucking smart, in my opinion," Exit remarks.

"Yeah, too smart for Ace and Killa," Gambit agrees.

"Who are Ace and Killa?"

"The Brawler sects of the Eleven-Quad gang are all run by different people, but Killa and Ace, you could say, are the leaders of all them, even if no one will admit it. If shit is going on with the Brawlers, they are usually the ones behind it," Grizzly answers.

"So, you don't think that they would be able to get their people out in time?"

"No. They too concerned with their corners and getting money. Whoever knows about us coming has to be by the hideout houses to tell them. It just doesn't make sense. Honestly, when Marcus thought it was your girl upstairs, it sounded like a reasonable explanation, but you were right when you said she never left the room. None of us would have given her what she needed to sound the alarm. Something is definitely off here. I just wish we could get to the bottom of it. I don't have the fucking resources to keep all these drug dens secure."

"Wait, what?" I turn to Gambit. "What does that mean?"

"We're looking for the people that attacked you, but I have to keep tabs on all the ones that we've already been at. If anyone shows back up or comes looking for the drugs that we stole, I'm the one who needs to know about it. It's a lot of territory to cover."

"Territory," I whisper.

There is no way this is about territory. "You don't think Marcus could just be wanting us to take over the Eleven-Quad territory?"

"No. I mean, what would he want with all this territory? We're an MC. We don't run an underground drug trade or anything like that."

I finish my beer and leave a tip for the bartenders. We don't have to pay for anything, but I always thought it's nice to show the servers gratitude.

"I see the gears turning in your head." Gambit puts a hand on my shoulder before I'm able to get up. "We're looking for her, Dare. We all are. Marcus wants to get her back as bad as the rest of us."

I nod once and get off the stool. I want to believe that shit. I know that I need to do some digging on my own, but I don't want to think that Marcus is intentionally dangling my daughter over my head just for him to expand his territory. Patch or not, he's a dead man if that's the case.

I slowly make my way up the stairs to my apartment, ready to fall into bed.

When I open the door, I expect to see Dharia still sleeping on the couch. Instead, I find her by my dresser, the only framed picture of Tia in her hand.

"What the fuck are you doing?" Irrational anger sweeps through me.

"I'm sorry. I wasn't stealing anything. I was just looking." She quickly sets the picture back on the dresser. It falls twice before her nervous hands can get it to stand up.

"Don't fucking touch shit that doesn't belong to you. I don't even know why I have to tell you something like that. Goddamn it." I knock her hands out of the way and put the photo where I want it. I stare at the picture for a few seconds while my anger ebbs. When I turn back to apologize, she's already moved to sit on the couch.

I pick up the photo and walk over to where she is. I sit next to her and hand the photo to her. "I'm sorry. I'm very edgy about this picture. It's my favorite one." I touch it tenderly like the cold glass would suddenly turn into the warm face of my daughter.

"This is Lisbeth then?" Dharia asks softly.

"No. This . . ." I hesitate before I tell her. This is a line. I haven't opened up to anyone about my family, so why the fuck do I feel so comfortable doing it with her? "This is Tia. My little girl."

"She's gorgeous. Those eyes, so expressive. I bet she's a handful," Dharia says as she carefully transfers the photo back into my hands.

"Oh, she's way more than a handful. I wouldn't have it any other way. I love her more than my next breath," I admit before I put the photo down next to me.

"She passed away?"

"No. She was kidnapped."

She gasps hard and puts a hand over her mouth. "Oh my God. That's so much worse."

I look at her in intrigue. Most would just offer their condolences. Others would tell me not to give up hope, but I had yet to hear anyone say that it's worse than being dead.

"What makes you say that?"

"The not knowing. I can't imagine how horrible that is. To know that your child is out there somewhere and not know if she's safe or needs help. To know she's probably looking for you and can't find you. At least with death, you know for sure, whatever you believe about the afterlife. If you believe in heaven, reincarnation, whatever it is, you know she has passed on and is in that next journey. But to be kidnapped . . . I can only imagine it must be pure torture."

I lean back in the love seat. "Sounds like you have some experience with it."

"No, I don't. I have no kids. But I've been around plenty of women who have lost theirs. I'm so sorry that happened to you. Lisbeth is her mother?"

"Yeah."

"How is she holding up with all this?" Dharia turns in my direction, genuinely interested in what I have to say.

"She's not holding up. The same bastards who kidnapped Tia killed her."

Her eyes close, and a tear falls down her cheek. I reach up with my hand and catch it with my finger. "Are you crying for me?" A wide range of emotions course through me. "I don't want your pity."

"Dare, I'm crying for your pain. I'm crying for whatever man you were before you had something as tragic as this happen to you all at once. I'm not pitying you. I'm hurting with you. No one deserves to go through the shit that you've had to go through. Bad man or not, no one deserves that." She taps my knee once before she leans back.

"Do you have any ideas, any leads on where she is?"

"No, I don't. Do you think I would be sitting here next to you if I had an idea of where your friends were keeping my little girl?" I get off the couch and walk briskly over to the kitchenette. What a fucking stupid question to ask.

I turn around to see her standing with her arms crossed in front of her and her eyes focused down. When she looks back up at me, her eyebrows are cinched in, and her lips are pressed together tight. "What are you talking about, my 'friends'?"

"Oh, for fuck's sake. Eleven-Quad. They have my kid. We just don't know which group of them or where. Why the hell do you think we're over here raiding everywhere?" I'm getting really tired of her denying that she had anything to do with Eleven-Quad. She may just be a lowly worker, but she worked for them.

"You're looking in the wrong place," she says and walks over to where I am.

"What?"

"Dare, Eleven-Quad doesn't have your kid."

My heart starts to beat faster. Is she finally telling me the information that I need? "Tell me what you know. Tell me where she is." I grab her arm hard and yank her closer to me.

She puts her hand on my hand that's grabbing her. "I don't know who has her, but I know it's not them. Eleven-Quad is nothing more than mercenaries. They go where they are told, sling what the fuck they are told to sling, and kill who they are told to kill. Ace and Killa are just puppets on strings."

This lines up with what Gambit and the rest of the boys were talking about downstairs. It's not something that the two of them would do. Not on their own. "Who controls them then?"

She looks down, and I see her jaws clenching through her cheeks.

"What is it? Tell me."

"Dare, I want you to find your little girl, but if I give you this information, then I'm screwing myself. They must have already figured out that y'all don't really know who the fuck is behind it, but if I tell you, they are going to know you had insider information. I'm the only insider. I go from being a captive to being a fucking traitor. I have my own family to think about." She doesn't look at me, but I can hear the pain in her voice.

"What are you talking about? I thought you had said you were small potatoes, that they don't care about you."

"They don't, but they have leverage against me." She puts her hands in her hair and combs it back. "I already told you that I don't use. I'm being forced to do this job to compensate for my brother Shaquan's debt."

She's paying off her brother's debt? Is *that* why she wouldn't tell me what she knew? If they figured out that she's helping me, they would go after her brother. "I thought you said he was in jail."

"He is. Do you think just because he's locked up that means they can't get to him?" She leans back and finally looks up at me. She stares at me like I'm stupid. "What rock do you live under? All these clubs and gangs have people on the inside."

"What makes you think that they would be able to get to him anyway? I mean, he could always talk to the guards about putting him in protective custody or something like that." I'm trying to think of anything that would get her to tell me the information she knows.

"Protective custody is for snitches. He would die there for sure." She shakes her head and turns around. I rush in front of her to stop her from walking off. I could threaten her, tell her that I would put her out, but I have a feeling that nothing I could do would get her to go against her brother.

"What if I found a way to protect him?"

She forces a laugh. "Dare, I know they will be able to get to Shaquan in jail. I tried to quit. I told them that I wasn't going to work for them anymore. I had a problem with what they were doing. I didn't even say I was going to the cops. Just told them I didn't want to pay off his debt that way. Two days later, I got photos of my brother being beaten and raped because I threatened to leave. What can you do to protect him? You got nothing out here. As long as I do what they say, they won't mess with him."

Fuck. That shit is tough. I don't know anyone inside that would be able to help us. But maybe my brothers did.

"What prison is he in?"

"Dade Correctional. Why?"

"If I can get something in motion to give him some backup in there, something where he wouldn't have to worry about being hurt, will you tell me?"

"I'd have to see the proof of it first." She raises her chin and tries to stare me down.

"I don't even know if the information you have is worth it. If it is, we'll move right away, but you have to tell me something today."

"You're asking me to trust that you're going to do the right thing." She shakes her head. I can see the indecision in her eyes.

"I'm trusting you to believe that I will do anything for Tia. This is my baby. I'm giving you my word that I will help your brother to the best of my abilities; call in every favor the club has to help your brother if you help me get Tia." I don't want to beg, but I will.

"Get me a plan, tell me how you're going to do it, and I'll tell you." She doesn't wait for me to reply. She simply turns and walks over to the couch. That's her final offer. I have to come up with something.

I leave her where she's sitting and get my ass downstairs. It's almost one thirty in the morning now, but I'm praying that the guys I need are awake. I see Gambit and Grizzly still sitting at the bar drinking and talking shit. I do my best to push down the fear that I have. I want to get her brother help, but I know my father would never agree to use any favors he has on her. He's selfish like that. I'm hoping that they'll go behind his back to help me out. It is as close to going against the president as I'm sure any of them have ever come. I don't know if they'll snitch on me the second I ask or if they'll help me.

I grab both of their shoulders.

"I thought you were upstairs tapping that ass. I guess thirty minutes ain't bad." Gambit laughs. "You gonna have to work on your stroke, though."

"I need you," I state. Both of them turn ready for business. "Privately," I add and walk back to the stairwell. They follow behind me without asking a question.

When we're inside the stairwell, I close the door and stand on the steps above them. I don't want to go upstairs until I know they're willing to hear me, at least out. The three of us have developed more of a bond than I would have thought possible. It's the only reason I even think to ask them.

"What's up, VP?" Grizzly asks.

"I'm about to ask the two of you to help me do something, something I want to be done without my father's knowledge."

They both look at each other. "Dare, we respect you as the VP, but we won't go against our president," Gambit bites out, and I see his hands balling into fists.

"I'm not asking you to go against him. I'm asking you to help me without getting everyone involved. It's nothing to do with him."

Grizzly pops his knuckles and looks up at me. "What do you want us to do?"

"Do you know anyone in Dade Correctional Prison?"

"Yeah, of course, we do. What does that have to do with anything?" Gambit asks.

"Would they protect someone in there if we asked them to?"

"Wait. We protecting people in the clink? I'm lost. Why?" Grizzly asks.

"Y'all going to keep this to yourself?" I look between them. Even if we couldn't get a plan together, I still didn't want them turning around and telling Marcus what's going on.

"Yeah," both of them answer.

"She knows something. Whoever the fuck she works for is holding her brother over her head. If we get the information, they'll know she snitched and will go after her brother. If we can come up with a plan to get him some backup in there, she'll help me."

"Fuck." Grizzly drags his hand down his scruffy face. "That's heavier than I thought you would say."

"Can you help me or not?" I ask, my patience fraying. I want to know what she knows.

"You need Apollo."

Well, there went that idea. "No, fuck no. He's not going to help me. He'll run straight to my father. Then she'll give us nothing. Just fucking forget it. I'll figure something else out on my own."

"Dare, hold up." Gambit grabs my arm before I can go upstairs. "Apollo is the only one that can push through favors in there. Especially these kinds of favors. He's not a jackass. Why do you think so many of us were pissed when your ass showed up and took his spot? He's an all right guy when you get past the asshole."

"Yeah, man. We want to help, but he really is the only one that can," Grizzly states from where he's standing.

"You think he'll keep this shit from Marcus?"

"Yeah, I think so. I don't see how helping someone in Dade will blow back on him," Grizzly replies.

"Fine, get him. I want this shit done now. And try to be quiet about it. I rather only the four of us know about it right now," I tell Grizzly, and he walks out.

"You really think she knows something?"

"I think she won't say anything if we can't protect her brother. I know she is stuck in a situation that she doesn't want to be in, and if we can give her a way out, she's going to do whatever we say."

Grizzly walks back in by himself.

"He said no, didn't he?"

"Chill. You told me to be quiet about it. Give him a minute," Grizzly counters.

A minute ticks by and then another.

The door finally opens, and Apollo walks in. "What's with all the cloak and dagger? I'm tired as fuck." He wipes the sleep out of his eyes and leans his forearm against the wall.

"Listen, we need some help, but really, you're the only one I know of who has the connections that we need. Marcus can't know about it," Gambit tells him quickly.

Apollo's eyes shoot to mine. His gaze pierces into me like fucking daggers. "You going against your fucking patch? I will rip your fucking face off," he growls. I take a step back, ready to fight him if I need to.

"I'm not going against the patch. I'm trying to figure the fuck out what's going on. I don't see there being any blowback from a protection detail."

Apollo's eyes squint, and he leans back. "Protection detail? What protection detail?"

I quickly explain to him the same thing I said to Gambit and Grizzly earlier.

"Yeah, I know a few people in there. What information do you think she has?"

"The real people who took Tia. At least, that's what she made it seem like."

"For real?" Apollo rubs the back of his neck. "A'ight, then. I'll put in a few calls in the morning. I won't be able to get in to see anyone until Thursday, but I can get him transferred to solitary until I do. My guys will watch his back when he gets out."

"That's it? You don't want nothing from me?"

"Bro, you saved my life. If I got it, it's yours. That shit's for life. As long as you don't go against the patch, we good."

"That's real. I appreciate that." I put my hand out and pull him into a man hug.

"Now, let's go find out what the little lady knows," Grizzly remarks from the side.

Finally, it feels like a door is opening, and I'm a step closer to Tia.

Chapter 22

I open the door to my apartment and see Dharia pacing back and forth. She stops and begins backing away when she sees that I brought other people with me.

"Easy, calm down."

"No, I don't care what you do to me. I'm *not* going to tell you anything." She moves until her back is against the wall.

"Easy, sweetheart. No one here is going to hurt you. We just want to talk to you about a few things. You can relax." Gambit slowly walks over and puts a hand out for her. "You don't have to worry about them, pretty. I'll keep those animals away."

"Could you get any more ridiculous?" Grizzly comments from behind him.

My eyes focus on where Gambit's hand is touching her, and I have to force myself to stay where I am. "Gambit," I bark out.

He spins around, startled.

"Hands off, brother." I look down at his hand, and a second later, he removes it.

"Oh, my bad." He laughs and backs away from her.

"Dharia, no one is here to hurt you. You asked me to get a plan. These guys are here to help me with that plan. You have my word." I put my hand out, and she hurries over to me.

"How are you going to help Shaquan?" she asks right away.

I turn to Apollo.

"I know quite a few guards and cons down there. I can get him transferred to solitary for a while, and when he gets released back into gen pop, my guys can watch his back. I can't do nothing about whatever is happening on this side, but while he's in there, I can have people watch out for him."

She turns to me, her eyes hard as if she's trying to figure out by looking into my eyes if I'm playing her. "Dare, this real? Don't mess with my family." Her head falls, and I can almost feel the tension rolling off her. "Please. It'll kill me if I do something to get him hurt again."

"It's real. I promise you."

She looks up with her eyes bouncing through the four of us. "Fine, ask me what you want to know."

"Why do you think Eleven-Quad doesn't have my kid?"

"Because they've been taken over. Eleven-Quad folded about six months ago."

"Bullshit!" Apollo jumps up at that. "We would have known some shit like that."

"There are still a few sects that are trying to hold their own, but besides them, they were all taken over. The place I was at was one of the last of the crews that were still operating on their own."

"Taken over . . . like they work for someone else?"

"Yeah," said Dharia. "They work for the same people I'm stuck with. Brutes MC."

"Oh fuck."

"Shit."

"Motherfucker."

The three of them behind me all curse out at the same time. I have no idea who Brutes MC is, but none of my guys seem to like them.

"Who are they?"

"Hold on. How do we know *she's* telling the truth? Who do you know there? Who do you work for?" Apollo asks Dharia.

"Breach is the one I'm supposed to report to directly. He keeps a running tally of how much I have left to work off. Luger and Mixie are the ones that deal with this kidnapping shit. They want to get into the kidnapping game. They think ransoms are much easier to get than trying to push product."

"Fucking hell. That sounds legit. Luger is the president of that club, and he always tries to find a come-up. If he's trying to get out of the drug game, it'll make sense that he's doing that. Eleven-

Quad would do the dirty work for them," Grizzly acknowledges.

"You know you are never going to be able to pay them back, right?" Apollo remarks. "They'll never let you or your brother out of that deal."

"I know. I just have to do what I have to do." Dharia leans against the wall.

"Why don't we like the Brutes?" I ask.

"The Brutes and Marcus have had a beef since he started this MC. They felt like he encroached on their space. They made a truce years ago, but tensions are still high between them."

"You think this is them coming for Marcus? That they're pushing him into breaking the truce?" I ask.

"Fuck, it would make sense," Apollo answers.

"OK, do you know of any other places that we would be able to go to find them?"

"I can't tell you where you'll find your kid, but I can tell you where the Brutes are holing up. If they have your daughter or any information about where your daughter is, then it will be there," Dharia replies.

"Where?" Apollo asks.

"Can I see one of your phones? I need to see a map. I only saw the locations on a map, not the exact addresses," she replies.

Gambit pulls out his phone and pulls up the map app. She zooms into areas near Jacksonville to point out a few places. Apollo takes down the information, and she continues. By the time she's finished, she has told us all about how the Brutes are trying to take over the state: the sex trade, the kidnapping trade, extortion. They want it all. That has to be the reason they came for me. They thought it would force Marcus out, that he would give up his territories to get Tia back.

By two thirty in the morning, Dharia has told us all that she knows.

"All right. We can use this information. I'll make my calls this morning to make sure your brother is safe. This is just a Band-Aid, though. Something else will need to be worked out, or they're not going to stop coming for him. You understand that, right?" Apollo tells Dharia.

"Yeah. I'll figure it out," she answers.

Part of me wants to tell her that *we'll* figure it out together, but I don't want that type of responsibility on my head. I've held up my side of the bargain, and that's all I'm going to do.

"OK, I'm going to get some shut-eye. We'll have to work on a way in." Gambit looks at me, "Dare, I know you don't want your father to know what's going on, but if this is them trying to come for him, we have to retaliate. We're going to need the whole club."

I knew it. The second they said that it was a long-standing beef between them, I knew there was no way that I would be able to work this behind my father's back. The Brutes didn't ask for a ransom, nor did they throw Tia in my face. It seems as if they are just waiting for us to challenge them. Once again, I'm going to have to go to my father for help.

"Yeah, I want to roll through today."

"Tonight would be better. They do most of their drops during the day, so more security. Nighttime, there are still a lot of them, but fewer. At least in the hideouts that I've stayed in," Dharia informs us.

We all look at her and nod our heads. She's right. Nighttime is better. I need to be patient just a little while longer.

"Get what we need together. I'm going to talk to my father first thing in the morning."

The three of them leave the room. I can barely stand still. There's no way I can sleep now. I walk over to the mini-fridge, pull out the Hennessey bottle, sit down on the small couch, and take a long drink.

"Thank you," Dharia speaks.

"What are you thanking me for? You gave me more information than I've gotten from anyone in months. I should be thanking you."

She comes over and sits down on the couch. "Dare, do you know how heavy this burden has been on me? To know the only thing I can do to help my brother is to work for the enemy and pray that they don't change their minds? I know that it might not fix everything. Hell, they might even find me and kill me, but to know that he has some help in there where I can't be, it's everything."

"I hear you. I'm happy that I can help, even if it's only just this." I put a hand on her leg and squeeze lightly. When she doesn't move away, I keep it there. I offer her the bottle of Hennessy. She tips her head back and, without touching her lips to the bottle, pours a shot into her mouth. She gulps it down, and a small drop sneaks past her bottom lip. She uses her finger to wipe it away, hands me the bottle, and I take another drink.

I lean toward her but stop myself. Why the fuck is everything that she does so fucking sexy?

"What are you going to do when you get free of the debt?" I ask her.

She leans her head to the side, her hair falling as she looks at me. "You just told me that I was never going to get out of it."

I shrug. "Well, if you could, what would you do if you were free?"

She sighs. "I'd live a simple life. I'm done with money. Maybe I'd own a bakery. I don't need to be rich or anything like that. I just want everyone to be safe and happy. My brother would be out of prison. He'd stay sober. I wouldn't have to worry about anything but my own little world. That's freedom to me. Peace." She smiles wide and looks at me, "What about you?"

"What about me?"

"What would you do if you were free?"

I don't comment on the fact that she can see that I'm a prisoner here, even if I'm one of the ones calling the shots. "If I could get out of here, I'd have Tia, and we'd go live somewhere in the fucking suburbs. Somewhere slow as fuck where she can run around in the backyard and grow. Where she doesn't have to worry about anything. I'd go anywhere where she'll be happy and safe."

"That is such a domestic thing to say." She laughs.

"What can I say? I'm just your average man."

"Yeah, right. An average man who can basically do whatever he wants." She laughs and takes the bottle from me for another drink.

"Sometimes doing whatever I want is fun. Other times, it can get old," I reply as I watch her gulp down her mouthful. She hands the bottle back to me, and I take another long drink. The alcohol is making me bolder.

"I bet," she replies.

I know she feels me on her leg. She could have pushed me off. She could have gotten up, but she stays and lets me touch on her. I look down at the wife beater that she's wearing and can see her nipples are erect through the thin material. She wants this as much as I do. Right now, it feels like I would do anything to have her riding my cock, but I don't want to make her feel like she doesn't have a choice. From what she's told me about her time with the Brutes, I don't want her to be forced to do anything she doesn't want to do. She doesn't deserve any of that shit, but I have to know if she wants this as much as I do.

"What do you want? Right now, what do you want?" My hand pushes up her leg a little more, and she stills slightly.

"I think I should be asking you that." There is no more laughter in her voice. Her hands are pressing into the couch, and she is looking at me with those big hazel eyes, waiting for my answer.

I shouldn't. I fucking shouldn't.

"Fuck it." I lean forward and press my lips to hers once. I wait to see if she's going to push me off or hit me. Instead, she just stays still. I press another kiss to her mouth, and she follows me back this time when I try to move away. Her arms wrap around my neck, and she kisses me with as much passion as I'm giving her. The soft, slow kisses quickly transform into desperate need. I tug her legs so that she is lying as best she can under me. I press against her hard and continue to kiss her.

She pushes my head up for a second, her hands on each side of my face. "What's your real name?" she asks out of breath, her hips still slightly swaying back and forth.

"Darius," I answer right away. I want to get back to kissing her.

She leans up and begins kissing me again. I roll against her, and she arches her head back as a low moan floats out of her mouth. It's the sexiest shit I've heard in months. As fucked up as it is, that one sound is sexier than anything that Star has ever done for me.

"Darius, you're driving me crazy." She runs her hands up into my shirt and lightly traces the divots of my muscles. Everything about her is soft.

"Fuck, I feel like I've been waiting forever for this shit. Hold on to me," I order her and dig my hands under her thighs. I pick her up, so her legs are around my waist. I rush over to the bed and drop her down on it. She's only wearing my clothes, so there's not a lot that I need to take off her.

"Condoms," she whispers, and I immediately pull some out of the side table. I show them to her to ease her mind.

I stand there for a second and just drink in the sight of her. Her hair fans out underneath her. Her skin is clear and smooth. So smooth, it looks like she was dipped in butter. Even her breasts look pretty as fuck . . . like a fucking doll. I kick off my pants, and part of me feels bad that I fucked Star last night, and now, I'm about to fuck Dharia, but there's no stopping this shit. My need for this woman is rushing through me like a fucking wrecking ball, destroying every last bit of logic I have left. I want her. I only hope real life is half as good as the fantasy.

She opens her legs for me, and I can see that she is trimmed but not shaved completely. I let my hand trail down her body and settle between her legs.

"Mmm . . . yes, Darius." Her back arches off the bed slightly, and I'm practically drooling at the sight of her. I bring my face down to her chest and suck in one of her peaked brown nipples. She cries out in pleasure as I suck hard and continue to rub against her cunt.

I let go of her nipple for a second to look up at her. Her eyes flutter open, and she bites her lips as she puts her hand on my head. This is all genuine. Nothing's rehearsed, not doing what she wants me to hear. She's as hot for this as I am for her.

"What do you want? Tell me what you want." I switch over to the other breast, making sure I pay the same amount of attention to it.

"Kiss me." Her voice strains, and she moans. "Kiss my pussy."

My eyebrows nearly go up to my hairline. It took me years to get Lisbeth to open up enough to tell me to do that to her. I like to think I can take cues as good as the next man, but something about a woman telling me exactly what she wants is a complete turn-on.

"With fucking pleasure." I kick off my briefs and pull her to the edge of the bed. Then I kneel on the ground next to the bed in front of her, place her legs on either side of my head, and dive in.

She gasps out the second my tongue swipes against her tight clit.

"Oh fuck." She grinds her pussy down on me, and I continue to devour her. I do the best that I can. I'm just now figuring out that I can't eat pussy the same way I used to. I have to learn new techniques since my tongue and jaw no longer want to do the same things that I used to do. I find a good rhythm going back and forth between sucking in as much of her juicy pussy as I can to flicking just the tip of my tongue against her clit. Her legs close tighter around my head, and I need to use my hands to keep them open.

"Suck right there. Right *there,*" she commands in a whisper. I do exactly as she demands and am rewarded by the sound of her screaming out my name in release.

"Oh my God, Darius. Mmmm." She trembles as she continues to come. She grabs her breasts and tugs on her nipples.

I love that shit. I quickly push up from the floor and get into position. I can't wait to get inside of her.

"Fuck, Dharia, you're sexy as fuck." I slide the condom on and press the tip of my cock against her folds.

I push in, but she stops me before I can go all the way in. "You gotta be easy," she pants.

"OK. Oh fuck, OK." I push in slow, and before I can even get the entire head of my cock in, my balls are already pulling up. It took everything in me to nut when I was with Star, but I can't even get all the way inside of this woman without wanting to come.

"Darius."

I push in some more, and the walls of her pussy squeeze me, urging me to pick up the pace. I find a slow pace and do my best not to make a fool out of myself. I know I won't be able to hold out for long.

I rock into her and let her legs wrap over my hips. I hold myself up on the bed and watch her face change with every thrust—the intense need. I want to watch her make these faces all day. "Come for me again. I need to see you coming on my dick."

"Oh fuck. Yes. Make me come, Darius. Fuck me hard."

Like a dog being let off my leash, I am more than happy to oblige. I grab hold of her waist and pump hard into her.

"Fuck, a little more. A little more." She talks to herself, and her hand sneaks between us, but I swipe it away. If she needs something more, *I'll* be the one to give it to her. I reach down the best I can and roll her clit between my fingers. She does need just a little bit more. After only a few strokes of my hand, her back is arching off the bed, and I can feel her walls pulsing with her orgasm.

"Oh my . . . oooh," she moans. I drop my face to her neck and suck hard on the sensitive skin there.

She squeals, and her entire body contracts hard. Her hands wrap around my back, and she holds on to me as I race to my own finish line.

"Motherfuck." I pull my face away from her and just let my head lie against her shoulder as I explode into her like a fucking bomb. It's the most intense orgasm I have ever had in my life. It feels like my whole body is tingling with the release. I suck in huge breaths and try to stop pumping into her, but even as I come, all I want is to get as deep into her as I can manage.

When it's all over, and I can force my arms to raise myself back up, I look down at her damp face, her messed up hair, and feeling the way she rubs her hands over my face in such a tender manner, and I know one absolute truth.

I'm in fucking trouble.

Chapter 23

I'm already up and ready to face whatever challenges today brings by five thirty in the morning. The first thing is talking to Marcus about the information that we got from Dharia. Then I hope that Apollo moves fast to help her brother so she can finally have a sense of peace about it.

I walk down the stairs and see that, for the most part, it's empty—all except Grizzly and Apollo, who are standing by the pool table talking to each other. Thc conversation looks to be a heated one.

"Apollo, everything good?" I ask as I walk toward them.

He waits until I get closer before he says anything. "Nah, things ain't good."

"Fuck, what happened?"

"Gambit went this morning on his own to check the place out on Third. It's just like Dharia said, except now, the motherfucker is stuck there. If he tries to run out, they'll see him and kill him. I don't think they're just going to wait for him to explain that he was only snooping around. We've been in contact with him via text, but this shit is bad. We need to get in there and get him out." Apollo grabs the back of his neck and pulls. "Bro, you need to go talk to Marcus, and you need to do it now."

"Yeah, I hear you. OK, get what you think we'll need. I'll try to make this as quick as possible."

"Honestly, it should be a no-contest decision. They used Eleven-Quad to make us look like fools. If they're the ones that sent that fucker in here to kill Apollo, then the Brutes have already broken the truce that we have. We have to retaliate. Marcus will see that. He has to," Grizzly explains. I know he's saying that to encourage me, but it sounds like he might have some doubts. Nothing is ever a sure-fire thing with Marcus.

I turn from the two of them and walk over to Marcus's space. He's usually entertaining a random woman most nights, but I don't know what he's like in the morning. I knock on his door and hear some groaning.

"Fuck off," he yells at the door.

I crack the door but don't look in. I don't want to see whatever he has going on in there. "Marcus, I need to talk to you. It's urgent."

"Ain't nothing urgent this early in the morning. Talk to me later."

"Marcus, now," I yell through the door.

I hear footsteps pounding on the ground, so I take a few steps back in case he comes out swinging. He pulls the door open hard. "What the fuck do you want, boy? I'm fucking sleeping."

"I need to talk to you. It's club business," hoping that's enough for him to get his head out of his ass.

"Fuck, you're the VP. Why don't you handle something on your own?"

"It's about the Brutes." The immediate anger that clouds his face is enough for me to know that he'll take this seriously.

"Get in church. Give me a second to put some clothes on."

I follow his instructions and wait for him in church. I have to make sure I think through everything that I'm about to say to the man. He has a way of throwing me off my game, and I need to stay levelheaded. So I sit on the small couch and do my best to keep myself calm.

The door swings open, and he steps in. "What the hell do you know about the Brutes, and why are you waking me up this early in the morning about it?"

"I know the Brutes have been playing us for a fool. I know that we're chasing our fucking tails trying to find the Eleven-Quad crew that attacked me, but it was really the Brutes the whole time. They have taken over Eleven-Quad. Those little gangbangers are just muscle for hire. We need to go after the Brutes if we're going to get the motherfuckers who did this. Have you heard anything from anyone? Demands? Ransoms? Gloating? *Anything?*"

He paces in front of me a few times as if in deep thought about what I just told him. I don't know what the hell there is for him to think about. I told him who we needed to go after, and it's like he's getting cold feet all of a sudden.

"Nah, I haven't heard anything. So how do you know it's the Brutes? You were sure the last time that it was Eleven-Quad that did that to you." He leans against the large table, crossing one foot in front of the other.

"I was right the last time. It was Eleven-Quad. We just didn't know that it wasn't them pulling the fucking strings. There's no use in trying to find the rest of Eleven-Quad because they aren't going to have anything for us. We need to go after the Brutes." I stare at him, and it's almost as if I can see the bullshit start to form in his mind.

"Look at this." He rushes over to the large safe that he has in the room and opens it. It's overflowing with cash and papers. More than I saw the last time that it was open in front of me. "Ever since we've been getting rid of those fuckers in Eleven-Quad, other high-level players have been reaching out to us. If we keep clearing the territory, we can think about expanding the club. Take this small piece of who we are and build it into a legacy.

That's the shit we need to be focusing on. Fuck the Brutes. We got a truce with them, and starting a war right now ain't good for business."

I launch myself out of the chair and slam the safe shut. Marcus only moved his hands out of the way by a small margin. "What the fuck don't you get? I didn't sign up for this fucking MC to make you money or be king of the fucking streets. I did it to find my kid," I yell at him.

"Darius, I don't know who the fuck you think you are—"

I cut him off and slam my hand against the safe behind him. "I'm fucking talking to you. They drew first blood. It's on us to retaliate . . . unless you're telling me that you're fine with someone disrespecting a member of your family? You're good with someone making your club the pussies of Florida? Is *that* the type of rep you want floating around in the streets? How many high-level players do you think will come looking for us then?" I sneer at him.

He smirks and pushes me back. My ass hits the table. I grip the hardwood to keep myself from punching him in the face.

"Look, I don't know what the fuck crawled up your ass, but I'm done with this conversation. I don't care what you think. I'm not going against Brutes MC. If they have your little girl, we'll get her another way."

I couldn't believe this shit. Grizzly was sure that he would say yes. He said we had to retaliate. The club thinks we must retaliate. "You don't care what I think, huh?" I ask Marcus.

"What the fuck are you doing?"

In the few weeks that I had been VP, I learned quite a few things, mainly about the code and what I could and couldn't do. One of the things that both Marcus and I could do is call church. So I open the door and stick my head out. Luckily, both Grizzly and Apollo are still outside. "Apollo, get everyone in here for church."

"What the fuck," Marcus yells from behind me.

"Right away," Apollo answers.

I turn back to look at my father. "If you don't care what I think, let's see what the rest of the Sinners think about you just letting another club run up in here and try to kill one of us. I remember there being a rule about traitors. What's the punishment for that?"

"I'm not a fucking traitor. You don't know what the fuck you're talking about." Marcus is seething mad. His entire mannerism changes as he paces back and forth at the head of the table like a caged lion.

I stand back and wait for the rest of the club to file into church. Once they do, I take my seat and wait for everyone else to do the same.

"Something up?" Creeper asks from his seat.

"Yeah, we got some information, and the president and I differ in opinion. So we need to take a vote."

"Fuck that. There will be no vote. *I'm* the president of this club, and what I say fucking goes," Marcus roars out at me.

"What you say goes when it has to do with anything besides going against the fucking patch," I yell back.

Bill stands up from where he's sitting. "Hold the fuck on, Dare. I don't have any idea what kind of shit we all just walked in on but don't go throwing those kinds of fucking accusations around." Bill has been with my father since the beginning, so, of course, he would try to protect him.

"I know it. I know what it means, and I know my father would never do nothing that would force him to go against the club, so I have something to bring to the table." I stare at Bill to see if he's going to say anything else. When he doesn't, I turn back to my father. "You want to tell them, or should I explain?"

Marcus drops down into his chair and puts a hand over his eyes like he has a headache. "I'm not telling them shit."

"Fine, I'll talk then." I lean forward so that my arms are resting against the table. "We received some information over the past few hours that we have been chasing our fucking tail. It's never been Eleven-Quad that was responsible for attacking my family and me. It was the Brutes."

A round of fucks and goddammits muttered through everyone.

"Apparently, they have been taking over the different crews in the Eleven-Quad gang. We've been going after the Brutes' lackeys. It's no wonder we haven't been finding anything. I think the same way we were going after Eleven-Quad, we need to go for the Brutes."

Creeper speaks up this time. "Whoa. We can't just do that. We've been at peace with them for almost a decade now. There's no reason for us to go after them."

"No reason?" I bang my hand down on the table. "Did you forget that one of these motherfuckers killed my wife and stole my kid? An attack on one of us is an attack on *all* of us. And if you say that I wasn't a member when this happened, we still have to remember that they sent someone into *your* home to kill Apollo. What if I weren't there to stop them? What if they went after one of *y'all's* family?" I look at Creeper. His ol' lady is right upstairs. "You think we should just let this shit go? That we should hide like scared dogs? I thought the fucking Sinners don't bow down to no man." I look at each one of them, playing on their pride.

"We need to retaliate. They have to know that they can't be allowed to fuck with us."

"So, what are you suggesting? That we just roll up to the front door and bust caps all over the place? That shit ain't going to work."

"We already have one location scoped out," Apollo offers up.

"What? How the fuck is that possible?" Marcus asks.

"When we got the information, Gambit went to go check it out." Of course, Apollo keeps things as vague as possible.

"Wait, wait. Where the fuck did we get all this information? Why are we just now hearing about it?" Trim squints and looks around the table, shaking his head like he doesn't believe what we say.

Apollo and Grizzly both look at me. This is where it might be a problem. "Dharia gave us the information."

"Dharia?" Marcus laughs. "That whore bitch we picked up at the Eleven-Quad den? Boy, I thought you actually had a fucking leg to stand on. So you expect me to launch a full assault because you getting stupid over some new pussy you found? Fuck out of here. This shit's over." Marcus gets up, and the rest of the table goes to follow his lead.

"It's not fucking over," I bark. "Her information is fucking accurate. You think I didn't check this shit out before I came to the table with it? Yes, I do expect you to act based on her say-so. She's the only one here that has been inside there. The only one that stands to lose something if they find out that she snitched on them."

"What does Gambit say?" Exit speaks up.

Apollo is the one to answer. "He says that it's crawling with Eleven-Quad members and that it's locked down tight. He also says he sees one of the cars that was here the day that bastard tried to gut me in their parking lot."

I look down and try to hide my smirk. Apollo knows what the fuck he's doing. With a positive sighting of known enemies, it will seem weak if we don't attack. I clear the emotion off my face and look up the table at everyone's faces.

"So the vote." I look at Marcus, waiting for him to deny what I know is going to happen.

"Fine. If you want to do this dumb shit, let's call a fucking vote. Who wants to roll up on the Brutes' clubhouse?"

We go around the table. Bill and Trim are the only ones who say nay.

Marcus stands up and plants his fists on the table. He leans toward me. "You want this shit to happen? *You* make it happen. If we lose a brother, it's on *your* fucking head."

He's letting me have the lead. Oh, fuck yes.

"I hear you. Let's get to work."

"Get the fuck out of here. Let me know when we're rolling out." Marcus leaves before all of us.

It doesn't matter. I'm more than ready to step up and lead us.

"Where are we going to hit?" Exit asks me as we walk out of church. I give him the address, and he pulls up some street maps on his phone. "Fuck. Could you have picked a worse fucking target? Maybe we need to hit another one of their safe houses first."

I grab Exit's kutte and wait for everyone to pass by. "We need to get in that one. Gambit is there. He's stuck."

"What the fuck?" His eyes go wide when he realizes this is more than just a hit. This is a rescue mission as well. He scratches the side of his face and looks at his phone again. "A'ight, I feel you. Let me do a drive-by to see if I can see an entrance."

"Make it happen, Exit."

He nods and takes off. I hear his bike roaring up before I make it across the floor.

"Grizzly, I need you to get everyone up to speed at what we're looking at. Creeper, make sure they have everything that they need." Both of them nod, and I turn to find Apollo.

"Apollo?"

"Yeah?"

I wave him over. What I have to ask isn't for everyone's ears. When he gets close enough, I ask him about Dharia's brother.

"I made the call as soon as I left the room. They put him in solitary at five this morning. They'll keep him there until I can get my other contacts set up. It might be a week or two, but he'll be safe."

I nod. "You trust these people?"

"Like brothers," he replies before he walks away to get ready for the fight to come.

I follow Creeper into the storage closet in the back so he can get me armed. It's not thirty minutes after Exit left that he returns. I'm surprised to see him so quickly.

"What the hell happened?" I meet him by the door as he walks in.

"We're fucked, that's what happened." He's out of breath and pulls out his phone.

Grizzly and Apollo walk up behind me to find out what the update is as well.

"What do you mean?"

He pulls up a bunch of photos on his phone, all of which showed the heavily secured safe house . . . except no one is outside. There's a landing above their parking lot, where Gambit is, but there's a high fence wall that he can't jump over. According to Exit, Gambit fell out of a tree and can no longer reach to pull himself back up. Of all the dumb-ass ways to get caught.

"Why can't he just go through here?" If there isn't anyone to see him, I don't understand how he's stuck.

"You see this here?" He points to a bunch of little boxes that look like security cameras, but they're low to the ground.

"Yeah, are they security cameras?"

"No, the security cameras are up there. These are motion detectors. They're all around the building, and these aren't the cheap ones either. This shit is military grade. I don't even want to know how they got some shit like this. The second Gambit jumps off this little canopy, they're going to be up his ass. We can't get in either. There's no way to sneak in, and they're not just going to open the door, so we can walk in."

"So how the fuck are we going to get in? We can't leave Gambit there," Grizzly states the fucking obvious.

I look up to the glass that is connected to my bedroom. Seems I'm going to have to find out if Dharia knows any more secrets.

Chapter 24

Apollo, Exit, and I walk up to my bedroom to find Dharia.

"Hey, everything all right?"

"Yeah, everything is good with your brother. He's safe, and we're working on a long-term solution." I grab her hand and pull her to one of the couches.

"Something else is up. Y'all wouldn't be up here looking like your dog just died if not."

"Yeah, one of the other members of the club is stuck at one of the locations you told us about yesterday, and Exit doesn't see any way in. Do you know of any back ways in or some way that we can get around the security system?"

She puts the tip of her nail into her mouth and bites down slightly before she shakes her head no. "I've never seen any back ways out, and I don't know any other way in."

"Fuck, we screwed then." Apollo pulls his phone from his pocket, probably to see if Gambit had sent any other texts.

"Wait. Do you know who's at that location?" Dharia asks.

"What do you mean? What does that have to do with anything?"

"Which of the Brutes are there? Do you know?"

"We weren't able to get inside, but we did get a few photos of the parking lot." Exit pulls out his phone and shows her the pictures that he took on his short recon.

"Breach is there." She exhales and sits back.

"OK?" I'm still not understanding what she's trying to tell us.

"That's your way in. Me."

"The fuck? No." The idea is wiped from my head the second that she says it. There's no way that I am going to send her in there with them—for what? To have them kill her the second she walks through the door?

"Dare, listen to me. It's the only way that you all will be able to get in. They are going to have to let you in."

"Bro, she's right. This is the only way." Exit shows me the photos again. "You see this right here? If she can get in and cause a distraction of some sort or even get them to open the door themselves, we can enter."

"How do you expect her to do that shit? This seems dangerous as fuck, with no guaranteed payoff." I push myself out of my seat and look at the three of them in the room. They can't seriously think this is a good idea.

"Dare, what other choice do we have?" Dharia shrugs and tries to smile at me.

"Why are you doing this? We don't know you from a fucking hole in the wall. Dare may be stuck on you, but I, for one, don't trust jack shit coming out of your mouth. Lucky for you, everything that you've said so far has been on point, but now, you're talking about sacrificing yourself. That shit seems weird for someone you just met a week or so ago," Exit states and leans back against the small table in the room.

"I'm doing this because I've seen those bastards use everyone that has come into their space for their own gain. I've watched them kill babies and rape women. Steal from people who can't afford it. Bully weaker people like my brother into doing shit that they have no business doing and then leaving them high and dry when they get caught. The Brutes are exactly what they sound like—the worst of the fucking worst. I'd rather help you than stay quiet about them. Either way, I'm sacrificing myself. Either I go back to working off a never-ending debt and having to try to ignore the shit that's going on around me, or I help you guys and maybe fuck up their plans for a while. Seems like a good choice to me." She moves her gaze over to Apollo. "All that matters is my brother is OK. That's all I want."

"Yeah, he's straight. You got my word on that," Apollo answers.

"Then let's do this. What do you need me to do?"

"What the fuck? When the fuck did we agree on this?" I ask, stepping in front of her, trying to figure out a way to get her to reconsider. I know what she's saying is the truth. This is the only way in, but I'm not sure I want to give her up. I'm tired of fucking losing people.

"Just now, brother, so let me get her set up." Exit reaches out for her, and she walks off with him. There is nothing that I can do about this besides make sure she has the best backup possible. If she is set to go in there to put in work for us, then I am dead set to do everything that we can to make sure that she makes it back out safely.

The ride to Breach's clubhouse is quicker than I would have imagined, but I enjoyed every fucking second of it. Dharia rides on the back of my bike, clutched to me the entire ride. Her hands were wandering around my body, squeezing on me as I handle the bike. I know I have to stay focused on what the hell we're doing, but her hands grabbing and squeezing my cock through my pants is doing a hell of a job distracting me. Every time I tell her to stop, she just laughs and does it again.

The plan is simple. She'll go inside the clubhouse, set off two smoke bombs that hopefully will get them to open the door, and either run out or give us the opportunity to run in. Their clubhouse has two buildings next to it. We can use the fire escapes of that building to get out of just running straight up in the open. Once the door opens, we can jump down and get in. That's the plan. Of course, some in the group don't believe that it will work.

"This is some bullshit. I'm too fucking old to be jumping off the side of damn buildings. If she's able to get in and do what the fuck you think she's going to do, then I'll rush the front when y'all start to get in," Marcus complains. He doesn't want to go along with the plan I came up with, though his plan isn't bad either. If half of us come from above and the other half come from the side, then it will be harder for them to stop the flood of us from entering.

"Good plan. Trim, Creeper, Exit, you three stay with Marcus and enter the front way. Grizzly, Apollo, and Mali, you come with me." They all nod, letting me know that they understand their assignments. Now, all we're waiting on is for Dharia to pull through. I grab her from my bike and push her away from the group so I can talk to her for a few seconds on my own. I'm still not happy about this shit, but I can appreciate what she's going through. She must be scared out of her mind.

"You sure you're good with this?"

"Yeah, Dare, this has to be done." I watch her swallow hard and look at the ground, her hand going to the gas mask clipped to my belt.

I pull her head back up so that she's looking at me. "No matter what happens, I'm getting you out of there. Once you pull that pin, toss it, then get down and cover your head. Don't move until it's over. Don't play fucking hero. Just get us in. You hear me?" I want to see that fire in her eyes. But instead, I only see fear. I can't stand it.

She lets out a ragged sigh, and every situation where she ends up dead starts playing in my mind. "Dharia."

She leans up and kisses me swiftly on the lips. I don't back away and don't give a fuck if the rest of the club sees. If we had the time, I would have a replay of last night right here on the pavement.

"I got this, Dare. Just be ready."

"We will." I leave her where she's standing and turn to the guys behind me. "Let's go. Exit, you have a location for us to leave our bikes?" He pulls up his phone and shows us the location of a Laundromat that attaches to the building we'll be using to scale down the fire escapes. We can park up on the opposite side of that, and the Brutes will never see us. The problem with that is if we have to be out in a hurry, we won't be able to get to our bikes. So we either have to take out everyone, or we'll be sitting ducks like Gambit stuck on the damn canopy.

We all jump on our rides and peel off in the opposite direction. I look over my shoulder one last time as I leave Dharia there in the dust. This plan will work or fail, based on what she's able to do. I just hope she's strong enough to get through this.

Chapter 25

Dharia

My heart is in my throat. When I told them that I'd be able to get them in, I meant it, and it sounded like a good plan, but now that I'm actually getting ready to do it, I have no idea if I can. The two smoke grenades are heavy in my sweater pockets. Creeper has some pretty innovative equipment. Instead of just the regular-looking smoke bombs, he created some that look like they're soda cans. I just have to pop the top and toss. If the Brutes check me, they'll only find that.

The plan is to wait fifteen minutes for them to get into position, and then I'll go into the clubhouse and open the two smoke grenades. They are supposed to sting but not kill. I've been in this clubhouse before. In fact, I spent two months sleeping in one of its corners, and I've never seen another way in or out. So it would make sense for them to open the doors to get the smoke out.

"You're going to do it. It's going to be fine." I encourage myself and look around to see if anyone is walking up the large walkway where the boys left me. "Fucking dumb bitch, you're going to get yourself killed." I push my hand through my hair. I'm walking into a suicide mission to help a bunch of bikers who stole me from another bunch of bikers. Talk about jumping from the pot into the fire.

The truth of the matter is, I'd do just about anything to make sure my brother's protected. It's my fault that he's in jail in the first place. He knew I needed money to finish school. Our mother is hooked on heroin and has been for most of our lives. I did my best to get good grades in high school, but even with a 3.7 GPA and the fact that we were poor as shit, there's not a lot of extra money set aside for poor Black kids from the ghetto. I had to work for every credit, took double shifts when I didn't have classes. I was completely burned out by my last year and still hadn't made enough money to pay for my last two semesters. My brother didn't want me to give up, and even though he was working to provide for us, the allure of easy money was too good to pass up.

Breach had offered him a deal where he would just mule some product from Jacksonville to Miami. A couple of hours and we would be able to pay for the whole year of tuition. He said he was only going to do it that one time. The Brutes gave me the tuition when he went on the job, and my school was paid before he even made it to the pickup spot. Shit was going great until he was on the way back. How the fuck was he supposed to know that the cops had set up a checkpoint because of a shoot-out at a local mall?

The judge wasn't trying to hear that this was his first offense or that the drugs didn't belong to him. There were no deals to be done. They just saw another hoodlum with drugs and threw the book at him. They gave him fifteen to twenty-five years, with the possibility of parole after fifteen years. He has only been in one year, and he was already being tormented by the assholes the Brutes had in lockup. He did what he had to do to get me through school, and I would do what I have to do to make sure that he's safe inside.

Fifteen minutes passed. Then I start walking to the small alleyway that I had been down a thousand times before. I didn't want to be here again. I'm hoping that today will be the last time I ever see this place. A high fence surrounds the area that goes out into the street, though no one comes down here because there's nothing but a salvage yard and a dead end this way. The building on the other side of the clubhouse that Dare and his club will use to climb down houses some of the city's homeless and new parolees. They are right in the middle of an area that no one wants to come near. Not even the fucking buses drive down this far.

With every step toward the door, my heart races until I can't hear anything but the sound of my blood rushing through my veins. Then a light flashes on, and even in the daylight, it's still bright enough to blind me for a second. They know I'm here before I make it to the door. I let my head fall back like I'm stretching my neck, and I can see Dare looking down from what looks like the eighth-floor fire escape.

Everyone is in position.

Now, it's just up to me. I bang my hand on the door and wait for it to open. Usually, I'm escorted by other members of the Brutes or the Eleven-Quad. I've never shown up by myself. Finally, the small door opens, and Sy, one of the prospects for the Brutes, looks me over.

"Girl, you got a fucking death wish? You know Breach is gonna have your ass."

"Is he going to have it out here, or you just wasting my fucking time?" I roll my eyes at him and cross my arms over my chest, trying to force as much attitude as I can without letting him see how badly I'm shaking.

"Yeah, I'll be sorry to see you go. Maybe he'll let me have you. I've been waiting to fuck that smart mouth of yours." Sy backs away from the door, and I hear a bunch of locks scraping against the metal door. I wonder if that's what a cell opening sounds like.

A large plume of smoke comes out of the door, and the pungent smell of weed wafts around me. I've never been one to indulge in smoking weed, but I do love the smell of it. So I inhale deeply and take a step inside—time to get this shit on the road.

"Where the fuck are you going?" Sy puts up a hand, pushing me directly on my chest. I stumble backward and look up at the tall man. His bald head is shiny and perfectly round. It reminds me of a Milk Dud. His beard is patchy but long. Everyone tries to pull off the Rick Ross look, but not everyone's blessed with those genetics. He licks his cracked lips and pushes me against the wall. Then he put my hands up and begins to pat me down.

"What you been doing? Hmm? We heard someone raided one of our drop points. We thought you was dead. I'm so fucking happy to see that you're not." He drags his hands down the front of my sweater as if he were trying to feel under my breasts. Instead, he's just squeezing on me. He moves his hand down to my pockets and pulls out one of the soda cans in there.

"I'm thirsty," I say before he asks me what it's for. He hands it back to me and continues his blatant groping.

"What you say, doll?"

I keep my mouth closed. The last fucking thing I need right now is to get into a fucking argument with him. He moves closer, and I almost turn away. His breath smells like pure shit, and he has the nerve to smile in my face with that rotten-ass tooth. If he would take care of his hygiene, he wouldn't look so fucking bad. He has smooth, brown skin that makes me think of Morris Chestnut. He has an okay body, tatted up and tall. He just always smells like three days' worth of sweaty ass.

"What do I say about what?"

"About you staying with me if Breach doesn't put a bullet in your head. I'm sure we can get some of your balance paid down a little more. Just let me have that sweet ass of yours. It'll only hurt for a day or two." He smirks, and I push by him. I can't be near him any longer.

"Breach, your bitch found her way back home," Sy calls out, and I do my best to locate him. Before I set off the smoke bombs, I need to find a place where I can hide. Right now, I'm completely exposed.

"Dharia, I'm so happy to see you. I know you have a fucking explanation about where the fuck all my product went." I turn to the left where Breach is standing, and my heart falls to my stomach. Behind him is a row of little boys. Children, I would guess, no older than 7 or 8. The Sinners will come in here to shoot up the place, and I have no way of letting them know that there are little kids in here. Fuck. How do I get them out of here?

"What the fuck is wrong with you? You got amnesia or some shit?" Breach pushes one of the little boys away and storms up to me. My eyes flit from side to side, trying to think of another option quickly. What the fuck can I do? Will the kids know to run if chaos breaks out? Fuck. What do I do?

Breach's large hand clamps down on my neck, and he shakes me once like a ragdoll. "When I'm fucking talking to you, you'd better answer. Where the fuck is our product?"

I gasp in a deep breath and try to pull at his hand. How the hell does he expect me to talk if he's squeezing the life out of me? I can't even swallow.

"You've been gone for more than a fucking week. You don't look like you got the shit beat out of you, so you better start talking fast, or I'm going to let Sy and the rest of the boys run through you. Then I'm going to call Mills and them down at Dade and have them do the same to your brother. They sweet on him, you know. He likes to fight back." Breach smiles, and I kick up, almost connecting with his dick. White spots start to dance behind my eyelids before he drops me down to the floor.

I heave in deep breaths. My lungs feel like they're on fire.

"The Heavy Sinners have it."

"What the fuck? What the fuck did you just say to me?" Breach grabs me by my hair and pulls my head back hard. I feel a chunk of hair yank out from the force of it. I hold his wrist to try to buffer it.

"The Heavy Sinners have it. They had their way with me already, and then they let me go."

He shakes his head and looks to the side, where a few Eleven-Quad are packaging up some blow. "You're lying. They not dumb enough to do that shit." He lets go of my hair, tossing me to the side.

"They are. In fact, they're getting ready to come in here any second."

He turns around, his grey eyes shooting daggers at me and his eyebrows scrunched together. "Bitch, you better come up with a different fucking story before I whore you out to the lowest bidder. Marcus wouldn't do that shit."

I quickly move to where the children are and subtly try my best to bunch them together behind me. They do it instinctively.

I clear my throat and talk loudly. Loud enough that everyone inside the clubhouse will hear me. "It's true. The Heavy Sinners MC is outside right now waiting to kill you." I need to get all of the Brutes and everyone else by the door. It's the only way.

"What the fuck is she talking about?"

"We got trouble?"

"Bullshit."

Club members and prospects start moving toward the only way out to see if what I'm saying is true.

"I don't see shit," Sy calls from the door.

I turn quickly to the kids behind. "Stay down and cover your mouths. Once it's all over, run until you're safe. Go home. Go somewhere safe," I whisper and hope that they understand. I'm toward the back of the clubhouse with a whole club of Brutes between me and the door. Once I set off these bombs, I'm going to be stuck here. It's the only option, though. I pull the soda cans out of my pockets and pop the tops. The sound of metal clanging on the floor doesn't draw any attention, but the fast-moving billowing plume of smoke causes everyone to turn around.

"What the fuck? Smoke, smoke!" Sy yells out, and I throw myself into the corner behind a couch. Then quickly, I pull the kids with me the best I can.

The bombs work like a fucking charm, and by the time I lift my head, I can't see a thing in front of me. The kids huddling next to me all start crying and screaming. My eyes are burning, but I do my best to blink through the smoke.

"Listen, you have to stay down. No matter what's going on, stay close to the floor. Don't move," I yell at them. I grab for any furniture I can, shove it in front of them, and pray it's enough.

"Find that bitch," Breach bellows out.

I need to get away from the kids. If they find me while I'm huddling with the boys, the kids are just going to be in the line of fire. So I make sure they're all down before I get on my hands and knees to crawl in the opposite direction.

"I can't fucking breathe," someone calls out, followed by a round of coughing.

Others are gagging and throwing up. The bombs are still blowing out smoke, and now, it's getting to be too much for me. I cough and fall to the side, trying to get away from the toxic air.

"No, don't open the fucking door," Breach screams again, but I don't know where he is. He sounds close, but I'm not sure.

"I can't breathe. We need to clear this shit out."

I fight the urge to pass out as I hear the sound of heavy locks grinding against metal. Finally, a gust of fresh air comes into the club . . . and then nothing.

I don't hear gunshots or people running. Just the birds outside chirping reminding me that today is business as usual. Dare has played me.

Chapter 26

Dare

"What the fuck is taking so long? I told you that bitch is just a fucking rat. You got us out here in the fucking open. They probably have another way out and are going to be on our ass any second. So this is what you get for letting your dick decide who to trust." Marcus's voice barks out of the speaker of my phone.

Apollo and Grizzly look at me. They're all thinking the same thing. The plan is blown. Dharia should have set off those bombs awhile ago. She could be in there right now snitching about our very location and what we're planning to do. If they find a way around us, there's nothing we can do besides die. Not to mention Gambit is still stuck on the fucking roof.

"Give it a few more minutes. She's going to do it." I speak loud enough that the phone on the ground can pick up what I'm saying.

"Dare, it's been more than enough time. We need to get the fuck out of here before they find out where the fuck we are. The plan is blown. We need to enter in a different way." Trim offers his opinion this time.

"Dare."

I look up at Apollo, who's trying to get my attention. "It's time to go," he mouths to me, not wanting the other half of the club to hear that it's only me that wants to wait. If Marcus knows that everyone is on the plan to get the fuck out of here, he'll call it.

A buzz sounds from Grizzly, and he plucks out his phone from his pants. "Smoke."

"What?"

"Gambit says he can see smoke from where he is. She just opened them."

Relief floods me, followed by fucking dread. If she set the bombs off, then why aren't they opening the door? What the fuck is happening in there? I'm itching to get the fuck down there and get her out.

"You hear that, Exit? Marcus? We got smoke. Be ready to move your asses," I direct before I hook the phone onto my kutte, leaving it on so I can hear them for as long as possible.

"Yeah, we fucking hear."

Now, people are moving around inside the building we're hiding on. Are they getting ready for their day? Maybe some of them are preparing for work. Some may be eating breakfast with their families. But I bet none of them realize there's about to be a shoot-out right next to their homes.

"Everyone, get your masks on." I slip mine on, watching as Apollo and Grizzly do the same.

"I can't fucking breathe. We need to clear this smoke," I hear someone scream from the door that opens from the side entrance. Then, finally, they're getting ready to open the door. The metal scrapes as the locks are turned and the door swings open.

"Move now," I hiss out, and suddenly, we're all running down the fire escape. The smoke is so thick that even when we make it to the last level, the man at the door can't see us. When I look to the left, I see a row of my brothers rushing along the side of the building with their guns drawn and ready to rush inside as well. It's been at least forty-five seconds since the door opened. We want the smoke to dissipate enough for us to go in but still be cloudy to hinder them.

"Grizzly, you got a shot?"

He pulls up his gun. I see him aim and fire. A bald-headed man gasps, then clutches his chest as blood seeps out of his fresh gunshot wound. He tries to talk for a second before he collapses right there in the doorway.

"Motherfucker, close the fucking doors—now!"

I hop down off the last level of the fire escape and lunge for the door. The body of the man who originally opened the door is slumped in an awkward position and stops the door from shutting. I grab the door, and Grizzly reaches over me to hold it open. I lean my head in slightly and fire two shots at the man who's trying to move the dead body out of the way.

Everyone has gas masks on, so I can't see faces.

"Stay low and look before you fucking shoot."

"Fuck that. Leave no fucking witnesses," Marcus booms out as he rushes through the door. The rest of us follow him in but break off so that we're not all bunched together. I scan the immediate area but can barely see anything. Thankfully, the masks make it so we can breathe.

"Dare, watch out!" I hear a muffled voice from the side. I turn my head just in time to see a heavyset motherfucker rushing me. He catches me directly in the side, and I go sprawling to the ground. He sticks his hand under my chin to rip off the gas mask, but I break his hold on me with my forearm. My gun skitters out of my grasp. I see where it went, but I can't get it. Sweat drips onto the plastic of my mask from his face. He hacks a few times but doesn't let me go. His eyes are bloodshot, and I see his chest heaving up and down. I grab the side of his head and push with all my might so that it slams against the hard brick wall that lines the inside of the club. The wall creates giant pockmarks on his cheek and forehead area. Then little trails of blood trickle down his face. He rages and tries to get out of my grasp, but I'm already pushing my upper body off the floor. I use my knee to dislodge him fully from on top of me, but he holds on to my arm and yanks me forward.

"You . . . fucking . . ." The man tries to talk, but the gas makes it hard for him to breathe. I throw my fist into his side, but it does nothing to him. There is just too much girth around his midsection for him to feel my punches. Instead of getting him farther away from me, it only allows him to grab hold of my kutte and slam me against the wall. He pushes his forearm into my neck and presses down, set on choking the life out of me. I try to turn my head, but I can't find anyone to help me. I hear gunfire, but I don't know who's coming up on top. I need to get this motherfucker off me. I reach out to the side and feel a floor lamp. I knock it to the floor, the body of it breaking into pieces next to us. Then I focus on his fucked-up face to keep myself conscious. My vision is slowly fading to black.

"Fuck," I groan out, but it sounds more like a gurgle than an actual word. I turn around and see the broken pieces of the lamp. I find the top part of it and grab it and see the very second when the bastard trying to break my neck notices, but it's too late for him to block it. I jab the top of it at the side of his face, the same side that I had already slammed into the wall. The hot lightbulb explodes, and he screams as his eyes fill with tiny fragments of glass and filament: his skin sears, and bloody tears flood from his eyes. Small shards of the lightbulb stick out of his eyelids.

"Ah, shit, my fucking eyes! Fuck," he cries and puts both his hands to his face, letting me go. I suck in a deep breath but don't let up. I bring the broken lamp up again and slam it down on his face. The socket where the lightbulb should have been slices into his already bloody face. The second time I hit him, he falls backward to the ground, and I bring the makeshift weapon up again. Again, I swing down with all my strength, and this time, the socket pushes into his eyeball and, finally, his brain. Thin grey liquid mixed with blood rolls down the side of his face, and his body seizes underneath me from the trauma to his brain.

One down, everyone else to go.

When I look to my side, I don't see any of my club mates around me. I hop over the small pieces of furniture and see bodies littered on the ground: a few Brutes, others with Eleven-Quad tats, but not one Sinner. Suddenly, I hear screams coming from the back someplace, and when I follow the sound, I see a hallway off the right side of the main area. I rush in that direction and pray that I'm not too fucking late. I rip the gas mask off my face. Finally, the smoke has cleared enough that I can breathe normally.

"Get the fuck off her right now!"

"Fuck you. I'm not doing shit. If I'm going, this bitch is coming with me," someone yells.

"Apollo," I call for him, but he doesn't answer. Instead, Gambit is the one that answers. When the fuck did he get in here? He must have run in when we started shooting.

People are down another hallway, and the group of them are all crowded around a door.

"Move, fuck, move out of the way." I push my way through everyone.

My breath catches, and I go to charge the piece of shit that's holding Dharia as a human shield.

"No," Grizzly says and grabs hold of my arm. "The gun."

I lean to the side and see a gun pressed right to the back of her head. There's barely any part of his body that isn't in some way shielded by her small frame. "We got you, Dharia. Everything is going to be fine." I try to keep my voice calm.

"Breach, there's no fucking way that you're getting out of this. Why don't you put the fucking gun down, and let's talk about this?" Creeper says from the far left of the room, his gun drawn and ready to fire.

"This motherfucker is Breach?" I'm so fucking happy to hear it. I was worried that someone else might have killed him before I get the fucking chance.

"Talk? Who the fuck you think you fooling? I know damn well how this shit ends. I have to say I'm fucking impressed, though. A plan like this is something I wouldn't expect y'all to come up with, especially from Marcus."

I don't turn to look for my father, but I log that information for later.

"You fucked with the Sinners. What did you think was going to happen? We were going to sit down for a drink? Nah, you come for us, and we kill all of you." I reach over to Grizzly and pull the extra gun tucked into the back of his pants.

I disengage the safety, aim, and wait for my opening. Gambit is on one side, Creeper on the other. Grizzly, Apollo, and I are dead center. Unless this motherfucker learns how to fly in the next few minutes, he's a fucking dead man.

"Come for you? What the fuck are you talking about?" He leans his head farther to the side, and I see Gambit flinch. I've seen how sure-handed Gambit is. If there is anyone in here I trust to take this shot, it's him.

"You had your little baby thugs come into my house, and they killed my wife and took my kid. Did you think that shit wasn't going to come back to bite you in the ass? Now, I want to know where Tia is. That's why you're going—"

Breach cuts me off. He sticks his head out a little farther. "Hold the fuck on. What the hell are you talking about? We—"

A loud blast, followed by a bright flash of light, explodes by my head. An instant, high-pitched beep erupts in my ear, and Bill's gun is still smoking at the side of my head.

I lean to the side, and around me is a lightning storm of bullets flying. I drop down, cover my head, and press my fingers to my ear, trying to get my hearing to come back. When I look forward, flashbacks of Lisbeth slice through any pain I may feel right now.

No, no . . . "Dharia," I scream for her as she lays in a pool of blood.

"I'm OK," she yells back.

A large body drops down on top of her, and the bullets suddenly stop.

"Oh shit. Fuck," Grizzly moans.

"Get him down. Shit. We gotta stop that bleeding." When I roll on my back, I see Grizzly's dark blue shirt turning brown with blood.

Creeper is on him right away, pressing QuikBloc and gauze on his abdomen.

Gambit rushes over to Dharia and lifts the dead Breach off her. Then she darts over to me.

"Can you get him fixed up?" I ask Creeper as I stand up.

"Not here. I need to call Doc. He'll live if we can keep this bleeding under control and get him sewn up, but we got to move right away."

"I'm straight, Dare. It's good," Grizzly says from the floor, cringing as Creeper continues to pack his wound.

"Can you ride?"

"For sure. Let's go." Grizzly tries to get up on his own, but he yells out in pain when he bends his midsection, his dark brown skin taking on a greyish hue.

"Trim, Gambit, both of you stay right next to him. If he fucking falls, you better be close enough to catch him," I order.

"We got it."

"Yeah. We need to get the fuck out of here right the hell now," Trim states.

"What's going on?"

"Five-Oh."

Everything goes quiet, and sure enough, in the distance, I hear sirens. So that's what the fuck happens when you have a gunfight first thing in the fucking morning. "Shit, let's move."

Dharia grabs hold of my hand, and we run out of the room. We get to the main room, and she suddenly lets go of my hand.

"Dharia, we have to go," I yell back at her as the rest of the club runs for their bikes. Apollo and Mali are the only ones that stay behind to wait for me.

"Wait, they're still here."

Who the fuck is still here? We don't have time for this shit. The last thing we need is to get caught in the middle of a fucking bloodbath by the cops. I watch Dharia run toward the back of the club, bend down behind a couch, and a second later, a group of kids come running out from behind it.

"What the fuck? Who are they?"

"I don't know. Breach had them." Her eyes open wide, "Oh God, wait." She runs in the opposite direction back toward the rooms we just left.

"Dharia, no. We can't fucking wait."

"Dare, we going to get fucking caught. Leave her," Apollo shouts from behind me. I look from him back to where Dharia ran off, then back again.

The sirens get louder, and it sounds like they're coming from the direction we need to go to get our bikes. We're already fucked.

"She didn't leave us." I couldn't do it. So I take off in the direction she went, Apollo and Mali right behind me. She yanks at a file cabinet with all her might.

"What the fuck are you doing? Are you crazy? You don't hear those motherfucking sirens?"

The drawer that she pulls on finally opens. There's a cloth bag in the corner. She empties it and starts shoving papers into the bag.

"What the hell is this?" I grab her shoulder and try to lift her, but she yanks away.

"Your answers," she screams back at me. "Help me."

Is this something about Tia? Those are the only answers that I'm looking for. I bend down and stuff the remaining papers in the bag, and then we race to the front and out of the clubhouse.

"Shit, we're going to be boxed in," Apollo growls out.

He's right. The cops are already a block away from the Laundromat where we parked our bikes.

"Fuck. Run the other way."

"That way," Mali points.

"There's nothing over there. We can't hide in the junkyard." Apollo looks down the block again at the trail of police cars racing on their way to us.

"Trust me." Mali grabs hold of me, and we all start running toward the dead end. Finally, we find one of the many holes in the fence that will lead us into the junkyard and follow Mali.

"Where the fuck are you taking us? We're sitting ducks in here." I keep Dharia close to me as she clutches the large bag she has slung over her shoulder.

Mali runs to the other side of the junkyard. Lined up, ready to be demolished or stripped, are broken-down cars.

He runs to the first one, opens the hood, then shuts it quickly. Then immediately, he moves to the next one. The next three, he passes over without looking.

"You think you can get one of these pieces of shit to work?"

"Absolutely. Most of the cars will run with some work. People just don't want to put in the work. We don't need it to work for long. A couple of miles will do." He stops at a Camry, opens the hood, looks around for a second before slamming the hood down, jumps into the front seat, and leans down. A second later, the lights turn on, followed by the sound of the car sputtering to life. The entire frame shakes like it might break apart at any second, but as he said, we only need it for a few miles.

"Good shit, Mali." I hit the top of the car and immediately regret it when the car lets out a loud squeal. This shit *really* is on its last legs.

We all get in, and Mali successfully navigates the dangerous junkyard until we're on the other side, a good three blocks over from where all the cops are. We'll come back later for our bikes.

By the time we make it out to the street, we can barely hear the sirens anymore, and I finally take a deep breath. I lay my head back and try to stop my brain from racing a million miles a minute. I hope Grizzly is OK. I hope those kids can get away, and I hope none of the Sinners are caught by the cops. Lastly, I hope Bill has a good fucking explanation for what he did.

Chapter 27

The ride back to the clubhouse is quite eventful. The car stalled twice, shook enough to rattle my brain, and left a trail of black smoke every time we accelerated at a green light. If we all weren't so on edge, it would have been funny.

We successfully got away from the Brutes' clubhouse without anyone catching us . . . or so we thought. However, when we pull up at the clubhouse, we notice a dark blue Dodge Charger is parked right out front.

"Fuck. That's the jakes," Apollo growls from his seat.

Do they know it was us? How the fuck did they get here so fast? Fuck. I peer out the window, trying to get a feel of the situation. I see Detective Pearson step around the car and start talking to Marcus, who is still standing outside. Maybe this is just about me.

"Mali, we're going to get out, and you're going to take this hunk of shit somewhere and get rid of it. Apollo, you get Dharia back into the clubhouse.

Dharia, put whatever is in the bag in my room. I'll talk to the detective."

"You got it," Apollo responds.

Dharia nods but doesn't let go of my hand. Mali stops the car, and we get out. Apollo practically has to pull Dharia away from me. Detective Pearson starts in my direction, and the rest of the members of the club walk inside.

"Mr. Heavy, your father here was telling me that your club was just on a little early-morning ride. I expected to see your bike." He tilts his head and searches me for anything that might look out of order. My gun and the gas mask are tucked into at the back of my pants, so he can't readily see it, but I can tell he's fishing for something.

"Yeah, my bike needs a bit of maintenance, so I had to leave it and get another ride home," I answer quickly. "Something happening that I need to know about?" He's never come here before, so, why, all of a sudden, is he here now?

The smug look he had on his face seconds ago drops off, and he puts his hands in his pockets. Something is wrong. Something is really wrong.

"What is it?"

"Look, I know it's been a shit road for you, and it might not seem like I'm out there working for you, but I am. But unfortunately, someone down at Central fucked up."

I take a step closer because I still don't understand what the hell he's talking about. Yet, everything inside of me says that I'm going to have to fuck him up before he steps foot off Sinners' property. "Come again? What the fuck does that mean?"

"Dare, you good?" Gambit stands by the door.

"Yeah, I'm good. But, Detective, I'm going to need you to tell me exactly what the fuck that means because I'm not getting it."

He steps back and sighs, not out of annoyance but fear. "There's a procedure that must be followed at every arrest, every questioning. If it isn't, all the evidence that was gathered for the case will be thrown out."

It feels like my heart is freezing in my chest. There is no way he is saying what I think he's saying. "What the fuck? What the fuck are you talking about?" I take another step toward him, but before I can move any closer, Gambit has an arm around my waist and holds me back.

"One of the officers thought we had a search warrant. He found the gun in the house, but we weren't supposed to have searched it. As a result, it was ruled as an illegal seizure, so it can't be used, and any other evidence from then on is inadmissible as well."

"Oh fuck, what the fuck?" Gambit says from behind me, but I just stare at the detective and wait for him to tell me he's fucking around. This can't be fucking happening.

"The judge ruled this evening that the case was thrown out. So the man that killed your wife will get off due to a technicality. I'm so sorry, Mr. Heavy."

Seconds feel like hours as my brain puts together the words that just came out of his mouth.

I close my eyes and shake my head. This is wrong. This is all wrong. Visions of Lisbeth screaming and fighting for her life play on a continuous, sped-up loop in my head. *So the bastard who did this is free . . . because they fucked up?*

"You son of a bitch. *You* did this. My family never meant shit to you. You let this shit happen." I do my best to rush him. I just want to feel his face exploding against my fist, but Gambit is still holding me back.

"Dare, listen to me. We'll get him. I'll get a tail on him right now. The bastard won't last the week. You'll get your revenge. You have my word on that," Gambit says directly in my ear so the detective can't hear him.

"I'm so sorry. I have to ask that you stay away from him. Try not to make more trouble than you need right now," the detective instructs, then turns to walk away. He at least has the tact to leave with his head hung low. When all this first happened, I believed in the system. I just knew that they were all out there fighting to get justice for the victims. Now, I know it's never going to happen. Sometimes, you just have to get justice the old-fashioned way . . . an eye for an eye.

Gambit pulls me inside, and my blood feels like acid in my veins. Everything is falling to pieces around me. I'm stuck in this MC that I never wanted to be in. The man who killed my wife is about to be out and back to his old life in a matter of hours. The only lead about where my daughter might be is dead because someone has a happy trigger finger. No, I'm tired of the fucking procedures. Tired of doing shit the right way.

Gambit closes the door behind me and stays to ensure that the good detective is indeed on his way.

"Grizzly is in the back with Doc Hudson. He says that it'll be a few days until Grizzly's up, but he should be OK," Trim tells me. My brain registers it, but I'm focused on only one thing.

"Dare, I hate to fucking admit it, but this was a good hit. Your girl did good." Someone, I think it's Exit, mentions.

The second I'm within reach, I yank my arm back and smash my fist across Bill's face. I hit him with such a force that he lifts clear off the ground before he crumbles to it.

"Oh shit."

I jump on him like a crazed animal, furiously punching him. Even when blood spews out of his mouth, I don't stop. He puts his hands up to guard his face, but that doesn't stop me.

"Darius, get the fuck off." Marcus reaches around to grab me by my neck and yanks me back. I turn in his grasp, no longer trying to fight the man on the ground but now trying to fight the man who brought me into this in the first place. I uppercut Marcus on the side of his gut. It knocks the wind out of him. He's already brought me in close enough that he can't keep his distance while I land blow after blow into his midsection. I hear bones break and Marcus howl in pain. He pulls me in and wraps me up like a boxer. Fuck that. I pull my head back and crack it into his face as hard as I can. The blow dazes him for a second, but it's all I need. I quickly grab him by the back of his neck and bring his face down as I launch my knee up.

"Darius, no, stop!" Dharia's voice floats through the air, and the fog of anger lifts for a brief second.

"You crazy son of a bitch," Bill screams at me from the floor where he's still trying to recover.

Marcus moves back a few steps, and I see his hand going toward his side. Then in a flash, both of us have our guns drawn and pointed at each other.

"What the fuck?"

"Goddammit."

The next second, every club member has their weapon drawn and pointed. Even in my rage-induced craze, I notice the power shift. Anyone that goes against the president should get shot down. I know it. It's one of the many rules that they all drilled into my head. It's what Marcus drilled into my head. Yet, here we both stand, guns drawn at each other, and the club is split with some pointing guns at him and others pointing guns at me.

The most fucking surprising of all . . . Apollo has his gun drawn on my father.

"You do have a fucking death wish," Marcus wheezes out.

"Maybe, but I'm taking you with me—that I fucking guarantee."

"Darius, what are you doing? How much of your family are you willing to give up? We have work to do. Stop this." Dharia's soft voice floats through the air, but I don't know where she is. I could give two shits about my father dying. That son of a bitch needs to be put out of his fucking misery. Apollo, Gambit, and Exit might have been my enemy when I first walked through those doors, but they have become more my family than anyone has ever been other than my mother.

I drop my gun, and so does everyone else. I turn in Bill's direction, and Apollo stands in front of me.

"Dare, he's had enough."

"Why did you shoot him?"

"What?" Bill hawks up bloody mucus and spits it on the floor. "What in the shit are you talking about now?"

"Breach. He was talking. Giving us answers, and you fired the shot that killed him. Why the fuck would you do some shit like that unless you have something to hide? Was it you who orchestrated this shit?" I speak over Apollo's shoulder.

"Boy, you're fucking crazy." Bill waves his hand but doesn't answer.

"Yes, that's correct. I *am* fucking crazy. Let's not test just how fucking crazy I am unless you ready to die."

"You threatening me, motherfucker?" Bill steps forward, blood speckles shooting out of his mouth and landing on my face.

"Threat? No, Bill. I'm *telling* you. Listen good, you old fuck. I. Will. Fucking. End. You." Apollo pushes me back again.

"I didn't do shit that we weren't there to do. The motherfucker was the enemy. My president told me to leave no fucking witnesses. I shot him. What don't *you* understand?"

I groan in frustration. He's going to stand there and act like what he did wasn't suspect as fuck.

"Why did you wait to fire until he was about to tell us about who ordered the hit on Darius? You didn't have a clear shot." Gambit is the one to speak up this time. "The fact that Dharia's head wasn't blown off is pure luck."

"Dharia?" Bill scrunches his face like he smells something bad. "Since fucking when do we give a fuck about that cunt? She's just a bitch. She can be replaced," he replies.

I lunge, but Apollo still has a grip on me.

"What the fuck are you hiding? Did you do this shit? Did you destroy my fucking life to get more funds for the club?" I lean to the other side of Apollo as I speak.

"What . . . no," Bill stutters, and my mind surges forward with more questions. I hit a nerve.

"How fucking convenient is it that as soon as all this shit starts to go down, we get an influx of people wanting us to work shit for them, and that our cash fucking triples?" I hiss at him.

"What?" Apollo asks in front of me.

I take a step back so I can look at him. "Oh, y'all don't know? That safe is stuffed. Not with singles either. It's stuffed to the fucking brim with lots of cash." I move Apollo out of the way and look at Bill again. Now the rest of the club is looking too. They don't know.

"What's he talking about?" Creeper asks.

"It doesn't matter what the fuck he's talking about. Bill ain't did shit but what he was supposed to do. Don't come in here losing your shit because your life is shit. We the ones fucking helping you. You've been nothing but problems since I brought you here. Fuck, I should have left Apollo as VP. At least he doesn't stir the shit as much as you." Marcus tosses his hand in the air, helps Bill up, and they walk away, probably to get patched up.

I rake my eyes over the crowd. No one says a word, but I can tell they are all thinking the same thing. They want to know if they've been played. I'm inclined to think the answer is yes.

The adrenaline is now leaving my system, and my body feels as if I just ran a fucking marathon. Dharia rushes over to me. She grabs my arm and drags me toward the stairs.

The second I get up to my apartment, I collapse. I'm not fucking built for this. My fucking face feels like someone is smashing his foot into it, and my hands are shaking like leaves.

Dharia leaves me against the door and runs to the bathroom. When she comes back, she has a wet washrag. She drops down to the ground and begins cleaning me off.

"Why are you still here?" I ask, my voice a gritty whisper.

"What?"

"Breach is dead. He's the one you owed, right? You're free. So, why are you still here?" What are her intentions? I just can't take trusting someone who's going to turn on me later.

"Darius, you and I both know this isn't over. Breach may be gone, but the rest of the Brutes aren't just going to let me be. Besides, I'm not going to leave you. Like I told you downstairs, we got work to do. We need to find Tia." She puts a soft hand on my face and caresses my cheek. Her hazel eyes blossom with fire and determination. There is something else there, something I don't deserve . . . adoration. Her touch is full of care and strength, but I feel like every swipe of her fingers breaks me down further.

Pressure builds in my chest so intense that it feels like I can't breathe. My head is spinning, and my body feels so weak.

I drop my head to my hands, and the constant torturous movie of my little girl being dragged out of my sight is too much to bear. A strangled sob forces its way out of my mouth. Tears I've kept locked up spill down my cheeks.

Warm arms immediately wrap around me. I let her embrace and support me. She doesn't realize her arms are the only things keeping me together.

Chapter 28

Dharia

I don't think I have ever seen someone with so much mental anguish before.

Mania. It's the only way I can explain what happened to Darius downstairs. He swung at everyone that got close to him, determined to beat down his father and Bill.

I hold Dare until he cried himself out. I try to kiss the pain away, and before I know it, he's fucking me right there on the floor by the door. I don't mind. It's a release we both desperately need. After we have our fill, I help him to the bed and hope some rest is just what he needs. I lay down next to him. It's nothing sexual. I just don't want him to feel alone. I can't say that I love him because I'm not there yet, but I feel for him. He's doing his damnedest to get his family back, and I can respect that.

I've been with other men in my life, but what seems to draw me to Dare more than any of the others is his power . . . his ability to lead without even trying. I saw what happened downstairs. The members turned on their own president to back him. I don't know shit about this family, but I know a fair bit from the Brutes. No one goes against the fucking president. Dare already has the club behind him without asking for it.

That type of power is sexy as fuck.

By eight that night, I'm restless and hungry. I take out a few slices of bread and make myself a peanut butter and jelly sandwich. If I stay here with him, I need to talk to him about getting some non processed food. I can make a meal if I have the ingredients. I also need to speak with him about clothes. Right now, all I have is some clothes that Creeper's ol' lady donated to me.

"Where's mine?"

I spin in shock. "Fucking hell, Dare. When the fuck did you wake up?" I catch my breath before I turn around and start making him a sandwich as well.

"I woke up when your sexy ass got out of bed." He turns over and folds his hands behind his head, showing off his toned chest and chiseled abs. The man has the body of a king. I do my best not to stare. The last thing I need is for him to get a big head.

"How are you feeling?" I ask as I open the small fridge and pull out two bottles of water.

He leans up and drags his hand over his face. He groans and closes his eyes. "Like I just come from a fucking war. Those bastards downstairs probably trying to figure out a way to get me committed."

I laugh slightly. "You did lose your shit a little." I walk over to him with the food, and he takes it from my hand. He makes a space so that I can sit, and then he presents the food in front of me when I'm comfortable.

"I need this to be over. One way or another, I need all of this shit to be over."

He's talking about his little girl. I hope that whatever I managed to pull out of the file cabinets is enough to help.

When I was working for the Brutes, every time they came back from a drop site with cash, I had to input the amount in ledgers. They did everything on paper, thinking that they could destroy that quicker than anything on a computer. The Brutes were like a little fucking corporation. They had files on who they worked with, new opportunities, and, most importantly, all their assets. I hope that something in the pile of papers I took from the Brutes' hideout would be enough to help Dare find his daughter.

"Dare, I know shit is fucked up, but you gotta have faith. We're going to find her."

He clenches his jaws and pops his knuckles. "In what condition? It's been months. I don't know what they're doing to her. These assholes aren't running a day care. What's she going to be like when I get her home? Can she survive it? I'm out here on the outside, and I can barely handle it mentally."

I need to give him something to do. He's spiraling. Soon, he'll be in that dark place where he's trying to kill everyone around him. "You want to look through the papers? See what we have there?"

His eyes dart to the chair, where the large canvas bag is still stuffed with paperwork. It might take hours to go through it all. "Fuck yes. What is it?"

I wipe the crumbs off my mouth and go for the bag. I drag it on the floor rather than pick it up. Then I take out a large handful of documents and put them on the bed in front of Dare.

He scans it but shakes his head. "What am I looking at? Seems like it's ledgers."

"Yeah. I didn't have time to keep everything separated, so it's all jumbled. Right now, this is going to be like finding a needle in a haystack." I let him know so that he doesn't get frustrated. He nods his head and begins making piles like he's been looking through ledgers for years, a peek at what he was like when he worked as an account manager in the business firm he told me about.

After about an hour of scanning through numerous sheets of paper, my eyes begin to cross.

Suddenly, someone knocks on the door, and I internally thank God for the interruption.

"Come in," Darius calls out.

Apollo stands in the doorway, his eyes wary.

"Don't worry. I'm done trying to shoot people today." Dare pushes himself off the bed, careful not to disturb the piles of papers he's already gone through.

"Fucking hell, I'm happy to hear that shit." Apollo walks in, closing the door behind him. He looks fresh and alert like he just finished taking a shower.

"Something going on?" I ask.

"I drew the short stick. The guys want to find out if this crazy motherfucker is going to come down and party."

"Party? Are you fucking serious? How the hell are we thinking about partying right now?" Dare questions.

"Bro, you know Marcus. Any excuse to get a girl on his dick, he's gonna take it. Besides, this may be a good thing. Keep the jakes off our case. If we up in here lying low, they going to think we have something to hide. So it's better if we act like business as usual."

"Whatever. Give me a minute, and I'll be down, only to show face, though. I got shit to do up here."

Darius walks over to the bathroom, and I hear the shower going.

"You know, when you first got here, I thought for sure you were going to fuck his head up even more."

I turn when I realize Apollo is talking to me. A first. The guys never speak to me one on one.

"Now, I'm starting to think you may be the only thing keeping him sane." He tilts his head slightly before he turns and walks out the door.

Can he tell that I feel that way too? That in the whole year I've spent trying just to survive with the Brutes to being taken by the Sinners to making sure my brother is OK, Dare is probably the only piece that makes me feel like there's a chance of normalcy.

This shit is crazy. My ass is falling for a fucking biker.

I shake my head and look around the small apartment that has somehow become more of a home than I've had in a while.

The splash of water against the tub floor draws my attention. I find myself walking toward the bathroom like Icarus to the sun. I stand in the doorway and just watch him, my desire ramping up at the sight of his hard body naked and wet. I watch as his hands roam over his body and cock. I bite my lip to keep myself from moaning with need. Fuck, the man is so damn sexy and talented.

Darius is a perfect lover. Not only does he last longer than five minutes, but he also takes direction and doesn't get pissed about it. He eats pussy like it's a five-course meal, and he knows when I need it hard and when I want it sweet. I couldn't ask for more in the sex department.

"I can open the curtain if you need a better view." He chuckles, and his deep voice squeezes at my core. Now, he turns so that his back is facing me, and even his ass is sexy.

Fuck it.

I reach down and pull off my shirt and sweater. Then my bottoms. I'm in the shower with him before he can turn around.

"Shit," he mutters when he realizes that I'm naked and touching on him. I lift myself the best I can and attack his mouth with mine. I moan when he slides his tongue into my mouth. I can feel the slight dip on the side of the muscle where a bullet must have gone through. He turns us around so that my back is against the shower wall. I suck his lip into my mouth and bite down.

A deep groan vibrates through his chest as he smashes me hard against the wall. I release his lips, and my hands quickly swipe down his body.

"Dare, I need you."

"Tell me." He pushes his hand down and grabs my ass right under the crease and spreads the cheeks apart so he can slide his finger to the opening of my pussy.

I moan loudly and try to push down so I can feel him inside me.

"I need you so bad. I need to come. Make me come, Dare. It's so intense." I pant and turn my head to prevent the spray of the water from going into my mouth. He bends down and sucks on the wet skin of my throat.

I latch my arms around his neck, my hands resting on his upper back. Then when he starts to swirl his finger right at the opening of my slit, I dig my nails into his back out of desperation. He's driving me crazy.

"Fuck, Dharia. You're going to be the death of me. I know it." In one quick motion, like I don't weigh anything, he picks me up so that I can wrap my legs around his waist. He lets my back lean heavily against the wall and takes a step back. He grabs hold of his thick cock and rubs it against my clit. The head is pushing against my opening but not going in as he rubs it back and forth from my hole up to my clit, then back down again . . . over and over until I'm so bound up with the urge to come that when he slams into me, my pussy immediately clamps down on him, and I'm spasming with my release.

"Oh my God." I do my best to hold on to him, but my body has a mind of its own, and I can no longer stay up. He takes over, holding me with both hands and slams me up and down his long cock.

I let my head fall back against the wall and just enjoy the ride. He leans his head down, and the water splashes off his broad shoulders.

"Dharia, this shit feels too good. Shit." He groans as he grinds deep enough inside that it causes me to lose my breath. I finally get some strength back in my limbs, and I hold on to his forearms and use them to come back on him with more force. My pussy squeezes and releases him with every stroke. It's not like anything I've ever felt before.

"Just the tip. Go shallow, babe," I whisper. I love feeling that broad head at the very beginning of my slit. Immediately, he does what I ask, lifting me all the way up so that only the tip of his cock is inside of me.

"Fuck, goddammit, that shit feels so good." He grips my ass so tight that it feels like he's breaking skin as he quickly pumps just the tip of his dick inside of me. "I need to go deeper. It's so fucking sensitive. I . . . fuck." His eyes drop from mine down to his cock glistening with both water and my slippery juices.

"No, wait, babe, please; a little more. Oh God, a little more." I feel my orgasm gathering with a scary intensity. Once I feel it take off, I grab the back of his neck and force his eyes back to mine. The primal beast inside of him that wants nothing more than to wreck all my walls is there staring back at me.

"Now . . . Darius, now."

"Thank fuck," he grunts out as he pounds as deep as he can get. I scream out my release, and he grinds deep inside of me.

"Mmm, yes, Darius. Fuck me," I moan out as my core clenches tight, and hot wave after wave of my climax washes over me. It makes me feel like every inch of my skin is tingling.

"Dharia, hold on. I need . . . Fuck." He grits out and drops me down to my feet.

I don't know what he needs, but part of me knows that it's going to be earth-shattering, and I'm ready for whatever he wants to give me.

My legs don't hold me at all, but it doesn't matter. Dare turns me around and bends me over so that my hands are on the edge of the tub. He lines himself up and slams into me. I scream out and instinctively try to get away, but I'm stuck between him and the wall. There is nowhere for him to go, and he is so deep I can do nothing but scream. He's right on the edge of pain. His size and his speed are more than I've ever experienced before.

"Dharia, shit's so fucking good," he groans as he pounds into me without abandon. I turn my head slightly and can see the look of intense determination. He's racing to the end. He is fucking me like his life depends on it.

My legs shake like leaves as my pussy takes the punishment he's giving me.

"Darius," I scream out and quickly raise my hand to my throbbing clit. The pain and desperation flowing through him seep into me, and all I want now is to come again. I rub fast and hard, keeping up with his thrusts. Then I let out a deep, guttural wail as my muscles jerk and contract with yet another orgasm.

"I can't hold . . . shit . . . I'm so deep . . . inside. I'm going to come inside." He pants hard. It's my warning, but I'm too far gone to care right now. He slams deeper into me one more time, his upper body curling forward as his cock throbs and pulses his cum deep inside my walls.

"Dharia, fuck," he moans and keeps himself pressed inside of me so hard, my head smashes against the wall.

I don't know if it's twenty seconds or twenty minutes, but he slowly pulls out of me. I slide down to the floor, and he leans his hand against the wall as he catches his breath, his cock in his hand.

I curl into a ball and just let the water wash over me.

"Dharia." He calls for me, completely out of breath.

"Dharia died. Please come back later," I mutter, and he laughs. Then he bends down and swats me on the ass.

"Come on, get up."

"Don't wanna." I play. I try to straighten my legs, but I would rather just stay lying in a ball in the tub. Much more comfortable.

"Woman, move your ass. I'm not going to leave you in the tub." He turns and shuts off the water. The sudden absence of that warm spray amplifies how fucking cold it is in the room. I shiver and sit up. He helps me out of the tub. I grab a towel and rush straight to the bed, then dive under the blankets to get warm.

"You're going to sleep?" he asks, surprised.

"After that, I'm going into a coma." I let my eyes flutter closed. "Why, what's up?"

"Nothing. I thought you would come down and party with the rest of us."

I sit up at that remark, completely focused. "You want me to come down? You told me not to come down."

"Yeah, that was before. I doubt any of the guys will fuck with you now, and they aren't going to let anyone else fuck with you either. You don't have to. It's just a bunch of women dancing and the rest of the people that want to get in good with the Sinners." He shrugs and pulls out a shirt from the drawer and some jeans. Then he slips into his boxer briefs before he puts on the rest of his clothes. "I won't be down long anyway. I just want people to see my face and check on Grizzly. I'll be up in a bit." He rubs some lotion on his arms and face, picks up his kutte from the coatrack by the door, and walks out without another word.

I lay back down on the bed, but I can't sleep now. He's never asked me to join him before. I wrap the towel around my body, walk over to the two-way window, and press the small button that shows me what's happening downstairs. Like always, the Sinners have a rager of a party going on. It looks like it could be fun. If he wants me to be there, I guess I could go. I smile—but right before I turn, I see something that lights a fire under my ass. A stripper wearing a bright white outfit, long dark hair, and plump lips puts on a show, and it looks like it's solely for Dare. If there's one thing I don't do, it's share.

Chapter 29

Dare

The first stop I make when I get downstairs is to check on Grizzly. I knock on the back door to see three women in the small room with him. Two of them are smoking a joint while the other is sitting next to the couch where he's lying.

"Dare, what's going on, brother? Everything set?"

"Yeah, we good. So what the hell do you think you're doing? Didn't the doctor tell you that you need to take it easy?"

He chuckles and pulls up the girl that's sitting on the sofa. "Oh, don't worry. I'm not going to do any work."

I roll my eyes. "Look, before you get your due relaxation, I just want to let you know that I really appreciate you putting yourself on the line like that. I know this shit is not what any of you signed up for, but I appreciate it."

"Dare, this is *exactly* what we signed up for. You're my brother. I'm going to go through hell if it means that I can help or protect you. But give me a few days to get on my feet, and I'll be right back at your side."

"I know it. That's real." I lean over him and bump his fist. I don't know where the hell his hands have been. "Now, it looks like you have some business to handle."

"Yeah, I got an extra one if you want. I'm not selfish."

I turn and walk out. The last thing I want is one of those women in there. My woman is upstairs, sleeping.

Like always, the stage is set up, and the strippers are doing their best to get as many tips as possible. Some new faces are there. One seems to be a real fucking acrobat on the pole. I find myself stopping midstride when she does what looked like a triple flip to land in a split on the stage. Twenties and fifties rain in her direction. Even I peel off a few bills for that shit.

I find Trim sitting on the left side of the room in front of two strippers. I need to talk to him as well. I want to talk to everyone, but I doubt I will tonight. "Trim, you got a second?"

"Uhh . . . Mmm-hmm." His head turns in my direction, but he has yet to take his eyes of the woman shaking her ass in front of him. I understand. I mean, why the fuck would he want to talk to me when he has a woman showing him what her entire pussy looks like? I'm sure he could paint a picture by memory at this point.

I clap him on the back and laugh. "Fuck it. Thanks for today. Have fun."

"Yeah, yeah. No problem," he answers, completely unfazed by what I just said.

I get a beer from the bar and find an empty lounge couch to sit in. I'm bored already. My eyes take in the beautiful women around me, and even though some of them arouse me, none of them hold my attention for too long. The only one I keep looking at is the circus chick at the other end of the room. She's bending in ways I'm not sure I have ever seen anyone bend in. I'm a bit afraid that she'll pop a joint out of place or some shit.

The music changes, and the entire crowd of people who aren't up on stage dance and sing out the song. The strippers take a second, and all change out. What a shame the circus woman is gone. I turn my head to the front to see Star in a bright white outfit standing right in front of me. Her silver high heels are reflective and shimmer with every move of her body. She has bands that crisscross up her thick thighs and a dainty silver chain around her belly. She works the pole like she's auditioning for a lead role–a lead role in my personal movie. I know she's going to be pissed when she finds out that I'm not going to be fucking her tonight . . . or any other night, that is, while Dharia sticks around.

My dick jumps at the thought of Dharia sleeping in my bed, her tight cunt warm and waiting for me.

Gambit comes and sits down on the other side of the couch with me. "You really think Bill had something to do with this?"

I hadn't expected him to come out with that. No one else seems to want to talk about it. "Don't you? The timing of that shot is suspicious. Breach seemed like he was about to tell us something, and Bill didn't want him to."

"Fuck, man, that's not what I want to hear. Bill has been like a fucking mentor to each of us. He's been with Marcus from the start." Gambit looks truly upset by this, but the truth is the truth. "Anyway, I just wanted you to know I already set up a tail on the man who killed your wife. I think you need to lie low for a couple of days, but then whenever you're ready, just let me know, and we'll get it set up."

"Lie low? Why the fuck would I want to do that shit?" I turn to look at him like he's crazy.

"Bro, they just let him out. If he ends up dead right away, of course, the first person they gonna think did it is you. You the one he wronged. They going to know it's revenge."

I hear what he's saying. I understand it, but that doesn't stop my brain from telling me to get up right now and kill him before he gets a good night's sleep. Whether they think it's me, I don't care. The only thing stopping me is that I want to get a few supplies together for what I plan for him and some pointers from Creeper. So yeah, I can let him taste freedom for a few hours . . . until I end his life.

"I'll be seeing him tomorrow."

"Dare, I really—"

"Tomorrow," I bark at him. He nods his head once and walks away.

When I turn my head back to the stage, the song is already almost done. Star rubs her clit, the indent of the ring I know she has there shows through the fabric of her thong panties. Money flies at her, but she doesn't pay anyone any attention. She only has eyes for me. The second the song is over, she's climbing down off the stage, gathering up her cash, and walking in my direction. Of course.

She comes and sits down next to me on the couch, draping one hand behind my neck and the other on my chest. She leans against me and presses her lips close to my ear. She licks up the shell of it, and I lean away slightly.

"I was hoping you would be here to party tonight. I need you so bad," she whines in my ear.

"Sorry, Star, that's not happening." I tap her knee and hope that'll be enough to get her to move on. I should have known it wouldn't, though.

"What? Why not?" She frowns, but when she backs up and looks at my face, her solemn expression turns into a naughty one. "Oh, I get it. You want me to beg, baby? You want me to tell you how much I've been thinking about you deep inside of me, pushing all the way to the very bottom of my pussy? You want me to tell you how I've had to get myself off a dozen times since you last fucked me, and every time I did, I screamed your name? Dare, my pussy is yours. Fuck me, please."

I lean away from her. Any other time I would have had her bent over this couch and rail into her, but now, this shit just sounds pathetic.

"Star, how many times do I have to tell you? We ain't nothing. We were never anything to each other. We fucked a few times, and you act like you're a fucking junkie. I don't want your pussy. I don't even want to be in your company. There are dozens of other men here. Go find one of them." I move over so that she is no longer leaning on me and just in time too. When I look up, I see Dharia standing over us, that crazy fire burning hot in her eyes. She doesn't even glance in Star's direction.

"You look like you need some entertainment." She moves my leg over and settles herself right on my lap.

"What the fuck? Bitch, don't you see me sitting here?"

Dharia's head snaps toward Star. "No, I don't see you sitting here. I see my man and some skank who's just about to fuck off."

Oh shit.

"*Your* man? Fuck out of here with that. I've been fucking him for the past few weeks. That's *my* dick. You better go take your girl-next-door ass to one of the prospects who are more your style, bitch."

Dharia stands up from my lap and gets right in Star's face. "Oh, you were? No wonder he was so pent-up when he finally got deep inside *my* tight pussy. Your twat is so used the fuck up there's no way he could hit bottom. But that's OK. I'll be taking care of him from now on. You're dismissed."

I should have stopped it, but I'm mesmerized.

"You skanky bitch," Star yells and pulls back her hand.

"Do it. I fucking dare you to lay one nasty-ass finger on me. I promise you it'll be the last fucking thing you ever do." Dharia gets farther into Star's face, waiting for the stripper to make her next move.

"Star, you need to get out of here," I say from where I'm sitting.

"What?" Star turns her face and looks at me.

I pull Dharia so that she's sitting down on my lap again where she belongs.

"Yeah, we don't want your clingy ass in here no more. So you can go and don't come back."

She opens her mouth to say something, but I've already given my order. Gambit, Trim, and a few hang-arounds grab her and physically remove her from the club. I see tears streaming down her face, but she brought this down on herself. I told her ass not to get attached.

"Am I going to have to do this shit again?"

"What the hell is that supposed to mean?"

"Look, I'm not trying to lock you down if that's not what you want, but I'm not going to do this back-and-forth shit. If you want to stick your dick in everything that walks—"

I grab the back of her neck and kiss her. Of course, she's jealous. I love that shit. "I'm done with all this shit. If you're trying to be down with me, then I'm with you."

"That's what I thought." She wraps her arms around my neck and bends down to kiss me.

Chapter 30

"Do you really need to do this?" Dharia asks.

"Don't question me."

"What the hell do you mean, 'Don't question me'? You're telling me you're about to go kill someone, and you don't think I should question you?" Exasperated, she throws her hands up in the air.

We woke up this morning to a knock on the door. Creeper is ready to get this show on the road. Gambit had an associate of his follow Shade Wills to a motel where he stayed all night with a woman. She would be the last woman he ever lies with. He killed my wife, so there's no way that I'm just going to let him get off scot-free. I spoke with Creeper last night about helping me with some of the "technical" aspects. I want Shade to suffer for a very long time.

"You think I should let the man who raped and murdered my wife walk this earth? That I should give up because the system fucking failed? Nah, I'm not doing that shit. What I'm going to do is I'm going to get my own justice."

She sits down on the bed like the world is on her shoulders. "Everyone will know it's you. Even Gambit told you that. They're going to know that you were the one who killed him. You want to end up in jail too? What about Tia?"

"If I have to fucking get locked up, then so be it. I don't give a fuck anymore," I yell out and knock the pile of papers that we already looked through last night on the floor. "I don't care. I'm never going to have what I had before. I've been trying so fucking hard to get it back, but it's not going to happen. I may never find Tia. She's probably dead by now. So no, I'll never get it back, but I can kill those who took it from me."

"He's in there," Gambit whispers as we make our way around the building, keeping low so that no one will see us sneaking into one of the few motel rooms. He's in the shitty part of town. The motel is known for prostitution and drugs, so it's doubtful anyone would even notice us walking in, but we still want to keep a low profile.

When we get to the door, we hear groans and a woman screaming out inside. Shade is in there fucking while we're standing out here trying to break into his room. He'll be completely off guard. Perfect.

"Masks up," Gambit says as he presses the crowbar into the side of the door, and it pops open.

"What the fuck?" Shade turns, trying to pull his dick out of the woman and grab for his gun at the same time, but Gambit trains his gun on him, so he doesn't move.

The woman opens her mouth to scream, but my gun is already pointed at her. "Don't fucking think about it. We don't want you."

Creeper pulls out his phone and takes several pictures of the woman. I have no idea what for.

"You even think about saying anything about what you *think* you saw here, I promise you we *will* come for you, and we'll make it hurt worse than anything you've ever felt in your life."

The woman nods, quickly gets out of the bed, throws on her short dress, and bolts out of the door with her shoes and her purse in her hands. The crack pipe is still on the dresser where she left it.

"Do you know who the fuck you're sticking up? You're all dead. I don't know who the fuck you are, but you're dead men."

Once Creeper secures the door behind us, I pull down my mask so he can see my face.

My hand shakes with the weight of the gun. All I want is to pull the trigger to rid the world of this piece of shit, but he made Lisbeth suffer. He deserves the same.

"The bed, Creeper." Creeper and Gambit move fast and tie Shade down to the bed, spread eagle and balls out naked. They stuff his nasty boxers into his mouth and then tape it shut so he can't scream.

"Do you remember who I am?" I ask him while Creeper goes over to the table with the bag containing the tools I asked him to bring for me. I don't know what to do with half the shit he has in there, but that is precisely why I brought him along. I spent so many years trying to be a good man when I was bred to be the worst. It's time that I embrace that to the fullest.

"Yeah, I'm sure you do. I bet you weren't expecting to see me again." I see a pack of cigarettes on the table and pull out the lighter. I play with it, letting the flame heat up the small piece of metal while I stare at the man who raped my woman.

Shade groans and pulls on the restraints, but he doesn't budge.

"Did you think because the cops fucked up that you weren't going to get what was coming to you?"

He continues to moan, but I don't understand anything that he's saying. My brain has already started speaking for him.

"You want to warm him up first. If you go straight to the intense shit, he'll go into shock and die," Creeper says as he comes back and stands next to me.

"Bro, I'm with you, but I'm gonna chill in the bathroom for this part. My pure mind can't handle this." Gambit walks off, leaving just the three of us in the room.

Warm him up, huh?

I look down at the lighter I've been flicking. Then I walk over to where Shade is and stare straight into his face as I flick off the safety on the lighter. I turn it so the flame is the highest it can go. I strike the lighter near his sides, but I don't touch him. His skin turns a bright red and begins to bubble before I move on to the other side.

"You didn't know her, but Lisbeth was a good woman. She didn't deserve what you did to her." I press the fire near his skin over and over until tears start to stream down his face. It isn't enough.

"Have you ever felt like you had the whole world sitting on your chest, like you just couldn't breathe? That's how I felt when y'all had me pinned to the ground, and you violated my wife." I walk over to the table and pull out a pair of pliers. I look at Creeper, and he pats his sides.

Then I walk back over to Shade and press the pliers to his side right where the raw skin covers his ribs. I don't push them through the skin, but I force them in deep enough where the pliers can grab his rib bone through the skin. Once I'm sure I have a good grip, I squeeze with all my strength. His bone pops and cracks under the pressure. It sounds like cracking open a walnut. Now that he's felt actual pain, Shade bucks and screams through the gag. I swear it sounds like he is asking me for mercy, but I am far from done.

I try to use everything that Creeper has in that bag. After about an hour of beating the shit out of Shade, he starts to fade.

"He's not going to last much longer," Creeper informs me.

"So the fuck what? You got a soft spot for him or something?"

"No. You can do whatever the fuck you want to do with him. But if you want to ask him anything, now's the time."

Shit, he's right. Maybe this bastard has some information on Tia.

I go up to Shade's face and lean over to the side so he can hear me. During the past hour, I used a razor blade to slice off his ear slowly . . . painful but not a lot of blood.

"You already know you're going to die, but I can stop all your pain now, or we can figure out a way to make this go on a lot longer. Now, I'm going to ask you some questions, and if you give me the wrong answers, I'm going to hand you over to the true master of pain over there. I'm just a novice at this shit. You understand?"

Shade slowly nods his head.

I rip the tape off fast, but he doesn't even flinch. "Where's my daughter?"

He whimpers, his head slowly moving from side to side. He doesn't know. "You *do* know. You're fucking lying." I take the lighter and press the flame to his hand. He yells out, but I slam my free hand over his mouth.

"I'm going to ask you again, where did you take my daughter?"

"I don't know. I didn't . . . I swear."

I look at Creeper to see what his opinion is. He nods his head to let me know that he thinks Shade's telling the truth.

Another idea pops into my head. I took a photo for Gambit to put through a form recognition software of the paperwork that Dharia brought. It didn't return anything, but maybe Shade would be able to tell me what it means.

"What do these numbers mean?" I show him the picture.

He mumbles something, but I can't understand.

"What?" I move nearer, and Creeper gets closer to watch my back.

"Initials, age, height, race, zip code, club number, price."

I turn the photo around, and now that he said that, it all clicks in my head. This isn't just a numbering system but a brief demographic profile.

Shit, the location of where Tia is could be right there on those papers at the clubhouse.

"I'm done. Let's go." I rush over to the table and pull out a long hunting knife from the bag. Shade already closed his eyes when I turn back, his mouth moving quickly. The motherfucker is praying. His eyes open when I stand over him. A slight smirk passes over his lips, and I bring the knife down square into his chest. I stand over him and wait until he's no longer breathing. He and his buddies made the mistake of thinking I was dead. I would make sure that he is.

"We have to get back right now. What do we do about the body?" I ask, anxious to leave.

"My people are already downstairs waiting for us to leave. They'll clean up everything. It'll be like no one was here."

I nod and call for Gambit.

"Oh, what the fuck?" He gags the second he steps out of the bathroom and sees the destruction I've inflicted on Shade.

"Focus. I need you to get on the jack and call the club. Tell the guys that I need every last one of them to go through the papers that Dharia has and find any of them that have the serial number that starts with the letters TH." He instantly does what I ask and walks out of the motel room. I have to change. I was the one beating the hell out of Shade, so I have blood splatter all over me. I quickly wash and change into the extra set of clothes that Creeper insisted I bring. When I walk out of the bathroom, he's throwing a strong-smelling liquid around the room.

"What the fuck is that?" I cover my nose.

"For the fingerprints."

The man thinks of everything. "Good shit. Let's get out of here." A second later, he gathers his supplies, and we walk out of the motel room like nothing happened. A group of people who are stumbling along and pulling out crack pipes walks by us. They walk directly into the room we just left like it's theirs. They must be the people that Creeper called to clean up the room. They play druggies well. I would have never guessed. Creeper doesn't say a word, and we jump on our bikes and get the hell out of Dodge.

With Shade put out of his misery, one wrong in my life has finally been avenged. Now, it's time to rectify the other. I just know I'll find Tia. I have to.

Chapter 31

I don't think I have ever pushed my bike that fast in my life. It's like I have the winning lottery ticket at home. I secure my bike in the parking lot and don't even wait for Gambit or Creeper to get in behind me. I just run into the clubhouse. I don't see anyone in the main area, so I run in a full sprint straight upstairs. Everyone turns their heads the very second that I burst into the room. All my boys are there, including Grizzly's fucked-up ass, looking like a little assembly line sorting through papers.

"These are the ones that we found so far. You figured it out." Dharia rushes over to me with a small stack of papers in her hand.

I can't stop myself from smiling as I take the stack from her hand.

According to the code that Shade gave me, the first two pages of the THs were too old. One is 16 while the other is 22.

The third page shines like the golden ticket from Willy Wonka himself.

Her initials, the right age, the right height, the right race, and the zip code followed by the word "offer." I don't know what that part means, but this is the map I need to get her.

"This is it," I hear myself say out loud.

"What?" Everyone stops what they're doing and walks over to where I am.

"Are you sure?"

"Fuck yes."

"Let me get my piece."

I press the page to my head and cover my face with it. I don't even have her yet, and I feel like I'm breaking apart. Is this *really* it?

"Let's go." I pull the sheet down, and everyone is already following me out. They don't care that there's no plan and that we don't know what we're walking into. They are just following me into the fray because we're family.

I put out a hand and stop Grizzly.

"Brother, I need you to stay back."

"Fuck outta here. I'm coming. Who the hell is going to watch your back? You're so little." He chuckles and tries to walk around me, but I stop him again.

"Grizzly, you know damn well I want you behind me when we get this shit done, but you're already jacked. I need you to stay here. You'll be no fucking good to us if you get stuck or can't get in or out like we need to. So stay back and watch over the clubhouse, and if something happens, let us know. Keep the women safe. Last line of defense, man."

"Dare, I can—"

"That's an order, brother." I see the disappointment in his eyes. If there is one thing I know, it's that Grizzly is probably as invested in this as anyone besides me can be. But I can't have him getting further hurt. One bullet taken because of me is enough.

"You got it, VP," he concedes and stays back.

I pull him in for a quick bro hug before I rush out the door and make my way downstairs.

"Do you have the address of where we're going?" Exit asks.

I tell him the zip code. According to the map that Dharia gave us earlier, there is only one safe house in that area, but I don't know if it's an old Eleven-Quad safe house or one that belongs to the Brutes.

It doesn't matter who it belongs to. No one is going to stop me from getting my daughter.

I grab what I need and look at who's there with me. Someone's missing.

I walk over to Marcus's room and see that the motherfucker is still in his pajamas.

"What the fuck? Why aren't you dressed?"

"Why the fuck would I be getting dressed?" His eyes blink rapidly as he gives me a blank look.

"They didn't tell you? Whatever. It doesn't matter. Get dressed. I need all hands on deck. I found Tia." I smile wide. If there's ever a time in my life that I thought my father would be happy for me, it would be the day I said those words. But instead, he flips his hands in the air and walks toward his TV.

"No, you didn't," he retorts matter-of-factly.

"Yes, I did. Why aren't you more excited about the fact that I've found your granddaughter? This is what I've been fighting for the last couple of months."

"Dare, I promise you, you didn't find her."

"How the fuck do you know that? Do *you* have her or something?" I bare my teeth and take a menacing step in his direction. He seems so sure that I haven't found her. *Too* sure, in fact.

"Where the fuck would I hide her? You see a baby around here?"

"Then if you don't have her, get off your ass and help me get her back. That was *your* word, that you would do whatever the fuck you could to help me find her. Now that I have, you're dragging your fucking feet." I think about what could cause him not to want me to find her. "I'm not going to leave the club once I have her back. I'm staying a Sinner."

"No shit. You thought I was going to let you leave? Don't be fucking stupid," he scoffs and looks at me. "Fine. If you want to waste your fucking time chasing ghosts, I'll go for the fucking ride. I ain't got shit to do no ways." He stands up and begins stripping out of his clothes. I leave the room at that. We'll soon be on the way, and I'll have my baby in my arms by this evening.

"This shit is off," Exit says through the phone as we're halfway to the location. He rode ahead to check out the site before we got there.

"What do you mean?"

"Bro, there are no clubhouses around here and nothing that even remotely looks like something Eleven-Quad would have owned. This shit looks like the houses you see in the movies and shit. Marcus is right. She's not here."

My heart drops to my stomach. Another fucking dead end.

I pull my bike over and take a few deep breaths so that I don't go off the fucking deep end.

"I don't care if we have to peek through every fucking window. We're going to check this shit out."

There weren't many homes in the location that Dharia showed us, but Exit's right. These are more like little mansions than drug dens or biker clubs. In fact, I don't see one bike in the area.

"What you want us to do?" Apollo asks as he rides up next to me.

"We canvas on foot. Do what we have to do to find her."

He nods and races off. I follow behind, praying that the Lord helps me with this. I don't think I can handle another failure.

By the time we make it to the small town, my head's pounding with a migraine. I'm so fucking tense right now, but it's not going to stop me. Only five houses are in the area.

It won't be long now until we figure out if Tia is here.

My heart feels like it's beating out of my chest. I have to swallow hard to keep myself from throwing up because of my nerves.

"She's here; I know it," I whisper to myself. They always talk about the "maternal instinct," but fathers get that shit too. It's like I can feel her close by. Like my heart is synced with hers.

We start at the first home. It has a lot of security, but the guys don't see anything out of the ordinary. An older couple sits in their family room, and the woman reads a book while the man flips through the newspaper. No children running around. I leave Mali and Trim at this one to give it a thorough look-through. We make our way to the next house, thankful that so far, no one has come out of their home wondering what a bunch of Black dudes is doing running from yard to yard. It's hard to be sneaky in the middle of the fucking afternoon.

This next house looks empty. The lights are off, and no car is in the driveway. I leave Exit and Bill there to check over that one. The third house is smack-dab in the middle of the large cul-de-sac of homes. It has a high-tech security system in the windows, and a woman in the kitchen moves from side to side as if she was dancing. I can't hear any music, though. She puts something in the oven before she twirls over to the large sink and begins to wash something. I'm about to leave someone here to go over this house while I move on to the next when Apollo comes darting out from the other side of the home.

"It's this one," he whispers happily. I rarely see Apollo smiling.

"What? You see her?" I grab him and try to force my heart to slow down.

"No, I don't see her, but I see someone better. Come on. We got to get in there."

"What the fuck is going on?" Marcus asks from the back. He hasn't been overly interested in anything that we're doing. He's only here because the club expects him to be.

I call Exit and tell him to get over here with everyone else. In the next minute, we're all pressed against the large building.

"The doors are reinforced, but there's a cellar door on the other side that I can break in. We can enter that way."

I nod. I'd fly at this point if he told me that's the only way to get in. I don't know who's in there, but if Apollo says this is the place, I'm going to trust him.

Exit quickly breaks into the cellar. Then the group of us rush into the basement before anyone can see us. The back of the home is nothing but trees and empty land, so I'm reasonably confident that no one will catch on that we're here.

We push through the cellar, and I'm the first one out the door that leads to the inside of the house. I follow behind Apollo as he crouches low and quickly makes his way toward the back of the house. Creeper, Mali, and Trim go in the opposite direction to make sure that we won't be pinned down. We have no way of knowing how many people are here or even if we just walked into a trap. I'm going purely off trust . . . trust in my brothers and trust in this patch.

"Apollo, where the hell are we?" Marcus whispers angrily.

"My home," a deep voice booms out to the side, and I quickly draw my weapon to point it in that direction.

It feels like my soul is being ripped out of my body for the second time in my life. Standing right in front of me is a large man with deep bronze skin, cornrows, and a long scar from the bottom of his eye to the side of his mouth.

"What the fuck?"

"Oh shit."

"Fuck."

Everyone next to me immediately draws their weapons and moves in his direction.

"Who's that?" My voice sounds unfamiliar. My slur is more pronounced than it's been in a while.

"That's Luger, the president of the Brutes MC," Apollo grits out and stands in front of me.

Luger is holding my heart. He is holding everything I have in his hands. Tia plays with his hair as if he were a family member instead of the man who stole her . . . instead of the man who's holding a gun to her back . . .

Chapter 32

"Tia?" I call out, and her little head swings in my direction.

The brightest fucking smile I've ever seen—and one I never thought I would see again—erupts on her face. "Daddy, Daddy!" She reaches for me, but Luger shushes her and bounces her on his hip.

"You motherfuckers broke into the wrong fucking house," he growls out.

"Just give me my kid."

"Can't do that. She's been paid for. Deal already made. She doesn't belong to you anymore. Now, get the fuck out of here before you have to see her die. And in case you think I won't, I've done much worse." He smirks as he bends close to her and kisses her on the cheek. He's a fucking psychopath.

"She's mine. I don't know who you paid, but it wasn't me. Tia is mine. I'm not leaving without her."

"Marcus, this is frustrating." Luger talks to my father. "I told you if there were any problems, everything we discussed would be void. I don't have time for this. Get your fucking people out of my house now, and I'll only kill this little one for your offenses."

"What?" Apollo takes a few steps away.

"What are you talking about? What offenses?"

"Oh, how could I be so rude? Seems like you don't know what you got in exchange for a princess like Tia. You got a piece of the pie. The Heavy Sinners are set to run all of Northern Florida. Your father got you to join the club, his legacy. He cleared out all the Eleven-Quad members that didn't fall in line, with your help, I'm assuming. He gave Tia as payment. He said he would keep you chasing your tail. How did his tail end up in my home, Marcus?" He directs his questions to my father again.

A loud hum descends on me. I feel numb. I've been trusting this man at least to some extent to help me find my kid—and he *knew* where she was this entire time.

"You're a fucking liar. I would never do no shit like that. He's my son. That's my granddaughter. You just want to break apart our ranks." My father barrels through the crowd with his gun raised, but Luger lifts Tia and puts her in front of his head and chest.

"Ah. Ah. Ah . . . You wouldn't want to kill this so-called granddaughter, would you? Isn't she special to you?" Luger asks.

"Daddy, go home. Daddy, please!" Tia begins to wail and reach out for me. The tension in the air is undeniable and too thick for her to ignore any longer.

"It's OK, baby. Daddy's here. Close your eyes, OK? Shhh." I do my best to calm her. I can't even bring myself to pull up my gun. I feel like such a fucking fool.

"What about *this* one? Isn't *she* special to you?" Creeper stumbles into the room. The woman I saw dancing in the kitchen is gagged and bleeding from her head. He has one hand behind her back and is pushing her into the room. The cocky smile that was on Luger's face disappears.

"I told your dumb ass to get in the motherfucking safe, you stupid bitch," he screams at her before he sighs and turns back to my father, still using my baby as a shield. "Tell your man to let my ol' lady go. Tell him to let her go, and I'll let you walk out of here with your entire crew intact, but I can't give you the kid. I was promised a life. It's the principal of the matter."

"Creeper, let her go," Marcus orders.

Creeper doesn't move. His eyes dart to mine. He's no longer taking orders from the old man.

"What deal was made?" I ask, my voice cracking.

"There is no fucking deal. He's playing you. Don't be such a fucking dumb ass," my father screams in my face.

"Oh, am I? Marcus, you should know better than that. Did you think I wouldn't have proof?" Luger sneers as he backs toward one of the bookcases near his giant TV.

The group of us slowly make our way toward him, spreading out around the room in case he's about to pull something out of the bookcase that could kill us all.

Instead, he pulls out a small flash drive.

"What the fuck is that? Don't do this shit." Marcus takes another step forward, but Apollo puts his hand out to stop him.

"What the fuck are you doing? Get your fucking hands off me. *I'm* the leader of this fucking club. What *I* say goes." Now, instead of pointing his gun at Luger, Marcus points it at Apollo.

A hiss followed by a popping sound echoes through the room, and on the large-screen TV, a color video shows Marcus and Luger sitting down with drinks in their hands. Luger must have a hidden camera in whatever room they were in.

"Now, Marcus, we've done what you needed. I don't understand why you had to go through all this shit to get your son to join. If he didn't want in, fuck him," Luger says.

"He's the only son I got. My club is going to stay with my family. That shit means more than anything. This was the only way to get him to join. I've already handled his boss. Any day now,

he should be delivering the bad news to Darius. I want him to have no fucking way but straight into the club," Marcus sneers as he brings the glass to his mouth and takes a swig. "That shit was almost fucked up, though. Your people damn near killed him. I told you to hurt him—not *put a bullet in his head."*

"We put a bullet in his jaw. He'll live." Luger puts his glass on the table. "What about the little one? You know he's going to come for her. I'd never rest until I found my *kid."*

"I'm banking on it. We'll use it to run through all the Eleven-Quad. By the time he's through searching for this little girl, there will be none left but those loyal to us."

"Us? What makes you think I'm going along with this arrangement?"

Marcus leans forward in his chair. "Because you and I both know that together, we can take over this entire fucking state. Hell, the entire East Coast. This money we making now is nothing compared to what we going to make when we start running everything. We'll be unstoppable."

"Not everyone in your club is going to feel the same way. I don't play shit safe. So that's going to be an issue."

"Who?" He laughs like it's the biggest joke in the world. "Apollo? He won't be in a position to question anything soon. Bill is too fucking blind to see

what's in front of his face. Creeper just does as he's told. Trust me, none of them going to do shit." Marcus chuckles before he raises the glass to his mouth and takes another drink.

"This is bullshit," Marcus says, looking around the room. He's sweating, and his eyes are darting from side to side. "You don't understand. This isn't what it looks—"

A loud boom, followed by a flash, erupts from behind me.

Marcus's head whips back. Flesh and brains erupt in a liquid halo before his body crumbles to the floor and shit rolls down his leg.

I turn my head and see the smoking barrel of Bill's gun.

"Traitors fucking die," he snarls.

Tia screams, the woman Creeper is holding screams, and the rest of the club looks at Marcus's body dumbfounded and in shock. Bill has been with my father since the very beginning. So if there is anyone to take Marcus out, it *isn't* supposed to be him. At least that's what we all thought.

"Well . . . fuck," Luger says as he shuffles my squirming daughter in his arms, careful of the gun he's holding.

I don't feel not one twinge of pain for the dead man on the floor. If anything, I only regret that it wasn't me who put the bullet in his head.

"Let my daughter go," I demand, bringing my attention to the problem at hand.

"I can't do that. There's a deal—"

"I made no fucking deal with you. The man you dealt with is dead on your hardwood floor. You were promised a life. There it is, right there." I point at Marcus.

"You're right. Seems there's been a sudden change in leadership among the Sinners. Darius, I think we should talk. I think we could have a great partnership. Your father thought so. Let's do this the right way." He puts Tia on the floor. "Let my woman go, and I'll give you Tia. I didn't want to hurt her anyway. It was your father's idea that I use her as a leash for you."

"Creeper, do it. Give me Tia now."

The world slows to a snail's pace as my little girl runs to me with big tears streaming down her little face, wearing a pretty dress and slippers that light up with every step straight into my arms.

If I could open my chest and stick her in there, I would.

Creeper lets the woman go, and she runs to Luger, who shoves her behind his body.

"When do you want to discuss the deal?" he asks.

"Fuck you and the deal. I want nothing to do with it," I spit out at the man.

"Ah, but you're not the only member of the club, are you?"

I turn slightly to see the rest of the men behind me. Apollo pulls out a knife and slowly makes his way over to my dead father. He quickly slices off the tag that says *President,* walks over to me, and slams it into my chest.

They could have killed me right there. I was an outsider, just a pawn my father used to get what he wanted, but they all were still standing behind me. "The Sinners will have nothing to do with your fucking deal," I repeat, including everyone.

He nods his head like he's impressed. "I see. You did hear the part where I said I was taking over the entire state, right? The Brutes will be the strongest club on the East Coast. You think we going to leave your little MC standing? If you're not with us, you're against us."

If we don't take this deal, we're guaranteed to have an enemy we may not be able to beat.

I push Tia behind me and smirk at the man in front of me. "Come after the Sinners if you want. I fucking dare you to do it. We're not the same club my father thought he was lord over. We'll see who walks out of hell alive." I push back, trying to get to the door. We outnumbered Luger, but I don't want to be here any longer than we need to be. Mali is down on the ground pulling the kutte off Marcus. He's a traitor. He doesn't deserve to keep the patch, even in death.

"I guess we'll be seeing you soon, Dare." Luger glares at me.

"Bet on it," I reply.

We rush out of the house and straight to our bikes. I clutch Tia to my chest to ride out, pulling over once we get far enough away that I feel Luger won't be following us. I nearly topple over, trying to get off my bike.

"Oh, Tia, my baby, Tia." I hug her and cry unashamedly. I keep pulling her back and looking her over. I don't know what happened, but she doesn't look any worse for wear. She's clean. Looks to be a good weight and seems to remember who I am. I keep thinking she's just going to disappear. All this time searching for her, fearing the absolute worst, and she, more or less, seems perfect.

She cocks her head to the side and observes my face. She isn't crying anymore. The horrible scene she just witnessed is now far away from her mind.

"Daddy. We go fast. Don't be scared." She reaches up and kisses the tears from my cheek, and all I can do is thank God that she's finally here.

I don't care what comes after or who we have to fight. All that matters is my Tia is home.

Epilogue

Three Months Later . . .

"This is the second fucking time that one of our drops has been hit. It has to be the Brutes," Bill says from his chair at the table.

"Bullshit. We haven't even heard a peep from them for months. So why would they go for our small drops? If they want to wipe us out, they could do it in one shot. That just doesn't make any sense," Apollo remarks from his seat, the new, or I guess you can say, "returning" VP of the club.

"You think it's a new player that's coming for us?" I look at the burned money that Gambit was able to pick up from the scene. My life as president of the MC started the very second I walked into the clubhouse after my father was killed.

I never realized how much fucking shit went into running a club, although, I have to say, the old man made it look easy. One of the first things I did was commission the building of a family home behind the clubhouse. I hate that our families are stuck in the small apartments upstairs. I checked the other rooms, and most of them are much smaller than mine.

Dharia's in charge of getting what we need for the new place. Every day with her feels easy and right. She's my little bit of normal in this new fucked-up world that I now live in. Plus, she is a godsend for Tia. She and Tia became close friends very quickly. Of course, there are days when Tia still misses her mom, but Dharia is always there to console her, no matter how long it takes. She doesn't get frustrated or angry. She is just there.

I promoted Grizzly to SAA, and he takes that shit seriously. That man has my back every day. No matter what I need, he's there. He was pissed when he found out that my father was behind everything.

Now that my father is gone, his underhanded deals and people he wronged are all coming out of the woodwork. Most recently, we have an unknown enemy targeting our small-time drug operation. We are barely getting it back off the ground, and it's been hit twice in the past month. That shit won't do. If they think it's that easy to break through our defenses, it'll be open fucking season on the Sinners.

"I think it could be anyone. What you want to do, Dare?" Apollo asks me.

I lean back in the chair. "I think it's time we remind everyone who the Heavy Sinners fucking are. My father had the right idea. It's time we take it all."